Library of Southern Civilization
Lewis P. Simpson, Editor

JUDITH BENSADDI
A Tale
and
SECLUSAVAL
A Sequel

The University Library, Washington and Lee University

Henry Ruffner

JUDITH BENSADDI

—••❧ A Tale ❧••—

and

SECLUSAVAL

Or the Sequel to the Tale of Judith Bensaddi

By

HENRY RUFFNER

Edited, and with an Introduction, by

J. MICHAEL PEMBERTON

Louisiana State University Press / Baton Rouge and London

LIBRARY OF CONGRESS CATALOGING IN PUBLICATION DATA

Ruffner, Henry, 1790–1861.
    Judith Bensaddi: A tale; and, Seclusaval, or, The
sequel to the tale of Judith Bensaddi.
    (Library of Southern civilization)
    Bibliography: p.
    I. Pemberton, J. Michael.   II. Ruffner, Henry, 1790–
1861. Seclusaval. 1983.   III. Title.   IV. Series.
PS2736.R44J8   1983   813'.3   83-9858
ISBN 0-8071-1129-5

In Memoriam
RICHARD BEALE DAVIS
1908–1981
Master Scholar, Master Teacher

Contents

Acknowledgments

I might not have discovered the memorable *Judith Bensaddi* had it not been for the amazing bibliographic recall and capable direction of the late Richard Beale Davis, Distinguished Service Professor at the University of Tennessee and recipient of the final National Book Award in History. Professor Davis recognized the importance of this unusual work of fiction and encouraged my work on a new edition of it. For helpful comments on the manuscript I am grateful to Professor Davis and to my colleague William C. Robinson. I am also grateful to the Research Grants Committee at the University of Alabama in Huntsville for awarding a grant to initiate the research. To my graduate assistants at the University of Tennessee, Knoxville, Candace Powell, Diane Brown, and Nancy Evans, I owe thanks for their interest and for painstaking legwork cheerfully done. To Don Haymes, graduate of the Harvard Divinity School, I am especially grateful for insight into Ruffner's place in American religious history generally and Presbyterianism specifically. To my wife, Nancy, I am indeed indebted for her patience in reading the manuscript and in listening to ruminations about this project over a six-year period.

JUDITH BENSADDI
A Tale
and
SECLUSAVAL
A Sequel

Introduction

Recalling in the early twentieth century the contents of the 1839 volume of the *Southern Literary Messenger*, the journal's historian notes that among pieces by Henry Wadsworth Longfellow, William Cullen Bryant, and William Gilmore Simms, a short novel titled *Judith Bensaddi* "took everyone by surprise."[1] Based on the novel's contemporary reviews, the surprise to the *Messenger*'s readers was clearly a welcome one, for the novel was later reprinted in the journal by popular demand. *Judith Bensaddi* offered its readers a poignant love story—based on an actual incident—set in a distinctly southern locale, with the popular topics of slavery, education, and rugged natural beauty added to its basic plot of star-crossed love. This tale, however, went far beyond what might have been expected by exploring an issue that few had dared to consider aloud: marriage between a Jew and a Gentile. In fact, the first version of *Judith Bensaddi* (1828) has been cited as the earliest work of American fiction to deal with this delicate religious and social problem.[2]

Yet *Judith Bensaddi* was not the product of a northerner or a rabbi; rather it was written by a liberal southerner from western Virginia accustomed to controversy and to the exposition of strongly defined views on moral issues. He was the Reverend Dr. Henry Ruffner, Presbyterian minister and sixth president of what is now Washington and Lee University. If Ruffner's contemporaries were caught un-

1. Benjamin Blake Minor, *The Southern Literary Messenger, 1834–1864* (New York: Neale, 1905), 72.
2. Curtis Carroll Davis, "*Judith Bensaddi* and the Reverend Doctor Henry Ruffner: The Earliest Appearance in American Fiction of the Jewish Problem?" *Publications of the American Jewish Historical Society*, XXXIX (1949), 115–42. Charles Brockden Brown's earlier *Arthur Mervyn* (1800) does not qualify as a "first" in this category, because the Jewish background of Mervyn's betrothed, Achsa Fielding, is in no way viewed as an obstacle to their marriage.

awares by *Judith Bensaddi*, modern readers are equally likely to be startled by this work, especially if they are familiar with the more courtly, apologetic romances of postbellum Virginia novelists such as Thomas Nelson Page. One of the more unusual works of fiction written by an antebellum southerner, *Judith Bensaddi* is both predictable in its use of accepted sentimental formulas and refreshing in its deviation from the positions expected of upper-class southerners in the 1830s and 1840s. For example, in addition to his sympathetic working of the "unthinkable" intermarriage question, Ruffner creates a nonplantation agricultural community reminiscent of the social utopian principles of Henri Saint-Simon. He also demonstrates that an entreprenurial yeoman of natural talents could, with an education, be as financially successful without slavery as a slaveholding tidewater aristocrat. Some of the most engaging passages of *Judith Bensaddi* are devoted to Ruffner's unusually detailed and loving description of the area around Rockbridge County, Virginia. In fact, Richard Beale Davis, eminent historian of early Virginia's social and cultural life, has maintained that in addition to its literary qualities this novel merits a modern edition because of its important place in the travel and descriptive literature of Virginia.[3]

That the novel never saw publication as a separate volume, that Ruffner was only a talented amateur in fiction, that his reputation was obscured late in life by controversy, have all contributed to its neglect by scholars in literature, history, social studies, and Jewish studies. A more readable twentieth-century edition of *Judith Bensaddi* may well add even more evidence to the hypothesis that there was often a maverick quality to southern fiction before Harriet Beecher Stowe, which suggests more insight among antebellum southerners than is evident from reading the material of the later "moonlight-and-magnolias" variety.[4] A reading of *Judith Bensaddi* also serves as an introduction to Henry Ruffner, "one of the ripest

3. Richard Beale Davis, "The Valley of Virginia in Early American Literature," in Davis, *Literature and Society in Early Virginia, 1608–1840* (Baton Rouge: Louisiana State University Press, 1973), 271.

4. Among Ruffner's southern contemporaries were several novelists who often took critical positions on aspects of southern life, *e.g.*, George Tucker, *The Valley of Shenandoah* (1824), John Pendleton Kennedy, *Swallow Barn* (1832), and Beverley Tucker, *The Partisan Leader* (1836).

scholars in Virginia," whose numerous contributions to Virginia and West Virginia life have been generally overlooked by modern southern historians.[5]

Ruffner's emphasis in *Judith Bensaddi* on geographical description, agriculture, educational concerns, mineralogy, and religious issues was almost inevitable given his background, interests, and life's work. The narrator-hero in the novel, William Garame, is much less an image of his real-life counterpart than he is a reflection of many of Ruffner's personal experiences and preoccupations. Certain elements of the tale also suggest Ruffner's criticism of and hopes for his own state and, more broadly, the South. A review of the highlights of Ruffner's life will provide further insight into *Judith Bensaddi*.[6]

Henry Ruffner was descended from a line of dynamic pioneers on the Virginia frontier whose physical vitality and innovative outlook were well known and respected. The Ruffner stock was German-Swiss Mennonite in origin, and the family had come to the Shenandoah Valley from Lancaster County, Pennsylvania. Peter, the first of the American Ruffners, settled in Virginia as a result of his father-in-law's gift to him of a royal patent for a large tract in what is now Page County. He extended his holdings several times over the years and at his death in 1788 was "one of the largest land-holders and most prosperous farmers in the Shenandoah Valley."[7]

One of Peter's four sons, Joseph, Henry's grandfather, developed a variety of skills in addition to that of farming. On his 1,200 acres of land he built saw and grist mills and became a hauler of bear skins from the backwoods to the market town of Fredericksburg. In 1793 Joseph moved westward to the untamed Kanawha country, where he

5. Elizabeth Preston Allan, "Notes on William Alexander Caruthers," *William and Mary Quarterly*, 2nd ser., IX (1929), 295.

6. There is no full-length biography of Henry Ruffner, but a number of sources provide the biographical data presented here: *Dictionary of American Biography*, XVI, 217–18; William Henry Ruffner, "The Ruffners: Henry. First Article," *West Virginia Historical Magazine*, Vol. II, No. 2, pp. 60–74, and "The Ruffners: Henry. Second Article," Vol. II, No. 3, pp. 36–44; Samuel S. Britt, Jr., "Henry Ruffner, Nineteenth-Century Educator," (Ph.D. dissertation, University of Arizona, 1962); Walter Javan Frazer, "William Henry Ruffner: A Liberal in the Old and New South," (Ph.D. dissertation, University of Tennessee, 1970).

7. Frazer, "William Henry Ruffner," 2.

bought some 500 acres and a salt spring five miles north of what is now Charleston, West Virginia, at Kanawha Salines. By the end of 1795 all of Joseph's family except David, his oldest son, had moved to the remote Kanawha outpost. David, Henry Ruffner's father, remained in Page County to supervise the still-active Ruffner mills. The next year David and his wife, the former Ann Brumbach, daughter of a Mennonite minister, moved to his father's home within the relative security of the Clendennin blockhouse. With them they brought their six-year-old son, Henry, born January 16, 1790.

On the death of his father in 1803, David received various properties, including an interest in the salt spring, whose potential had not been developed during his father's life. With his brother Joseph, David began in 1808 the arduous labor required to begin salt production, and until the 1850s the Ruffner saltworks was a major supplier to the meat-packing center of Cincinnati. Over the years the Ruffners used their wealth and ingenuity to improve both the salt-making process and social conditions in Kanawha County.

By 1814 David Ruffner had become the sole proprietor of the saltworks, and with his son, Henry, as a helper he instituted a number of innovations. David first substituted locally mined coal for the wood formerly used to heat the salt brine in the evaporation process. Henry suggested a novel method, using steam, to make removal of the coal cinders from the grate bars easier. The Ruffners also developed new methods to achieve deeper drilling for brine; these included the use of a steel drill bit with casing and tubing to draw the salt water to the surface. The well, which eventually reached a depth of seventy-eight feet through stone, became a model for similar operations, and the tools and methods developed for it were precursors of those to be used in the yet unknown petroleum industry.[8]

David Ruffner represented a cultural departure from most of his German neighbors, and it was this disparity, along with his inventiveness, that formed a role model for Henry in later life. As well as being athletic, David, unlike most others in his region, was a believer in education and books. Even as a teenager, he maintained a

8. Gerald Forbes, "The Civil War and the Beginning of the Oil Industry in West Virginia," *West Virginia History*, VIII (1947), 383–84.

personal library and subscribed to newspapers. His interest in culture was complemented by a variety of civic and political commitments, including four decades as a magistrate in Kanawha County and several terms in the Virginia House of Delegates. He was also intrumental in founding several area schools and churches, though he himself was not of a strong religious inclination. Like his father, Henry Ruffner was to become a strong-willed individual, an imaginative innovator and reformer, devoted to the concept that education and hard work were the keys to worldly success for the struggling people of western Virginia.

Most of Henry Ruffner's early years were taken up with three interests: helping his father on the farm and at the saltworks, reading every book he could lay hands on, and participating in the boyhood sports usual to the region, such as fishing and raccoon hunting. While always physically active, Henry Ruffner was too sober minded and intellectually inclined to remain merely a sportsman or gentleman farmer. With his father's influence and his own rich intelligence, he was destined for loftier pursuits.

Ruffner began to discover his future vocations while a student in the newly founded classical academy of the Reverend Dr. John McElhenney at Lewisburg. During his student days at the academy, from 1809 to 1811, Ruffner was introduced to the two most vital forces of his life: education and Presbyterianism. McElhenny, a Presbyterian minister and graduate of Washington College, founded his academy on the crest of a rising local interest in the Presbyterian Church and a need for basic academic training. His influence was credited with turning young Henry Ruffner from being a self-styled "infidel" into a Calvinist with a passion for learning and what Ruffner later called a "restless imagination."

Ruffner began his college studies at McElhenney's alma mater in Lexington, in May, 1812. Washington College had begun as Liberty Hall Academy near Timber Ridge Church outside Lexington in 1776 with a grant from George Washington of one hundred shares of the James River Company. It was to become Washington and Lee University in 1870, soon after the presidency of Robert E. Lee. A voracious reader from childhood, Ruffner finished Washington College's four-year curriculum in less than a year and a half, graduating summa cum laude in the fall of 1813.

Ruffner's later scholarly reputation rests less on the quality of the curriculum at the college when he was a student there than on his own perceptiveness and hard work. Dr. William Alexander Caruthers, physician and novelist, suggested the dubious value of the courses at Washington College as late as 1820. "We got a little Latin and less Greek. Mathematics of which the measure would be the even root of a negative quantity. Physics on the homeopathic principle. Textbook Belles Lettres and superficial Philosophies. Yet the libraries of the Literary Societies provided good reading to occupy the leisure afforded by the curriculum."[9] Ruffner was exposed, at least, to a number of disciplines in which he would take a continuing interest: ancient and modern languages, mathematics, geography, astronomy, natural philosophy, and logic. Too, it was Henry Ruffner's later personal efforts and scholarly abilities that were in large measure responsible for the dramatic upgrading of the college's reputation for teaching and scholarship.

During his student years at Washington College, Ruffner taught courses at the grammar school connected with the college and developed an absorbing interest in theology. He studied this subject under the school's president, George A. Baxter, during the year after his graduation. During that time, at President Baxter's request, he also taught the language classes of the ailing Professor Daniel Blain at the college. Ruffner found teaching classical languages to college students to be rewarding. It was an experience whose lasting significance he could not have appreciated at the time.

In the fall of 1814 he began a year of travel through the eastern states and western territories, developing an eye for geographical detail and a love of exploration he would later express in a variety of works, including *Judith Bensaddi*. Ruffner's domestic grand tour helped him appreciate the rugged beauty and economic potential of his own region. Whether he consciously realized it or not, Ruffner's later-published adulations of western Virginia and the Shenandoah

9. Quoted in Allan, "Notes on William Alexander Caruther," 294–95.

Valley were as promotional in their own way as the early writings of Virginia's first "salesman," Captain John Smith.

Ready now to satisfy the helping instinct he had long nurtured, Ruffner returned to Lexington in Rockbridge County, where he was licensed to preach by the Lexington Presbytery on October 8, 1815. He immediately turned west to the Kanawha country, where he apparently thrived in the role of missionary to the impoverished and often unruly mountaineers. For much of his life "Ruffner held to the Jeffersonian ideal of a society in which the yeomanry would play a dominant part, but he contended that the yeomen must have the knowledge and discernment that would guide them to wise decisions and protect them from 'deceptious demogogues.'"[10] Ruffner willingly accepted the main currents of the Jacksonian era while despising its foolish excesses. His love of and respect for the western Virginia mountain yeomanry as well as his belief that they could flourish with guidance is frequently made clear in *Judith Bensaddi*. Ruffner also believed that education could channel the native vitality of the yeoman and significantly raise his social and economic status. On this point, C. C. Pearson has suggested that "as an exponent of its energy and hard sense and of its views on education, antebellum western Virginia had no better representative than Henry Ruffner."[11]

During his missionary days Ruffner preached at the Charleston courthouse and managed to organize two churches and a school intended primarily for the mountaineers. Ruffner began the school, Mercer Academy, in 1816, paying for much of its construction himself. He also served, without pay, as its first instructor. This type of generosity is fictionally repeated by the educated yeoman, William Garame, in *Seclusaval*, when he helps to found a school for mountain girls in the area of his model agricultural community. In developing his idealized Seclusaval, Henry Ruffner no doubt recalled David Ruffner's building of a town in the early 1830s near his saltworks. At Kanawha Salines numerous opportunities for work and commerce

---

10. Ollinger Crenshaw, *General Lee's College: The Rise and Growth of Washington and Lee University* (New York: Random House, 1969), 58.
11. *DAB*, XVI, 218.

drew a variety of laborers and merchants; yet David Ruffner's community differed from Henry's in that the latter is meant to be free of the boomtown vices that often plagued what was later to become Malden, West Virginia.

In March, 1819, Ruffner married Sarah Montgomery Lyle, daughter of militia captain William Lyle, a land-wealthy farmer, businessman, and the sheriff for Rockbridge County. Henry had met Sally Lyle during his student days at Washington College, and their union produced four children, one of whom, William Henry (1824–1908), became the first superintendent of education in Virginia and earned the appellation Horace Mann of the South. In the 1870s it was William Henry who was to institutionalize his father's earlier plan for a system of publicly supported schools in Virginia.

While reasonably satisfied with his success as a missionary and teacher, Ruffner changed his apparent career path shortly after his marriage. The ailing professor for whom Ruffner had substituted at Washington College died, and President Baxter, remembering Ruffner's highly competent teaching, offered him the professorship of ancient languages. Hoping to combine his love of scholarship with his more divine calling, Ruffner accepted. This appointment initiated a thirty-year relationship between Ruffner and the school, during which he served by turns as professor of languages, professor of mathematics, acting president, and finally, president and professor of moral philosophy.

During his presidency, from 1836 to 1848, Ruffner tirelessly pushed the college toward academic excellence. Toward that end, his normal weekday schedule put him at his office desk at 5 A.M. and rarely home before 9 P.M. or later. Teaching on Saturdays and preaching on Sundays were additions to an already strenuous work load. His college responsibilities and the need for some attention to business interests left all too little time for the needs of his family and contributed to a nervous condition that afflicted him later in life. In fact, one of the regrets of his last years was that he had set aside his early ministerial call to take up the rigors of a college professorship and presidency.

Until the last two, conflict-torn years of his presidency, however, there was general agreement that Ruffner had been the best choice as president. Prior to Ruffner's tenure, the college's reputation for scholarship had been pale in comparison with that of "Mr. Jefferson's university" in Charlottesville. Then, too, before Ruffner's installation as president, several men who held the office had had brief and decidedly unsuccessful incumbencies. Thus he had several opportunities to develop administrative expertise and upgrade the curriculum as acting president.

The college made numerous advances during Ruffner's presidency, and he was personally responsible for a variety of innovations. Despite the school's close connection with the Presbyterian Church, he insisted that it disavow sectarianism in its curriculum and choice of faculty and students. Because of his commitment to education for the disadvantaged, he admitted a number of "poor scholars" to the school each year. He worked vigorously to reverse the long-standing trends in lax discipline among the students and the overly generous marks awarded them by the professors. Science received more emphasis, and all the courses, most of which had been taught at low levels of sophistication, became more rigorous. Flying in the face of a currently accepted educational philosophy, Ruffner insisted that what the student learned was far more important than the mere exercise of his mental faculties. Finally, he instituted the then-novel concept of formal meetings of the college faculty, complete with minutes.

During his years as teacher and president, Ruffner maintained scholarly interests that further sated his curiosity and polished his widely known erudition. As often as his schedule allowed, he read scholarly and literary works in Latin, Greek, French, Spanish, German, and Italian. He also drafted a number of works on mathematics, mineralogy, political economy, and Hebrew grammar, which, according to his son William Henry, he never offered for publication. In the sciences he was regularly engaged in informal experimentation in astronomy, geology, ornamental horticulture, and more general aspects of agriculture, giving numerous lectures on agricultural reform to area farmers' groups. Ruffner earnestly believed that science was the pathway to wealth and that agriculture was much more a science than most believed. This opinion he shared with the earlier Virginia agricultural reformer, John Taylor of Caroline (1753–1824). A number of Ruffner's ideas about farming and landscaping appear graphically in *Seclusaval*, the sequel to *Judith Bensaddi*, including his belief that western Virginia was best suited to a pastoral mode of agricultural economy. If he could not, as he wished, persuade local farmers to take courses at the college, Ruffner was at least able to share his views through fiction.

Ruffner managed to maintain his reportedly eloquent and persuasive preaching skills by serving frequently in the pulpit at Timber Ridge Church, some seven miles from Lexington, and occasionally at churches in Fairfield and New Monmouth. He was well known for his ability to bring sinners into the fold and turn the intemperate from strong drink. On those Sundays when he did not preach at area churches, he gave lectures on Christianity and natural theology to students at Washington College. In his preaching and theological writing Ruffner attempted to balance reason with divine revelation, covering all with a mantle of functional scholarship. One of his earliest published works, *A Discourse Upon The Duration of Future Punishment* (1823), is embedded throughout with Biblical Greek and Hebrew phrases as well as translations.

A number of activities caused Ruffner's reputation to rise outside western Virginia. In 1838 he was awarded the Doctor of Divinity degree by Princeton. The honorary D.D. from this Presbyterian school was no doubt a result of the educational reforms initiated at Washington College during Ruffner's first two years as president as well as his scholarly publications in theology, which attracted widespread interest. In 1841 Ruffner became the chief figure at a multi-county educational convention in Virginia for which he wrote a major document promoting general public education.

The Proposed Plan for the Organization and Support of Common Schools in Virginia was based on a concept as yet unheard of in the state: district schools paid for by property taxes. Debated in the Virginia legislature, the plan was predictably attacked by the large landholders in the east, who considered education the perquisite of the wealthy. Despite continuing opposition, Ruffner's *Proposed Plan* was later adapted and instituted by William Henry after he became Virginia's superintendent of schools in 1870. In the early twentieth century a United States commissioner of education enthusiastically called Ruffner's 1841 essay "the most valuable document on general education issued by Virginia since the early days of Thomas Jefferson . . . [by] the most conspicuous leader of the progressive education public of the South at that early day."[12] It is no hyperbole to say that in the 1840s and 1850s Ruffner was the best-known and most-persistent voice in Virginia for state-supported schools.

In 1847 Ruffner wrote the work that earned him praise in the North and in western Virginia as well as undying enmity among the powerful eastern Virginia slaveholders. His *Address to the People of West Virginia* originated during a weeks-long debate sponsored by the well-known Franklin Society in Lexington. During the society's lengthy existence from 1800 to 1891, it counted among its membership such Virginians as Matthew Fontaine Maury, William Alexander Caruthers, Stonewall Jackson, and Robert E. Lee.[13] Ruffner's position in a February 27 speech given before the society was that Virginia should be partitioned at the Blue Ridge, with slavery to be confined to eastern Virginia and gradual emancipation, and possibly colonization, to begin in western Virginia as soon as possible. To demonstrate western Virginia's need to be free of slavery, Ruffner contrasted the economic vitality of the established free states to the decline of the older areas of slave states in which there were "too evident signs of stagnation or of positive decay—a sparse population—a slovenly cultivation spread out over vast fields that are wearing out, among others that are already worn out and desolate; villages and towns . . . often decaying . . . generally no manufacturing or even trades . . . commerce and navigation abandoned . . . to the people of the Free States" (*Address*, 12).

Although he probably never owned more than one slave at a time, Ruffner was himself an admitted practitioner of the peculiar institu-

12. *Report of the Commissioner of Education for the Year 1899–1900*, (Washington, D.C.: Government Printing Office, 1901), 437–38. Ruffner's *Proposed Plan* is discussed in some detail by Britt, "Henry Ruffner: Nineteenth-Century Educator."
13. Charles W. Turner, "The Franklin Society, 1800–1891," *Virginia Magazine of History and Biography*, LXVI (1958), 432–47.

tion. Had he not been a slaveowner, of course, Ruffner would have had little credibility with those whom he tried to persuade. His stated aversion to slavery was wisely based more on avowedly economic and sectional motives than on moral ones. He saw slavery as an inhibiting factor in the development of the yeomanry of his own section, since it drove many of the laboring class westward from the region and reduced interest in the industrial development desperately needed in western Virginia. The scholarly Ruffner used United States census data from 1790 through 1840 in his *Address* to demonstrate that the agricultural economy in the east had been enervated by a dependence on slavery and, with it, inefficient agricultural practices. Nine years earlier, in *Judith Bensaddi*, Ruffner dwelled on the shortsightedness of the abolitionists' arguments while favorably comparing southern agricultural slavery with the allegedly insidious English industrial variety, a common defensive posture among southerners of the 1840s and 1850s. The Edenic and progressive agricultural community of the fictional Seclusaval in *Judith Bensaddi* is intended to succeed without the taint of slavery, which even in western Virginia's "smaller doses, mix them as you will, are sure to sicken and debilitate the body politic" (*Address*, 15).

To argue against the institution of slavery on ethical or religious grounds alone, as the hated abolitionists had done, would have invited disaster despite what Ruffner might have personally believed. Looking back after twelve years at the episode of the Ruffner Pamphlet, as the *Address* was commonly called, Ruffner recalled: "No one, so far as I remember, took the abolitionist ground that slaveholding is a sin and ought for that reason to be abolished. With us it was merely a question of expediency and was argued with special reference to the interest of West[ern] Virginia."[14]

The timing of the Ruffner Pamphlet was highly unfortunate since the once-popular antislavery sentiment in eastern Virginia had generally evaporated after 1832 and had become muted in western Virginia by 1847. One student of the controversial document has called

---

14. *Kanawha Valley Star*, August 3, 1858, quoted in Charles Henry Ambler, *Sectionalism in Virginia from 1776 to 1861* (Chicago: University of Chicago Press, 1910), 245.

it "the last public effort in the Old Dominion to rekindle interest in this old Jeffersonian dream."[15] Although he had always repudiated what he called the "fanatical violence" of northern and British abolitionists, Ruffner was branded an abolitionist in the eastern newspapers because of his pamphlet. His early supporters in the West, those who had loudly called for a large press run of the *Address*, generally abandoned him after its publication.

Pleading poor health, Ruffner resigned the presidency of Washington College in June, 1848. Indeed, his formerly robust health had begun to decline, as had that of his wife, an arthritic, who died seven months after his resignation. There is little doubt, however, that the wave of criticism against Ruffner's antislavery stance hastened the end of his administration. His involvement in local disputes within the Presbyterian Church—where he had often been a peacemaker— and the neglect of his Kanawha properties were also contributing factors in his decision.

Ruffner's departure from Washington College, which awarded him the LL.D. in 1849, did not signal a retirement from either controversy or work. After Sally Ruffner's death, Henry went to Louisville, Kentucky, to participate in the ill-fated emancipation debate still active there. His involvement was invited and no doubt based on the widespread knowledge of the persuasiveness of the author of the Ruffner Pamphlet. While his Virginia support had effectively vanished, Ruffner's voice was still welcome in other southern locales, and until the Civil War, "Trans-Allegheny Ruffnerism continued to be a potent force."[16] Ruffner spent the summer of 1849 at the library of Lane Theological Seminary in Cincinnati. There he read widely for his most scholarly work, *The Fathers of the Desert*, a two-volume, critical history of monasticism published in 1852. Ruffner's interest in historical research had been enlivened through his activity as a member of the Virginia Historical Society.

He left Cincinnati for his beloved Kanawha mountains in 1850 with his second wife, the former Laura J. Kirby, and his oldest daugh-

15. William Gleason Bean, "The Ruffner Pamphlet of 1847: An Antislavery Aspect of Virginia Sectionalism," *Virginia Magazine of History and Biography*, LXI (1953), 275.
16. *Ibid.*, 282.

ter to take up farming once more. He had apparently forgotten the lesson he learned as a young man: the farmer's life ill suited his scholar's temperament. He soon put aside the plow and returned to the pulpit, this time at the church founded by his father in Malden. He held this position until a year before his death, putting the finishing touches on his "Early History of Washington College" and delivering the fruitless, though impassioned, "Union speech," in 1856. To the end, Ruffner maintained his pro-Union, antislavery position despite an ever-increasing hostility to such views. In his last months he continued to predict in the western papers the ultimate decline of what was to become a war-torn Virginia. Before his death on December 17, 1861, Ruffner saw one of his worst fears realized in Virginia's secession, but he failed to see two of his most cherished dreams attained: comprehensive public education and independence for western Virginia.

Ruffner's liberal idealism was upheld after his death by two members of his family. William Henry endured a strong barrage of criticism for his proposal that schools be built for black children as well as white. Henry's younger brother, General Lewis Ruffner, attempted unsuccessfully to promote racial harmony in the Kanawha area in the postbellum years, and Lewis's Yankee wife, Viola, earned her own measure of historical importance as the early teacher and benefactor of Booker T. Washington at Kanawha Salines. The liberalism of Henry Ruffner and his family seems tame by today's standards, but in its day and place it was unquestionably heretical. A twentieth-century commentator on Ruffner, Charles W. Dabney, suggests that while his contemporaries often criticized and even feared his apparently dangerous educational and social opinions, Ruffner was clearly a wise and patriotic man, merely ahead of his time.[17]

Remembering his pastoral colleague, a Virginia minister recalled his impression of Henry Ruffner in a passage that characterizes the air of unshakable resolve by which he was best known.

His appearance would have attracted the eye of any intelligent observer. He was six feet in height, erect, broad shouldered, with a deep chest, a coal-

17. Charles W. Dabney, *Universal Education in the South*, (2 vols.; Chapel Hill: University of North Carolina Press, 1936), I, 82.

black eye, and hair as dark. His face was always serious, calm and thoughtful. His manner was kind and gentle, though somewhat reserved. He was a
friend through good and evil report. He did not fear the face of man. Had
duty called him, he would have marched in a forlorn hope for the benefit of
church or country with as much deliberation as he walked to his class-
room. His modesty was proverbial. His charity was like the flowing
streams of his mountain home, widening and deepening as they advance.
Scandal stood abashed in his honest presence. In his stainless name, his
domestic, social, college and pastoral life, he was an Israelite indeed in
whom there were no guile. None ever merited better the doctorates conferred on him, and none ever bore so modestly the many notices of his literature and scholarship. He was a diligent student through a long life, and
his well-trained mind was stored with the most varied and accurate learning in all branches of science, literature and theology.[18]

Henry Ruffner's own account of a guileless Israelite in *Judith Bensaddi* had its stimulus in an incident related to him by his wife,
probably in 1827 or early 1828. Sally Ruffner received an evening visitor from Lexington, Dr. William Alexander Graham, a graduate of
Washington College and brother of a professor at the school. Ruffner
did not hear the "affecting tale" told Mrs. Ruffner by Graham until
after the visitor's departure, but its recitation caused him to rush ex-
citedly to his desk and compose a first draft of the brief 1828 version
of *Judith Bensaddi*. Even in the sketchy outlines of the biographical
account, Ruffner quickly saw potential for an attention-catching tale
with a universal moral, which to Ruffner's homiletic and didactic
point of view was the chief purpose of fiction.

While their length, plot details, and outcomes vary, the two versions of *Judith Bensaddi*, published in 1828 and 1839, are clearly indebted to Dr. Graham's personal story, whose essentials were later
recalled by William Henry Ruffner.

Dr. Graham took ship at some Southern port—Savannah perhaps—intending to disembark at some point convenient for reaching Lexington, Va. He
found among the passengers on the ship a brother and sister of the Jewish
race, whose home was in England & who were now travelling in the U.S.
They were interesting & cultivated people & the sister beautiful. Young
Graham, a gallant bachelor, was not slow in making the acquaintance of

18. Rev. John Leyburn [?], [1871?], quoted in Ruffner, "The Ruffners: Henry. *West Virginia Historical Magazine*, Vol. II, No. 3, p. 43.

this inviting looking pair, though it was sometime before he was informed of their Hebrew blood. The new friends seemed mutually pleased, & as the sailing packet was slow compared with a modern steamer there was a good prospect for a social voyage of several days. But alas! their newfound happiness was suddenly destroyed by a lurch of the vessel, by which the brother was thrown into the sea & drowned. The sister naturally became wild with grief & was so manifestly helpless that Graham not only did all in his power to soothe her but offered to go with her to New York & place her on some vessel bound for Liverpool. By the time this was accomplished, they were much interested in each other & agreed to correspond. Letters passed between them for a time, but no important event followed.[19]

In developing the character of the fictional William Garame, or Garay in the earlier version, Ruffner retained Dr. Graham's acknowledged gentility, education, and intellectual curiosity. The real Graham, unfortunately, was also something of a ne'er-do-well, whose checkered career included law, medicine, gold prospecting, and invention (a carbon dioxide fire extinguisher). Most of the positive values and experiences of young William Garame, however, can be more specifically compared with those of Henry Ruffner.

In addition to his adaptation of Dr. Graham's personal narrative, Ruffner, one of the most widely read Virginians of his day, made use of a variety of literary and traditional sources in the 1839 version of his story. Several rural characters in George Tucker's fictional critique of Virginia's social and economic weaknesses, *The Valley of Shenandoah* (1824), closely resemble some of Ruffner's minor figures. There is an obvious indebtedness to Sir Walter Scott's Jewish Rebecca in *Ivanhoe* (1820) and to Scott's use of symbolism in *The Talisman* (1825). Ruffner probably also knew *Harrington* (1817), by the English novelist Maria Edgeworth, whose attitude toward the Jew-Gentile intermarriage issue is even more ambiguous than Ruffner's. The bower-of-bliss motif of the wedding feast in Ruffner's *Seclusaval* sequel is most likely based on Edmund Spenser's English marriage song, *Epithalamion*. Ruffner's fascination with romantic "lofty crags" was hardly original. Curtis Carroll Davis has noted twenty-six literary quotations in *Judith Bensaddi* and has identified

19. Penciled manuscript dated "Lexington, Va., January 6, 1904," in the Historical Foundation of the Presbyterian and Reformed Churches, Montreat, N.C.

sources for sixteen of them, including works by Ovid, Homer, Milton, Shakespeare and Goldsmith.[20]

Even in works by Virginia writers, the problems of cross-cultural, or transracial, romance were not new, and Ruffner could look back to a short work by John Davis to find an early literary treatment of Virginia's most famous love story. Davis' *First Settlers of Virginia* (1805) is a fictional and historical rendering of the affair between Captain John Smith and Pocahontas. Whether Ruffner perceived the parallel between his own dark, exotic heroine and Smith's savior is debatable, but the symbolic union of the Old World and New World characters in both works is significant. The liberal Ruffner was certainly no xenophobe, and he populated his Seclusaval with an English gardener and French Hugenots as well as members of the native Virginia yeomanry.

In terms of sources, it would be pointless to make too much of the name Bensaddi except to suggest Ruffner's erudition. A reader and author of religious works, Ruffner may have known the allegorical tale *A Fragment of the Chronicles of Nathan Ben Saddi* (Philadelphia, 1758). This short piece turns on the unjust arrest of one Reverend Dr. Smith. It is perhaps only coincidence that the victimized father of Ruffner's Judith is also named Nathan. More likely, the scholarly Ruffner, who planned a Hebrew grammar, was familiar with the Hebrew word *t'saddi*, meaning "a righteous person," "a doer of good deeds." Ruffner could not have selected a more appropriate name for Judith, whose righteousness, generosity, and innocence are played against the vacillation and perfidiousness that often surround her.

In fact, it is Judith's virtue that detracts from her characterization. This enthusiastic but reflective Jewish woman is simply too good to be true. Her long-suffering disposition fails at first to persuade the indecisive Garame that her character transcends religious objections. Yet it is finally her many virtues, especially that of fidelity (her family motto), that win over the falsely proud Garame. While it is unlikely that Ruffner personally knew enough Jews to present what

20. "*Judith Bensaddi* and the Reverend Doctor Henry Ruffner," 142.

the modern reader would sense as a realistic portrayal of the details of Judith's Jewish nature, he undoubtedly knew much of the development of their history and their current status in his own region.

The positive reception given Ruffner's *Judith Bensaddi* is partly attributable to the generally low level of antisemitism that prevailed in the United States between the Revolution and the Civil War. During the antebellum period, there was a marked shift in the southern states away from the voting, property, and religious-oath laws that had so clearly discriminated against Jews in both southern and northern colonies. In the South the democratic impulses of the post-Revolutionary period led to enfranchisement for Jews in 1787 in Virginia, 1790 in South Carolina, and 1798 in Georgia. In those southern states where Jewish populations were small—North Carolina and Maryland—discriminatory statutes remained in effect somewhat longer.[21] (It was not until 1823 in Maryland, for example, that the tireless work of a Scotch Presbyterian, Thomas Kennedy, resulted in the passage of an antidiscrimination bill favoring the state's Jews.) Principally in the South's few urban areas, there even developed a durable attitude of friendly acceptance based on the broad variety of significant contributions made by Jewish citizens.

As a colony and later as a state, South Carolina was an American leader in tolerance toward its Jewish minority, especially in the period from 1800 to 1860. The Jews of South Carolina originally settled in the areas around Charleston and Georgetown, and many developed enviable reputations as legislators, lawyers, bankers, teachers, newspaper editors, and physicians. It would be difficult to label as simple coincidence that Ruffner's elusive Dr. La Motte of the Charleston area bears essentially the same name as the well-known Jacob De La Motta, a Jewish physician in practice after 1810 in Charleston.[22] While Ruffner surely knew Dr. De La Motta's reputation as a physician, he was no doubt also aware of his position as secretary of the Charleston Literary and Philosophical Society and

21. Leonard Dinnerstein and Mary Dale Palsson (eds.), *Jews in the South* (Baton Rouge: Louisiana State University Press, 1973), 5–6.

22. Barnett A. Elzas, *The Jews of South Carolina from the Earliest Time to the Present Day* (Philadelphia: Lippincott, 1905), 179–81.

his writings and lectures on scientific topics, which were printed in area newspapers.

Ruffner probably knew of the relatively small Beth Shalome Congregation in Richmond, and there is little doubt that he was familiar with the widely known Jewish community of Charleston. By 1820, this group constituted 5 percent of the white population of that city, and by 1800 its Beth Elohim Congregation was the largest Jewish community in America. The roots of this congregation, purely Orthodox until 1824, were clearly tied to the Iberian community of Bevis Marks in London, partly through the immigration of a small number of Portuguese Jews from London to Charleston and partly as a result of the Charleston group's strict adherence to the ritual of the London congregation.[23] That Ruffner's Judith Bensaddi and her brother, Eli, are from London and stop at the port cities of Savannah and Charleston on their southern travels is no accident of travel itinerary, for the well-read and widely traveled Ruffner was aware of the concentration of Jews in coastal cities as opposed to the more inland and rural areas like as his own. The open-mindedness of Judith on religious matters may be connected to the liberal Ruffner's probable approval of the well-publicized movement in 1824 of a portion of the Beth Elohim Congregation to reform the group's rigid orthodoxy. This event is of historical importance because it was the first effort in America toward Reform Judaism; and it would have pleased Ruffner, since it signified, in part, an effort to reduce hardened differences between Judaism and Christianity.[24]

In the antebellum period, to a far greater extent than today, the need for assimilation was a necessary reality from the Jewish point of view. Such was the case to avoid the vulnerability caused by their "strangeness," and the joining of Masonic orders as well as intermarriage were among the methods used to achieve this goal. Concern about intermarriage as an erosive factor in maintaining the integrity of the Jews as a people was less evident among American Jews of this period than it has been in the twentieth century. More likely to have

23. *Ibid.*, 131–32, 147.
24. See Morris U. Schappes (ed.), *A Documentary History of the Jews in the United States, 1654–1875* (New York: Schocken, 1971), 171–77.

been an urban than a rural phenomenon, intermarriages were apparently not uncommon, though actual conversions to Christianity seem to have been rare.[25] Despite what the modern reader may think of Ruffner's eventual—and offstage—conversion of Judith to Christianity, there were a number of conversion stories, circulated by missionaries in the South and elsewhere, that Ruffner likely knew.[26] Their purpose was that of using Jewish characters—genuine exotics in most of Virginia—to capture the imagination of the irreligious Gentiles on the southern frontier.

Ruffner's concern and sympathy with minority groups was not limited to the Jews, for his ideal community in the novel, Seclusaval, was to be heavily populated with imported French Hugenots—themselves an often-scorned, but industrious, minority in the South. Ruffner realized that if his dream of a slaveless society in the western rural South were to become a reality, such a social order would require the joint effort of all its diverse elements, regardless of their origins. It was his desire to halt the spread of the enslavement of the South's largest minority group, of course, that played a major role in prematurely ending Ruffner's career.

Henry Ruffner's apparently liberal attitude toward the Jews—one not always shared by his fellow rural southerners, as *Judith Bensaddi* makes painfully clear—reappears in the work of his son William Henry. Both as a minister and as superintendent of public education, William Henry kept in touch with the rabbis of several Virginia congregations. In his first report to the State Board of Public Education he devoted three pages to praise of the state's Jewish communities in their unfailing support of education, both in the public sector and through the various Hebrew schools across the state.[27]

25. Malcolm Stern suggests that until 1840 as much as 15 percent of the American Jewish population had intermarried, in "The Function of Genealogy in American Jewish History," in *Essays in American Jewish History* (Cincinnati: American Jewish Archives, 1958), 85. See also Bertram W. Korn, "Factors Bearing Upon the Survival of Judaism in the Ante-bellum Period," *American Jewish Historical Quarterly*, LXIII (1964), 343.

26. See, for example, "'The Converted Jew,' An Affecting Tale, 1821," in Joseph L. Blau and Salo W. Baron (eds.), *The Jews of the United States, 1790–1840: A Documentary History*, (3 vols.; New York: Columbia University Press, 1963), III, 711–13.

27. Herbert T. Ezekiel and Gaston Lichtenstein, *The History of the Jews of Richmond from 1769 to 1917* (Richmond, Va.: Herbert T. Ezekiel, 1917), 227.

The chief purpose of Ruffner's novel, of course, was not the propagation of the Gospel, for he reminds the reader in strong terms that Christ was a Jew, includes some unflattering portraits of "Christians," and has his protagonist decide to marry Judith even before he learns of her conversion. Actually, the thematic emphasis of *Judith Bensaddi* is not primarily religious; rather it is concerned with the validity of human instincts, the morality of the pure heart. Early in both versions of his "narrative somewhat instructive and affecting," Ruffner states his desire to demonstrate the importance of determined, positive action in the face of imagined barriers and "the blindness and weakness of human nature." This concept is closely related to a major element of sentimental fiction: "a belief in the spontaneous goodness and benevolence of man's original instincts."[28] It finally becomes clear to the wavering Garame that his instinctive and deep love for the beautiful and sensitive Judith can overpower his socially developed prejudices and artificial fears of her "racial" background. It is a credit to Ruffner's skill as a writer that despite the sentimental rhetoric used to develop the theme, he convincingly captures the reckless devotion, imagined slights, and paranoid jealousies that by turns are a part of Garame's passion. The novel's happy conclusion suggests Ruffner's secondary moral: suffering and virtue pay, eventually.

Less clearly articulated in the novel, but unquestionably present, is a second tale of love, that of Henry Ruffner for the mountainous terrain of western Virginia. When he speaks of his "habitual feeling of patriotism," Ruffner, like Jefferson, means his own region and specifically the valley of Virginia and the rugged Kanawha region. Country pleasures are favorably compared in the novel to the stifling artificiality of city life; the mountains are declared more wholesome than the tidal plains; and it is implied that Ruffner's poor mountaineers are more virtuous than the most fashionable aristocrats of the decaying tidewater establishment.

The grandeur of the valley of Virginia and the Blue Ridge Moun-

---

28. Herbert Ross Brown, *The Sentimental Novel in America, 1789–1860.* (Chapel Hill: University of North Carolina Press, 1940), 176.

tains has evoked enthusiastic response from travelers, novelists, and poets since its exploration by Governor Alexander Spotswood in 1716.[29] Its best known geological feature, the Natural Bridge, has been one of the area's major tourist attractions at least since Jefferson's description of it as the "most sublime of Nature's works."[30] The bridge, about thirteen miles from Ruffner's Lexington home, is given rapturous and detailed treatment in *Judith Bensaddi* as is the country around the twin peaks of the House Mountains, visible to Ruffner from the buildings of Washington College. Within a ten-mile radius of Ruffner's home in a bend of Buffalo Creek are numerous sites mentioned in the novel, including the Zollman estate, once known as Seclusaval.[31]

Because the majority of its characters, scenes, and attitudes are antithetical to those of the plantation country, it would be improper to classify *Judith Bensaddi* as a "plantation novel" like John Pendleton Kennedy's *Swallow Barn* (1832). Because of Ruffner's sectional orientation and because of the hero's excursions into the mountains of northern Georgia, North Carolina, and western South Carolina, even the label "Virginia novel" is questionable. In fact, Ruffner may have been one of the earliest writers of what might best be termed "southern Appalachian fiction," a genre whose inception is usually credited to Mary Noailles Murfress in the 1880s.

It would be difficult, using today's critical standards, to make a case for *Judith Bensaddi* as a well-wrought novel; by any criteria it is the work of an admitted amateur. It depends heavily on such devices of sentimental fiction as incredible coincidences, near misses, untimely deaths, didactic passages, and frequent outbursts of emotion; and its structure is marred by Ruffner's difficulty in meshing the love theme with his adulation of the mountain country. The thin plot is slow moving and burdened by lengthy interpolations, but

29. William Alexander Caruthers, Ruffner's contemporary, chronicled Spotswood's expedition and described the Blue Ridge in his novel *The Knights of the Golden Horseshoe* (1845), and it is likely that he had read Ruffner's description of the terrain in *Judith Bensaddi*.

30. Thomas Jefferson, *Notes on the State of Virginia*, ed. William Peden (1787; rpr. Chapel Hill: University of North Carolina Press, 1955), 24.

31. Davis, "*Judith Bensaddi* and the Reverend Doctor Henry Ruffner," 137.

what saves *Judith Bensaddi* in a literary sense is its local-color passages and the empathy the readers of Ruffner's day and ours have for the timeless emotions of its two chief characters.

What makes *Judith Bensaddi* most important, however, is not its literary qualities but its historical significance. Ruffner was willing to deal sympathetically with "the Jewish question" at a time and a place in which such an attitude was dangerous. Even the harshest twentieth-century commentator on the novel, Louis Harap, admits that "it is at least faithful to reality in its anti-Jewish attitudes" of the period.[32] Its widespread appeal to readers in both the North and the South suggests a great deal about the interests and tastes of the American reading public of the period.[33] Ruffner's sustained glorification of the Valley of Virginia is perhaps unmatched by any earlier account and few that follow. Finally, *Judith Bensaddi* suggests the hopes of a religious and educational leader in emerging western Virginia for political and economic parity of his struggling region with that of the more sophisticated East.

---

32. Louis Harap, *The Image of the Jew in American Literature* (Philadelphia: Jewish Publication Society of America, 1974), 76.

33. Davis, in *"Judith Bensaddi* and the Reverend Doctor Henry Ruffner," 136–39, summarizes several favorable reviews that suggest the novel was known at least as far north as New York and at least as far west as Huntsville, Alabama.

A Ruffner Checklist

Ruffner's works published during his lifetime span a period of almost four decades from 1822 to 1859. While he was not a prolific writer, his output was relatively steady given his numerous responsibilities, and he displayed an interest in a variety of subject areas. Only those works clearly attributable to Ruffner are cited here. Not included are sermons and regular contributions, published anonymously in area newspapers such as the *Kanawha Valley Star* and *Kanawha Republican*. A number of Ruffner's works were reprinted; only first instances of publication, however, are here noted. The only work published after Ruffner's death, the well-researched "Early History of Washington College" (1890), was originally to have appeared in the *Southern Literary Messenger*; but the editor ultimately rejected it because of the furor created by Ruffner's persistent pro-Union, anti-slavery stance.

Published Works

Address to the People of West Virginia Shewing That Slavery Is Injurious to the Public Welfare and That It May Be Gradually Abolished Without Detriment to the Rights and Interests of Slaveholders. By a Slaveholder of West Virginia. Lexington, Va.: R. C. Noel, 1847.

Annual Address Delivered Before the Franklin Society of Lexington on the 17th Day of January, 1838. Richmond, Va.: T. W. White, 1838.

Centennial Address Delivered at the Church of Timber Ridge in Rockbridge County, Virginia, October 3rd, 1856. Lexington, Va.: Smith and Fuller, 1857.

"Cincinnati Address Delivered at Washington College, June 28, 1838," *Southern Literary Messenger*, IV (1838), 792–96.

A Discourse Upon the Duration of Future Punishment. Richmond, Va.: N. Pollard, 1823.

"Early History of Washington College," *Washington and Lee University Historical Papers.* Baltimore: Washington and Lee University, 1890, pp. 1–150.

"The House Mountain in Virginia," *Souvenir* (Philadelphia), II (October 15, 1828), 126.

"Essays on the Early Language and Literature of England," *Southern Literary Messenger*, XIII (1847), 307–12, 373–80, 479–85.

The Fathers of the Desert; or, An Account of the Origin and Practice of Monkery Among Heathen Nations, Its Passage into the Church, and Some Wonderful Stories of the Fathers Concerning the Primitive Monks and Hermits. 2 vols.; New York: Baker and Scribner, 1850.

Inaugural Address By Henry Ruffner, President of Washington College, Virginia, Delivered on The Twenty-Second of February, 1837. Lexington, Virginia: [Board of Trustees], 1837.

"Judith Bensaddi: A Tale Founded on Fact," *Souvenir*, II (1828), 24–25, 33–36.

"Judith Bensaddi: A Tale, Revised and Enlarged by the Author" and "Seclusaval; or, the Sequel to the Tale of 'Judith Bensaddi,'" *Southern Literary Messenger*, V (1839), pp. 469–505 and 638–62, respectively.

"The Kanawha Mountains," *Southern Literary Messenger*, XXII (1856), 174–78.

"Kanawha Pieces. By an Old Man of Kanawha" [a series of fictional and autobiographical sketches], in the *Southern Literary Messenger*, XXII (1856): "The Sycamore and the Honey Locusts," 348–51, "Ben Newlan's Leap," 351–55, "Augustus Woodward," 355–59, "Little Bobby Willson," 359–63; and XXIII (1856): "The Disappointed Bridegroom," 47–50, and "A Screech," 50–54.

"Literary Recreations: Modern Magic," *Southern Literary Messenger*, VI (1840), 628–40.

"Literary Recreations: The Rescued Novice," *Southern Literary Messenger*, VI (1840), 804–11.

"Literary Recreations: The Yankee and the Duellist," *Southern Literary Messenger*, VI (1840), 733–36.

"Miracles Considered as an Evidence of Christianity." In *Lectures on the Evidence of Christianity*, edited by William Henry Ruffner. Charlottesville, Virginia: University of Virginia, 1852, pp. 60–107.

[With] J. D. Ewing and Francis H. Smith. "Memorial of the Rockbridge Agricultural Society on Common Schools." *Journal of the House of Delegates of Virginia, Session 1840–41*, Document No. 40. Richmond, Va.: Samuel Shepherd, 1840.

"Notes of a Tour from Virginia to Tennessee in the Months of July and August, 1838," *Southern Literary Messenger*, V (1839), 44–48, 137–41, 206–10, 269–73.

Outlines of a Plan for the Improvement of the Common Schools in Virginia, Prepared at the Request of the Kanawha Lyceum, in "Education Convention of Northwest Virginia [at Clarksburg, September 8–9, 1841]." *Journal of the House of Delegates of Virginia, Session 1841–42*, Document No. 7. Richmond, Va.: Samuel Sheperd, 1841.

The Predestinarian: A Treatise on the Decrees of God. Lexington, Va.: V. M. Mason, 1823.

Proposed Plan for the Organization and Support of Common Schools in Virginia, Prepared and Presented to the Legislature at the Request of a School Convention Held in Lexington on the Seventh Day of October, Eighteen Hundred and Forty-one, and Composed of Delegates from the Counties of Bath, Augusta, and Rockbridge. Journal of the House of Delegates of Virginia, Session 1841–42, Document No. 35. Richmond, Va.: Samuel Shepherd, 1841.

Review of Ellwood Fisher's Lecture on the North and the South. Louisville, Ky.: n.p. 1849.

Review of the Controversy Between the Methodists and Presbyterians in Central Virginia. Richmond, Va.: J. Macfarlan, 1829.

Strictures on a Book Entitled "An Apology for the Book of Psalms" by Gilbert McMaster, to Which Will Be Added Remarks on a Book Entitled "The Design and Use of the Book of Psalms" by Alexander Gordon. Lexington, Va.: V. M. Mason, 1822.

To the People of Virginia! John Letcher and His Antecedents. Read and Circulate. Richmond, Va.: Whig Book and Job Office, 1859.

Union Speech Delivered at Kanawha Salines [Virginia], on the Fourth of July, 1856. Cincinnati: Applegate, 1856.

Manuscripts

Three repositories house unpublished material relating to the Ruffner family. The majority of that material written by and about Henry Ruffner is at the Historical Foundation of the Presbyterian and Reformed Churches in Montreat, North Carolina. This collection, Papers of Henry Ruffner and William Henry Ruffner, was donated by the Reverend Robert F. Campbell, whose personal papers at Montreat also contain Ruffner material. Two collections in the West Virginia University Library in Morgantown, West Virginia, include Ruffner family material: the Roy Bird Cook Papers and the general genealogical materials collection. The McCormick Library at Washington and Lee University in Lexington, Virginia, houses a variety of Ruffner's sermons, lecture notes, and notebooks.

A Note on the Text

There are two distinct versions of *Judith Bensaddi* in serial form and
an unverified pamphlet edition of the second version reported by
William Henry Ruffner. The earlier serial version is a five-page
sketch published as the lead item in two 1828 numbers of a short-
lived literary journal, the *Souvenir* of Philadelphia. The second
version, "revised and enlarged by the author" to sixty-two pages of
six-point type, appeared in the more prestigious *Southern Literary
Messenger* in 1839. This version was later reprinted, probably without consultation with Ruffner, in the 1850 volume of the *Messenger*.
Though called a sequel because it appeared in a later number, the Seclusaval section is clearly an integral part of the second version of
Judith Bensaddi. In unpublished footnotes to his history of Washington and Lee University, Ollinger Crenshaw points out yet another
source, apparently identical to the *Messenger's* text, in the July and
August, 1839, numbers of the Lexington (Virginia) *Gazette*. The text
was reprinted in the March and April, 1871, numbers of the same
newspaper.

The present text, the *Messenger's* 1839 version, is altered only in
terms of the modernization of mechanics. In spelling, for example,
staid becomes *stayed*, and *vallies* is changed to *valleys*. Typographi-
cal errors are eliminated. Ruffner's untempered generosity with the
comma is restrained for modern taste and usage, and several painfully rambling sentences are partitioned. Archaic words or phrases
(for example, *whilst* and *one while*) are kept, and other changes that
might editorially dilute the flavor of Ruffner's style are avoided.

JUDITH BENSADDI
A TALE

Second edition, revised and enlarged
by the author

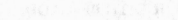

Preface to the Second Edition

Ten years ago the author heard at bedtime some extraordinary incidents that had befallen a young friend of his. The romantic character of these incidents so excited his fancy that he could not sleep until a tale was fabricated out of the materials and the mind had unburdened itself by putting its conceptions on paper. After a hasty revision this effusion of a restless imagination was sent to the press. It was published in a literary periodical of Philadelphia and, to the author's mortification, a good deal blurred by a foul typography. It was copied, errors and all, into several country papers, and in spite of defects, whether in authorship or typography, the natural interest of the story caused it to be considerably read and admired.

After some two or three years, the author's name accidentally leaked out and became generally known among his acquaintances, and it has been from that time sent abroad occasionally in connection with this sole specimen of his literary fancy work. Feeling some regard for his reputation as a writer, even in this unusual line, he has been induced now, after so long a time, to employ some of his leisure hours in preparing a corrected and enlarged edition. He has given more development to the chief incidents and characters, added some of a subordinate kind that are new, and interwoven some descriptions of natural objects with the narrative. Thus he has more than doubled its size and, he presumes to think, greatly increased the interest of the story. There is still in some parts a want of the careful finish and strict correction that are desirable even in the smallest work of taste and fancy. For remaining defects of whatever kind the author can offer no apology but either the want of genius for such compositions or, what is certainly true, the want of sufficient uninterrupted leisure amidst weighty cares and occupations to polish a work of literary amusement. He has found an agreeable relaxation from severer labors of the mind in this exercise of the imagination. Should any of his acquaintances think that the composition of a tale, however innocent in its tendency or serious in its effect, misbecomes the gravity of his office, he begs to be excused for this once and to be indulged in treating the only child of his fancy so far like a pet as to be allowed, after such long neglect, to give it a new dress and thus to let it go forth with better hopes to seek its fortune in the literary world.

Introductory Reflections

Sometimes a single incident at the outset of a man's career may determine the course and color of his after life. He may find himself placed unexpectedly in such critical circumstances that by a decision which cannot be delayed, he has the prospect of making, yet the apprehension of marring, his fortune during life.

An unlooked-for tide in his affairs may seem ready to bear him away to the islands of the happy, but he fears by the way some hidden rocks and quicksands by which all his hopes are in danger of being wrecked and engulfed forever. He stands upon the shore in trembling perplexity, strongly tempted yet afraid to embark. The tide of fortune begins to ebb, warning him that time and tide wait for no man and that procrastination will be the death of opportunity. He still hesitates, painfully suspended between the attractions of hope and the repulsive suggestions of fear. The tide is gone; the happy opportunity has fled; he discovers too late that the danger was imaginary and the offered good inestimable. Then does he bewail his indecision and reproach himself through life for the neglect of the golden opportunity. A bright and lively object had, like a heavenly meteor, flashed upon his sight and kindled his feelings to a glow. As it shone upon his enraptured vision, it invited him over the waters to its region of felicity, but when he delayed to answer the call, it vanished forever from his sight and left him weeping upon the desolate shore. His only consolation was that the result, though unfortunate, was not fatal and still left open to him the humble path of exertion and the ordinary prospects of life to which he had formerly looked. Reflection teaches him the salutary lesson that the accidental opportunity was an act of Divine Providence, throwing rare circumstances into conjunction to show man that his way is not in himself and that his own conduct in so extraordinary a case is evidence of weakness and fallibility which should humble him beneath the mighty hand that sways the destiny of man.

Such a critical tide of fortune once occurred in the affairs of my life. It gave occasion to these reflections and was of so rare and striking a character as to make a story somewhat interesting and instructive. I proceed to record it, not only for the entertainment but the admonition of the young reader, who should learn from it to act promptly as well as prudently in critical conjunctures and never to indulge any feeling in regard to human affairs to such excess as to disqualify himself for the exercise of a cool and dispassionate judgment. This is the lesson which I would now teach him from the most affecting portion of all my experiences.

II

A Student's Journey to the South

I was born and educated in Rockbridge, a county that lies in the great Valley of Virginia and derives its name from that famous curiosity, the Natural Bridge. My parents were respectable but in such moderate circumstances that they could afford me nothing more than a good education. Our residence was on the North River side near Lexington, the seat of Washington College, an institution which has never made an ostentatious display of its claims to public notice but which has nevertheless produced a large number of good scholars and excellent men. Here, of course, I pursued my liberal studies. We lived so near the village that I could attend all its schools without boarding away from home. This prevented in my case what often happens in others, a breach of domestic attachments by early absence and long association with scenes and persons at a distance from the parental domicile. All my pleasures during the freshness and ardor of youth were associated with home and kindred and the beautiful scenery of my birthplace.

Having by years of diligent application obtained a distinguished place among the graduates of my college, which does not bestow its honors with a lavish hand, I betook myself ambitiously, and I may add successfully, to a course of professional studies under a learned gentleman of the village, whose office I frequently visited while I kept my lodging at home. My industry was the more energetic because my worldly hopes depended on my personal exertions, and I was resolved to make up for my want of fortune by mental accomplishments and professional ability. Before I had finished the extensive task allotted to myself, I suffered a disheartening check upon my exertions. Excessive application to books gradually brought on me the symptoms of a consumption—the penalty often paid for literary ambition. Still, though aware of danger, I was loathe to quit my books. But the frequent cough and the hectic spot on a pale cheek alarmed my friends so much that they called in a physician to aid them with his authority in persuading me to desist. His warning voice, added to their anxious remonstrances, at length overcame my reluctance to quench the lamp of study. Yet I did it reluctantly, even when I knew that persistence would extinguish the lamp of life; so treacherous a guide is even the noblest passion and so needful of control. I consented, however, to fly from the sharp air of the mountains and to spend the approaching winter in the warm plains of the south. I promised also to abstain from all study and to apply myself wholly to the social pleasures and amusements which might cheer my drooping spirits and promote the restoration of my health.

When the chill winds of November admonished me to depart, I prepared to travel alone on horseback. My simple preparations being soon completed, I bade a sorrowful adieu to my friends and to the homestead of my youth where every object was pleasant and dear to my soul. Never had I felt so melancholy. My previous absences from home had been only short excursions for amusement. My local attachments were strong and unbroken; my little circle of kindred and friends was nearly all the world to me. My journey was a solitary one to a strange land; my disease I knew to be always insidious and often fatal. I was constitutionally subject to fits of mental dejection. How could I be otherwise than sad? I was in fact plunged into the deepest gulf of despondency. When I reached the top of the Blue Ridge, a lonely fugitive from home, breathing short from obstructed lungs, going far away for the first time, to live and, not improbably, to die among strangers, I turned to take what might be my last look over the woody hills and the cedar bluffs that bent the river half round my paternal home. I saw the smoke in bluish wreaths ascending from the peaceful nook. I began to weep—yes, though a man grown, I wept like a child when I waved my hand to bid the unutterable adieu to my native land and turned my horse's head down the southern declivity of the mountain.

I pursued my journey moping and sometimes despairing but occasionally interested, and the more so as I went farther on, with the new scenes through which I passed and the new aspects of human life that occurred to my observation. I arrived safely, though still in low health and spirits, at a village near the Savannah river, where I purposed to sojourn during the winter. The location was suitable in every respect; the climate was mild, the society good, and one of my former college mates was the most popular physician in the place. By him I was soon introduced into some of the most agreeable families in the town and neighborhood. Now I learned by experience what I had heard from the reports of travellers: how engaging are the charms of southern hospitality. My case seemed to excite as much sympathy among these benevolent strangers as if I had been of their own flesh and blood. They ministered to my diseased mind a thousand delicate and consoling attentions. My rustic backwardness in strange company was quickly subdued by their easy and open simplicity of manners—that true politeness which is not an imitation of conventional forms but an agreeable manifestation of kind feelings. New scenes, cheerful conversation, pleasant rides in the soft winter air, and all the nameless appliances of watchful benevolence to a drooping invalid soon turned the ebb of my health and spirits into reviving flow. My appetite was restored, my cough ceased, my respirations became free, the purple tinge of health revisited my cheek, and all the world again brightened around me. And what was not a recovered good but a positive and a delightful acquisition, I began to relish in a high degree the pleasures of society and was daily learning to act my part in company with a better grace and a more ready communicativeness than formerly. During my studious life, I took no pleasure in social parties but preferred to ramble alone for amusement in the green woods or on the wild cliffs and shady river banks about home or over the high mountains that border my native valley, from whose forest-crowned summits I could look out and see finer sights than "the cloud-capped towers and gorgeous places" of the artificial world. But now the experience of three months, devoted to the enjoyment of mixed society, had completely tapped a new fountain of pleasure in my soul; and the stream that flowed from it, if not so deep as some others, was yet so sweet and sparkling that I was resolved no more to neglect its pleasant entertainments. My new circle of hospitable friends had gained such a hold upon my affections that I felt, much less than I had anticipated, the weariness of a long absence from home. But still I did not forget my dear native mountains. In the solitude of my chamber I often longed for their whispering shades and mossy rivulets, but I could bear my absence without repining now because I hoped, ere long, to see them again as I had often seen them with delight, raising their green heads aloft in the vernal air and bathing them in the cerulean light of heaven.

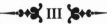

III

The Student's New Stage Acquaintances

To confirm my health and to enlarge my scanty knowledge of the world, I resolved to visit Charleston on my way home and thence to take a sea-voyage round to the Chesapeake. Accordingly, when spring began to smile over the woods and fields, I bade my southern friends an affectionate farewell and took a seat in the Charleston stage, which left the village two hours before sunrise. I found two other passengers within; but discovering by the starlight only that they were a man and a woman, I said nothing to them, and they said nothing to me until daylight. We seemed on both sides to feel a diffidence of venturing to address a stranger in the dark when we could not see even the color of his face. They once in a while spoke a few words to each other in a low and remarkably sweet tone of voice. This awakened in me a curiosity to see what manner of persons they were whose half whispered words sounded so musically. When the dawn began to disclose the personal appearance of my fellow travellers, I was struck with their beauty. They were evidently brother and sister, the one being a masculine likeness of the other. They were in the bloom of youth, with complexions between brown and fair, raven black locks, and eyes moderately large, not quite jetty black, but star-bright interpreters of intellect and feeling. Their faces were roundish oval, all the features in just proportion, and the expression of the whole, vivacious and benign. In person, they were well shaped, the limbs plump and rounded, their stature of the middle height, and the body inclining to fulness. Nothing else in their personal appearance struck me as remarkable until I saw them walk, and then I noticed an easy and graceful agility of movement, indicating muscular elasticity, sprightliness of mind, and, as I thought, a cultivated taste.

The young lady struck me at once, and indeed at all times, as the most beautiful gem of humanity that I had ever seen. At first I considered her, but rather doubtfully, as a brunette—a sweet pretty brunette—but when I looked at her in the open air and the full light of day, the ebony black of her flowing hair and the mild black of her lustrous eyes contrasted so strongly with the delicate hue of her complexion that I pronounced her so fair as to be only not florid. I endeavored to criticise every part of her person and features—but, except what I have mentioned, I discovered nothing in the superlative degree—her round forehead was not very round; her nose had no very marked character; her mouth was neither wider or narrower than common; her lips neither thick nor thin. The only striking circumstance about her mouth was a sort of tremulous vivacity of muscle, ready to catch and to express the slightest movements of the soul. As to her chin and cheeks, I could not say that they were or were not dimpled, for the play of her features made dimples appear and vanish alternately. Nor could I call her neck long and arched as the necks of beauties are usually described—this young lady's was neither long nor short, though it tapered a little. Her foot was not very small, not a withered Chinese foot, but in good proportion to the person which it had to support. As to other first appearances, my fellow passengers were genteelly but not showily dressed and had all the air of good breeding.

After several glances of curiosity had passed between us, we gave token of a willingness to try each other's conversation. We began with due caution, feeling our way with a short remark at a time on the weather, the road, and other such trivial matters. This foretaste proving satisfactory, we extended our remarks to subjects less trite, such as the features of the country and the condition of its inhabitants. Here too we mutually elicited observations, good in themselves and savoring of better yet in store. Encouraged by our progress thus far, we promptly advanced another degree and launched forth our thoughts into a bolder strain, making, in turn, little discourses on the effects of climate and geographical circumstances in modifying the character and pursuits of the population around us. Here we at least bordered upon the philosophical or got perhaps within its confines, yet none of us failed, not even the lady, young and beautiful and bright-eyed though she was. Her speeches thus far on in the conversation were neither many nor long, but they were music to the ear, intelligence to the understanding and to my heart; they were—I knew not the nature of the impression—it was something undefinable. It can only be suggested by comparison, and yet I am in doubt whether to say that it was refreshing as a crystal fountain in the shade when the fields glow with summer heat, or rather a genial warmth like that of the April sun when the zephyr breathes softly and the flowers are springing.

We soon dismissed all caution and reserve. We had found ourselves to be mutually agreeable and in a short time understood one another so well as to feel assured that nothing would be said or taken amiss, so we poured ourselves forth without measure and were soon flowing on with a full current of loquacity. My fellow travellers delighted me more than strangers had ever done. Their speech, so intellectual yet so modest, was set off with such sparkling vivacity, yet with such a kindliness of manner, that it raised in me the highest tide of social animation that I had experienced since my melancholy departure from home, or perhaps the highest that I had ever experienced.

But who were my new acquaintances? I had a great desire to know, but not the impertinence to ask. They spoke English with the perfect ease and idiom of well-educated natives of England or America, but in their persons differed from my notion of the Anglo-Saxon race. The course of our conversation, however, soon led us to speak of the people of different countries. I alluded to my Virginia mountaineers —they to their fellow cockneys and to London as their native city. Their name, Bensaddi, soon afterwards mentioned, sounded in my ears like an Italian name; and I shrewdly conjectured that their dark eyes and hair, with their brunettish complexion, were due to the influence of an Italian, perhaps of a Sicilian, sun upon their ancestors.

I was now curious to know the object and course of their travels. As if he had perceived my curiosity on the subject, the openhearted young gentleman took occasion to tell me the following particulars. The father, having some business with a planter in the West Indies, had sent his son to attend to it; the sister took a fancy to accompany him and had, after much pleading, obtained their father's consent that she might see the curiosities of nature in the torrid zone, and "the black man in the miseries of West Indian bondage, and the white man in the highest state of freedom, as he is in your happy country," said the young gentleman politely.

"Miss Bensaddi sees man in the extremes of slavery and freedom here," said I candidly.

"Not so far gone in the dark extreme of slavery," said he, "for West Indian bondage is worse than yours, though I confess that the mildest form of slavery is a degradation bitter to the feelings of mankind."

"Yes, sir, to us it would be intolerably galling, because we have the birthright and the sentiment of freedom. But happily for the poor Negroes, they have never known the state of freedom nor imbibed its sentiments; hence, they are not aggrieved by a sense of degradation and wrong. Born to slavery, they grow up with minds conformable to their condition and rarely, if left to themselves, brood over the hardships of their lot; but finding their parents, themselves, and nearly all their race placed in it by Divine Providence, their only thought is to make the best of a condition which is not without its comforts and advantages."

"Truly, sir, you have accounted for a fact which is little known in England and which both surprised and gratified us when we observed it in America. The slaves, in general, seem to be as contented and merry a set of beings as any in the world. They laugh, and sing, and dance, not to 'drive dull care away,' for dull care seems never to visit them. They seem to think that as they themselves belong to their master, he is bound to take their cares into the bargain; so they throw the vexatious pack upon his shoulders and leap for very lightness of heart at their deliverance."

"Now, brother," said the young lady playfully, "did not I tell you when we left Savannah that if you stayed much longer among these merry slaves you would renounce abolitionism and defend slavery as the best condition of poor laborers. You know what careworn wretches most of our hireling laborers and small jobbers are at home, especially the mechanics and manufacturers; how hard they must work for a scanty subsistence while they are healthy and strong;

how precarious their resources and how little they can hope to lay up for their future support; and, consequently, what a miserable prospect they have for the coming days of sickness and old age—having nothing better to rely on than the cold comfort of the parish hospital with a stinted dole of public charity often grudgingly administered. What a contrast to your lighthearted slaves who are sure of a competency without care on their part, a provision which they look to as their right and enjoy without the mortification of being dependents on charity. Thus released from the care of providing for themselves and their families, their only remaining care is how to get easily through the hours of labor and merrily through all the rest. Now, brother, have you not proved that we ought to renounce abolitionism?"

"Not yet, my sister. You have made an ingenious web of my argument and thrown it dexterously over my own head, but you have not so fastened the loopholes but that I can escape its entanglements. Everything that has length and breadth has two sides, you know. So has slavery and so has free labor. I turned up the bright side of slavery, and you showed the dark side of free labor. The contrast was strikingly advantageous to slavery—so you clapped, without further ceremony, this inference upon me as the conclusion of the whole matter. That was not fair—was it, sir?"

"You need not appeal, brother, for I acknowledge that I was too hasty. But, sir," said she, addressing me, "we are sincerely gratified at one result of our observations thus far in America. We have discovered that Negro slavery is not on all sides so dark and doleful as we had imagined. It has, indeed, some cheerful sunny spots, delightful to look upon. Brother, tell Mr. Garame of the pleasant scenes that we witnessed at Colonel P——'s, where we saw the Negro wedding. That sight would have convinced anyone that slaves might be happy in their slavery. It was an example in point—or what I have heard Doctor Magruder call an ocular demonstration. Do tell it, brother."

"Tell it yourself, Judith, for you enjoyed the sight fully as much as I did, and you probably remember the circumstances better."

A slight tinge of rose-colored modesty suffused her cheek as she hesitated a moment to answer.

"I fear that I should make a wearisome story of it—for, after all, it was but an humble scene of joy, felt by untutored hearts, and manifested in a way so unrefined as to afford little scope for entertaining description, especially when told to one who is so familiar with incidents of the kind as I suppose Mr. Garame is. Such pleasant passages in the experience of slaves often occur in this country, I presume. But they are almost unheard of in England, and I shall carry this one home in my memory for the edification of some friends there who have been lately filled with dismal ideas of American slavery and almost raging indignation against all slaveholders. We were fast catching the same dark colored views and feelings when we embarked for America. One object of our voyage was that we might see how the poor slaves lived and fared and what could or ought to be done for their relief, and we rejoice to find that, in some cases, nothing better can be done for them than to leave them in the undisturbed possession of their blessings."

"I am glad that you have found it so; but, Miss Bensaddi, I beg that you will favor me with an account of the Negro wedding. I know that the slaves in my part of the country have as light a task of labor and enjoy as many comforts as common laborers can well experience in any country or any condition and that they have both hearts and leisure to frolic as much as their white fellow laborers. But I am a stranger in these Southern parts and have had very limited opportunity of observing the condition of the slaves. You will, therefore, gratify me by giving a sketch of the wedding scene."

"Well, sir, an imperfect sketch is all that I can promise. We went by invitation to the hospitable mansion of Colonel P——. On approaching the house, we observed a large party of slaves before one of the quarters by the yard fence, and we were struck with their tidy apparel and joyous looks. Seeing us regard them with interest, Col. P—— remarked that they were to have a wedding among them that evening. When we expressed our pleasure at their appearance and our curiosity to observe their manners and customs, he told us that we could have the opportunity of witnessing the whole affair if we pleased, as some of his family always attended their marriage ceremonies, and that we could look in upon their supper and ball after the ceremony was over. We gladly embraced the offer and were much gratified with more than the novelty of the sight. These slaves had more comfortable accommodations and were more civilized than the West India slaves and, we thought, more also than the generality of slaves that we had seen in this country. The reason was that they had an excellent master. I never anywhere saw so gladsome a wedding party. There was, of course, nothing elegant or refined—but there was enough of finery in their dresses—indeed, a profusion of gay colors, and flaunting ribbons, and gewgaws in their bushy curls, with all which their simple fancies were mightily pleased. I was, myself, exceedingly gratified with the full hearted joy that sprang up in them and sprang out of them too when the fiddle and the dance gave free vent to the fountains of feeling within them. Merry jests started forth every instant, and jovial laughter burst in claps of delight from their souls. We looked through a window upon this scene of harmless mirth and of joy that gushed light and free from the hearts of nature's children; and we could but consider these outpourings of pleasure as a reward—if not a full one, still a real reward—bestowed peculiarly on them for their submissive toils at a master's bidding; and while I looked and reflected on what I saw, I felt a strange mixture of emotions. Tears trickled down my face—for what I could not tell—they might be tears of joy or tears of compassion or both together; and while the tears came, I sometimes found myself laughing, but whether out of diversion at their oddities or out of sympathy with their merriment, I do not know, for I seemed to have all sorts of incongruous feelings at the same time.

"The next day an incident occurred that gave us a still more touching proof of their happy condition. News arrived that their dear 'massa was 'lected to Congress.' Perhaps they did not exactly understand what this was, but they understood at least that it was some high honor, and they triumphed as if the honor were all their own. They could not contain their gladness—they shook each other by the hand—they came in a crowd to the door and sent in a request to see their master. When he came out and asked them kindly whether they wanted anything, their spokesman answered: 'Nothing, massa, only to tell you how we thank God that you be 'lected to Congress.'

'Well, boys,' said he with emotion, 'I am gratified to find that you are so rejoiced at it—and, boys, you need not go to work today; you must have an infair for the bride and bridegroom; so make ready for that.' 'Yes, massa, thank'ee, but we lef' a little to do in dat field; we'll go finish it—then we'll dress for the infair.' When they were retiring, one of them, as he passed near the window where we stood, said aloud to himself: 'God bless my good massa.'

"I thought," continued the young lady, wiping her eyes, "that next to the blessing of good parents to take care of us in childhood was the blessing which poor ignorant laborers have in a good master to direct their labors and to take care of all their interests."

"Now, sister," said the young gentleman, smiling, with a tear in his eye, "do you not see that you have become an advocate for slavery—quite a pleader and as earnest in the cause as a fee'd barrister?"

"If I am earnest, you must observe, brother Eli, that I am pleading only in a particular case; and if I advocate slavery, it is only in such cases as the one which I have described, where the master is discreet and humane and where the slaves are unfit for any higher condition than that of common laborers and are moreover contented with their situation, as in such cases they are likely to be. Then I believe that they are happier than they could be in a state of freedom. To abolish their slavery is then to abolish their best source of happiness—and what sort of philanthropy would that be?"

"There you are right, sister. I think, sir, that in this country at least, many cases exist in which the abolition of slavery would be a sorry boon, one for which the merry fellows whose happiness we had taken in charge would not thank our philanthropy, at least not after the experiment of freedom had taught them that they must now shoulder their own cares and still work or starve. And, sir, when we consider that the half of mankind does, and must, labor in poverty whether they be bond or free, the loss of human happiness through slavery will not appear to be of such mighty magnitude that the heart of a zealous abolitionist must needs burst in attempting to conceive it."

"Your zealous abolitionists," said I, "probably confine their attention to the evils of slavery and swell their conceptions by brooding over these alone until the miseries of bondage grow to an uncontainable magnitude before the imagination. These philanthropists would suffer a less painful distension of their sympathetic hearts if they would condescend to take an impartial view of all the facts and, in the fulness of their humanity, would allow their horror of slavery to be somewhat abated by a consideration of the exemption of the slave from some of the worst ills of poverty and some of the most corroding cares of life and by a consideration of some positive comforts which grow out of the relation between the slave and his master. Divine Providence has annexed to this relation some of the happy feelings which arise from the relation of parent and child. But even the filial feelings of a son or daughter may be destroyed by ill usage, much more the correspondent feeling of the slave. Notwithstanding the exceptions, however, the general fact in this country is that the slave is attached to his master and feels sensibly, almost every day of his life, that there is comfort in having such a protector and superintendent in his humble station as a poor laborer. But I suppose that some men are so violently philanthropic that they will not look at this side of the picture. Why, sir, in the same partial way of considering a subject, they might soon gather up a store of indignation against a higher character than the slaveholder. They have only to set their imaginations to brooding over the evils alone of any condition in life, even the highest and best, and they will soon engender in their minds, and nurse to maturity, a heavy indignation against the Disposer of our lot and raise their feelings to a sublime pitch of philanthropic blasphemy."

"Yes, sir," said the young lady with animation, "we know from experience how the dark-sided representations of slavery tend to inflame the imagination and to exasperate one's sympathy until the milk of human kindness is poisoned with gall and wormwood. When we left home we were beginning to consider slavery in America as made up of little else than knotty scourges, brutal oppression, and the heart-rending cries of mothers robbed of their children—of peccadillos punished with bloody lashes, and taskmasters wringing toil from every age and sex without reward and without mercy. I shudder now to think how exaggerated reports of this sort, often reiterated, so galled my humanity that I could almost wish to see the horrors of St. Domingo repeated on every set of slaveholders in America—such a bitter charity did I feel for African bondsmen. But I have learned a lesson from it, which I hope not soon to forget, and that is, never to let partial statements of human oppression work up my sympathy to rage, and never, if possible, in any case, to let a good feeling overrun the heart like a torrent and gather impurities by the violence of its course."

During this conversation my fair companion had gradually acquired a spirit and energy of expression, of which we all partook, but which in her bordered on the impassioned eloquence of enthusiasm. Her delicate frame had begun to dilate with swelling emotions and all her features to express the glowing fervor of thought. I began to expect from her a lofty outpouring of soul and would probably have been gratified if the coach had not stopped at the breakfast house so soon and turned the bold current of our conversation into the shallow and discursive channels of small talk.

I need not say that I was highly pleased with my fellow travellers. The subject of our last conversation was a serious one but well adapted to draw forth their moral sentiments and to try the strength of their reflective powers.

I have attempted to give the thoughts which they uttered and to imitate their style of expression, but there was an indescribable something in their manner, especially the sister's, which gave an extraordinary interest to their conversation. The brother's language was peculiarly witty and amusing and withal very sensible; but when Judith spoke—the soft melody of her voice, and after she became excited, its lively intonations, the kindling lustre of her eyes, the play of her expressive features, with the winning modesty of her manner and the undefinable eloquence of both her manner and her style—made all that she said go warm and animating to the heart as if an ethereal fire had penetrated to the sources of animation and given an exhilarating impulse to all the principles of life. Not to admire such a person with such a mind, I considered impossible.

"I could love her," said I to myself, when I got out of the stage and saw her trip gracefully into the house. "Yes, I could love her with all my heart—but how rash and vain were that for me, her accidental companion for a day! I must not indulge this amatory propensity. The warmth of so delicious a passion might solace and delight me today, only to afflict me with aching regret and hopeless longings after she will have left me tomorrow. I must close my breast against this dangerous Cupid. I see him now with bended bow and malicious eye, watching for an avenue to my heart."

So said I to myself, but I was a sheer novice in the mysteries of love. Ovid may teach the signs and rules to the inexperienced, but we shall be still unwise till nature shall, by actual experience, teach us the interpretation.

IV

The Student's Description of a Bridge

After resuming our seats in the coach, we began to speak of our journey to Charleston and our ulterior courses of travel. My free-hearted companions promptly communicated their plans. They would spend a few days in Charleston and then take a packet and go to Norfolk by sea. They would thus avoid the disagreeable route by stage through the tame sand flats and miry swamps of the Carolinas, disagreeable at all seasons, they had been told, but most so in the watery month of March. From Norfolk they would visit Washington, Philadelphia, and so on to Boston, where they intended to embark finally for England.

My heart gave a leap, a higher one than necessary I thought, when I heard of the days in Charleston and the voyage to Norfolk.

"Your route to Norfolk," said I to Mr. Bensaddi, "coincides at all points with mine, and if mutually agreeable, I should be glad of your company all the way."

"Very agreeable, I assure you, and I esteem it a fortunate circumstance that we shall have your company so far."

His pleased look confirmed his complimentary declaration, and my instinctive glance (or was it accidental?) at Miss Judith's face caught the smiling token of her satisfaction as it played over her beautiful features. But what did that signify? Travellers generally like company though it be not particularly agreeable—but for all that, when the smile was caught playing so sweetly over her countenance, I felt it glide down immediately into my heart and, nestling there, produce a series of agreeable little titillations. But Mr. Bensaddi thus continued:

"We are total strangers in this country—we have not a single acquaintance nigher than Boston. To meet with a companion every way agreeable is very gratifying to a land traveller and particularly so to a voyager. One who has travelled much feels this pleasure the more sensibly because he has been annoyed with accidental companionships which not only plague him for an hour but stick and grow to him like barnacles and make heavy sailing for the poor wight whether it be on land or water. I am the more inclined, therefore, to stick like a barnacle myself when I fall in with a choice companion. I wish your route coincided with ours all the way."

"I wish so too, Mr. Bensaddi, but my route from Norfolk leads me westward to Richmond and thence still westward to my home in the mountains. I should be much pleased if your curiosity led you to visit my native valley; its scenery is fine and well worthy of a traveller's attention."

"I should delight to visit the Natural Bridge," said Judith, with kindling eyes. "Is that near your residence?"

"Within fifteen miles, and that single object would reward a trip to the mountains."

"Writers describe it as a great curiosity, but I have a very imperfect conception of it. Do, if you please, give us a full description. You are doubtless familiarly acquainted with its appearance and can describe it better than travellers who have taken but one hasty look."

The brother joined earnestly in the request.

"Do, if you please," said the beautiful sister again.

How could I refuse? Yet, I professed, as in modesty bound, that I was not a good describer; and I added what was true, that no description could do justice to this singular object, which refused to confer a just impression of its beautiful magnificence through language or painting and demanded that all who would enjoy the delightful conception should come personally and do homage in its own rocky abode. Hence it comes to pass that no visitor of common sensibility ever viewed it attentively without acknowledging that the reality exceeded all that he had conceived or anticipated.

"Well, sir, that only increases our desire to know something more of an object so interesting and which we cannot visit. We will make allowance for the inadequacy of all description and still thank you for improving our notions of so rare a curiosity, of which, at present, we have very obscure conceptions from accounts defective in themselves and imperfectly remembered."

"Well then, sir, I will make the attempt. In the first place, imagine yourself to be travelling from the village of Lexington, southwestwardly, through a valley ten or twelve miles broad, separating two ranges of high mountains and presenting a surface broken into every variety of hill, dale and ravine. Twelve miles from the village you leave the main road and, after crossing the hill on the left, pursue the course of a brook which glides over a bed of solid limestone. Within two miles of the main road, you cross the brook a second time and go up an acclivity to an inn by the wayside. Here you find that the road continues to ascend the slope of a hill which gradually rises before you to the elevation of a mountain. Your course is west of south. A few yards beyond the inn your eye is drawn towards a vista between the forest-covered hill that you are ascending and a similar one on the left. This opening is made by a deep narrow glen through which you descry, at the distance of several miles, a portion of the high and many-formed blue ridge bounding the great valley on its southeastern side. Attracted by this, you may not be aware of anything remarkable about your feet, as you ascend the slope, until you observe that you are in the line of this deep glen and apparently at its head. Casting down your eyes, you discover a sudden break in the rocks by the roadside. The glen seems to terminate there in a deep, narrow chasm. You approach the margin a few yards from the road; perpendicular cliffs open to a fearful depth under your eyes as you lean forward and see at the bottom a small river which seems to issue from a cavern underneath the road. And passing between parallel cliffs, it is joined about a hundred yards below by the brook which falls to the bottom of the glen over a high bank of limestone. You turn about, towards the opposite side of the road, to observe whence the deeply sunk rivulet flows. There you discover the same or another dark wild glen with the tokens of a like chasm on that side. You go with breathless curiosity to the margin of this, which is about twenty yards from the other chasm. Here again parallel walls of rock crowned with evergreens open a passage for your eyes down and yet further down till you lean over the abrupt brow and with a shudder behold the same rivulet coming from the deep dusky ravine above and passing under the Natural Bridge. You might have crossed it unwittingly if you had kept your eyes directly upon the road as it continues to ascend the acclivity of the mountain.

"Desirous now to peep under the bridge, you return a few steps along the road, and passing by the side of the chasm among cedars and Arborvitae* trees that love such wild limestone cliffs, you find a projecting point of rock a little below the crown of the precipice and a few rods up stream from the bridge. Here you see the massive thickness of the bridge, thirty feet of solid stone, with the arch gracefully spanning this great mountain cleft, down into which you look with dizzy head and mute astonishment.

"As yet, you have seen only one side of the arch, which being on a lower level than your position, precludes a sight of its vault. Curiosity soon prompts you to descend that you may take an upward view. For this purpose, you must follow a path that conducts you south of the bridge to the place where the brook tumbles over the rocks. Here is the nearest place where the descent is practicable. Winding round the base of a crag near the bottom of the glen, you behold from beneath the trees that overshadow your path the high arch supported by its abutments, somewhat rude in appearance, but solid and everlasting as the mountain that supports them. Yet the form of the whole is so nearly symmetrical that you are impressed rather with the sublimity of the object. As you advance towards it, the perpendicular walls of rough rock enclose you on either hand and leave but a narrow space of sky visible between the cedar-topped crags overhead. The arch seems now to expand and elevate itself to receive you beneath its ample vault and to awe you into a due respect for its superb majesty. When you look around and observe near the bridge some forest trees of the ordinary size growing from the bottom of the glen and reaching with their tops the feet of others, which having fastened their roots in crevices of the wall, strive to reach the upper air, yet fail by far to attain the elevation of the arch, and when you look up to the arch itself, moving your eye slowly from side to

* *Thuja* or *thuya* is the botanical name of this beautiful evergreen. [Ruffner's note.]

55

side and from end to end over its spacious vault, it seems still to enlarge its amplitude and to rise heavenward until your breast labors with the grand conception. You think how centuries and millenniums have rolled over this changeless structure and how other centuries and millenniums are yet to roll over its undecaying solidity. You think of it as the emblem of its eternal Creator, and the puny works of man dwindle to insignificance before this cloven mountain from whose deep interior you look up and behold the everlasting rock that bends its glorious vault from crag to crag, seventy feet in span and two hundred feet above your head.

"When filled with these contemplations, you move to a point in the glen above the bridge where you see its beauty and magnificence under another aspect. The arch has apparently a different curvature and the opening beneath it a different, yet more beautiful, outline than it does when viewed from below. Shift your position to some other spot where, from under thick trees and beetling precipices, you can take another look. Now the same features appear under another form, and, as you move from side to side and farther or nearer, new transformations appear, such as you never observed in a work of art. You wonder how it is possible that one object, so simple in its general structure, should exhibit such an entertaining mutation of aspects, which are the more interesting because they put at fault the rules of perspective and consequently differ from the anticipated effects of your changes of position. If you study the cause of this, you will find perhaps that it arises from a general approach to regularity of structure, combined with deviations from it so various and so graceful that the visitor sees at every step some new and unexpected combination of forms and appearances, variable as the shifting scenes of the kaleidoscope, but all disclosing new features of beauty and sublimity, leaving on the mind the final impression that this singular curiosity is a wonderful specimen of Divine art, which has diverted its workmanship of formality but retained the graces of form and proportion in the general outline while it has left just so much of unfinished rudeness in the details as to cast an air of wild sublimity over the whole work."

Here I closed my lame description. After a pause, Judith started as from a reverie, emotion depicted in her face and lighting her fine eyes to a glow like that of the evening star. Turning to her brother, she said, "Oh, brother! how can we leave the continent where such an object may be seen and not go to enjoy the sight? I would cheerfully travel a thousand miles to see that bridge, so grand, so beautiful, Nature's sole specimen of divine art in the construction of a bridge. Is it not, Mr. Garame? Or does the world contain another?"

"I think you are right, Miss Bensaddi; though Humboldt describes a natural bridge in the Andes, it is not like ours. There is a solid arch, but very inferior, and also a broken arch, composed of loose rocks, which by a rare accident in falling down a deep narrow chasm got wedged together and continue firmly lodged against the sides at a great height from the bottom. The bridge itself is of difficult approach, and the bottom of the fissure is inaccessible."

"Oh, yes—now I remember to have read of it. That must be a wild place, but it is not comparable to your Natural Bridge. It has less appearance of design in its formation; it cannot impress you with such awe by its immoveable solidity nor with such admiration at its lofty proportions, struck off with Nature's careless but master hand. It is not very wonderful to see loose rocks caught midway down a great mountain cleft, though the scene be romantic enough. But to see a real bridge, built by Nature for a highway, skillfully designed for it, then cut without hands out of the solid mountain rock—defying all human power to shake it and human art to imitate its magnificence—springing its grand arch aloft—so mighty a mass, yet so high, so airy, so light. Oh, brother, can we not go to see it? I know that your time in America is limited, but if you will give me that sight, only for a day, you may hurry me as rapidly as you please over the rest of the journey."

"My dear sister, I would gladly afford you that pleasure and gladly enjoy it myself, but I am doubtful whether we can spare the time. Yet, if we have a quick passage to Norfolk, we may possibly run up to the mountains and snatch a glance at so wonderful a specimen of Nature's handiwork—or rather un-handiwork, for Nature works without hands, I believe. I will tell you, Mr. Garame, what sort of fancy your interesting description suggested to my mind. Methought that dame Nature must be sitting somewhere about that bridge, probably hidden in a thicket of cedars on a craggy point of the rocks, watching the visitors as they come and look and wonder and, when they turn to go away, sending an elfin breeze to whisper in their ears: 'Ye are pretty two-handed folks to be proud of *your* works, are ye not?'"

"Your pleasant fancy conveys a truth. When a man is under the bridge and thinks of himself and his fellow bipeds, it is with a feeling of humiliation that is salutary without being painful. But, Miss Judith, in relation to the inquiry which you made a while ago, I have another curiosity to mention—one of little notoriety as yet because it is hidden in the mountain wilds of Virginia—which may boast of having the only curiosity comparable to the Natural Bridge: that is, the Natural Tunnel among the Cumberland mountains in the southwestern angle of the State. Here, a small river flows between high mountains, along a narrow valley, which is suddenly closed by the junction of the mountains. But nature has cut a tunnel four or five hundred feet long through solid rock and, thus, given egress to the water. The arch of the tunnel is nearly regular, solid throughout, and of considerable span, but its elevation above the floor does not exceed forty or fifty feet. This tunnel would be a finer object if it were straight so as to let one see through its whole length at once. But such as it is, or as I have heard it described by an intelligent visitor (for I have not seen it), you will readily conceive that it is a rare and interesting curiosity and one that would be much visited if 'dame Nature' had not (as if jealous of showing too many of her works of *internal improvement*) hidden it among rugged mountains in a place remote from the great highways of travel."

These notices of the bridge and the tunnel, with some allusions to various particulars of my native country, awakened a lively interest in my fellow travellers. I saw it and was glad. Their eager inquiries about the scenery, the population, the literary institutions and state of society not only gratified my habitual feeling of patriotism but strengthened, while it gratified, a new feeling, as yet so undeveloped in the recesses of the heart or so concealed under the disguise of other feelings as to be unacknowledged even by consciousness. I knew only that I thought the bright-eyed beauty, who had been shining now for hours into mine eyes, to be the most bright eyed of beauties and to be, moreover, in mental qualities the most attractive vision that had ever realized itself to my perception. I may have conceived the like when fancy garnished some ideal picture of a lovely woman, but here seemed to be the living substance of what poets had taught me to imagine but experience had never taught me to expect in this iron age of degenerate humanity. True, this lovely creature did not appear to be exempt from defects of character. I could discover, on a few hours acquaintance, that she was subject to illapses of mental excitement bordering on enthusiasm; yet did she not lose in my view one feature of loveliness on account of this overexcitability, for here I acknowledged a point of agreement in our tempers.

I had called up prudence and set that dignified virtue to guard, with hundred eyes, the avenues of my heart against the insidious Cupid. "But, then," said something within me, "I have since discovered that she is not to be my companion for a day only, but for a whole quarter of a moon, and according to the proverb, 'Circumstances alter cases.'" "Well," said prudence faintly, "if they do alter cases, it is not always for the better. Does this new state of the case diminish either the probability of your falling in love or the danger of your falling afterwards into something less pleasant?" This remonstrance was so feebly uttered that prudence was evidently yielding to somnolence. Oh, thou drowsy Argus! What subtle enchanter had so soon drugged thy hundred eyes to sleep?

This I well remember, that I sought occasion to set forth to these strangers all that was attractive in my country and that in portraying its landscapes and whatever else might commend it to my fellow-travellers, my imagination then, more than ever before, bloomed with rich ideas, and my mouth shed forth every rising conception with a fluency of eloquent expression which I can but imperfectly recall in making this record.

Among other entertainments which my native land affords to the visitor, especially if his mind be imbued with the love of nature, I mentioned the fine views from the mountain tops; and I suggested that I had made some delightful excursions to the House Mountain near Lexington and could never forget the splendid prospects that its lofty summit spreads before the spectator.

This suggestion had the intended effect. My companions instantly besought me to describe my visits to the House Mountain. No longer coy, with memory and imagination on the wing, I was commencing a prelude to my story when the coach stopped for dinner and gave me the opportunity of arranging my thoughts a little. As soon as we resumed our journey, I was called on to proceed, which I did substantially as follows.

V

The Student's Account of His Visits
to the House Mountain

To make my description more intelligible, I shall begin with a general sketch of the Allegheny region of Virginia.

The Allegheny mountains consist of parallel ridges, casting off short spurs and sometimes long branches that vary from the general direction; but they always embrace rich valleys watered by clear streams that either murmur over pebbly beds or dash over rough rocks. To find their mother ocean they had to break their way through the ridges that run between them and the sea coast. Some of them, as the Powhatan or James River, have made several breaches through successive ridges, two thousand feet, more or less, in height.

The line of continued mountain nearest the sea is the Blue Ridge, which, beginning in Pennsylvania about the Susquehanna, increases in height, ruggedness and diversity of form until it stretches its vast length into the Carolinas, where, being joined by the chief Allegheny, it becomes the great father mountain of the system, the huge, wild, prolific source of a thousand rivers, that gather themselves together in the deep valleys and, with their several aggregations of water, run brawling and working their ways out in every direction to seek the common source and depository of all sublunary waters.

Between the Blue Ridge and the North Mountain lies the Great Valley, my native land, "the loveliest land on the face of the earth." (Here I detected a smile, instantly suppressed, on the faces of my auditors, but not a smile of contempt I was sure.)

The Valley is full twenty miles wide near the Potomac but narrows to twelve miles in Rockbridge, where it is infinitely diversified with mountain, hill, knoll, slope, vale, dell, ravine, cliff, rift, with every other modification of surface that is named and that is not named except plains and lakes, whereof we have none; but we have clear limestone springs gushing from forest-crowned hills and "giving drink to every beast of the field."

Westward of the Great Valley for many miles, the country is composed altogether of high mountains with narrow vales between. But here, and further west, fountains of health flow; a hundred mineral springs of different qualities, with a pure atmosphere, delightful summer weather, shady forests, beauty in the vale and sublimity in the mountain, all combine to invite the invalid for health and all for pleasure, who love either the charms of nature or the social enjoyments of a watering place. But enough of introduction. Now for the House Mountain.

This short isolated mountain is a conspicuous object in the picturesque landscape of Rockbridge. It stands about six miles west of Lexington, from whose inhabitants it hides the setting sun, and not infrequently turns the summer showers that usually come with the west wind. Being separated by deep vales from the North Mountain, the more lofty, it stands like an island of the air, with its huge body and sharp angles to cut the current of the winds asunder. Clouds are often driven against it, cloven in the midst, and carried streaming on to the right and left, with a space of blue sky between, similar in form to the evening shadow of the mountain when the light of departing day is in like manner cloven. Sometimes, however, a division of the cloud, after passing the town, will come bounding back in a current of air reflected from another mountain. It is not unusual to see a cloud move across the Great Valley in Rockbridge, shedding its contents by the way, strike the Blue Ridge, whirl about, and pursue another course until it is exhausted. The traveller, after the shower is passed and the clear sunshine has induced him to put away his cloak and umbrella, is surprised by the sudden return of the rain from the same quarter towards which he had seen it pass away.

What is called the House Mountain consists in fact of two oblong, parallel mountains, connected about midway of their height and rising upwards of 1500 feet above the surrounding country. The summit ridges are each about a mile long and resemble the roof of a house; the ends terminate in abrupt precipices; and all around huge buttresses, with their bases spread far out into the country, rise up against the sides and taper to points which terminate some hundreds of feet below the summit. These buttresses, or spurs of the mountain, are separated by vales which run up between them.

The students of our college make parties every summer to visit this mountain for the sake of the prospect. They set out in clear weather and spend the night on the mountain that they may enjoy the morning beauties of the scene, which are by far the most interesting. Now the ladies, too, have begun to adventure on this romantic enterprise. Last summer I had a delightful ride by moonlight with a party of them and their male friends. We pattered along while the whole country was hushed in sleep, through woods, by meadow sides, over hills, and up a vale that led to our object. The vale was at first broad and spread open its fields to catch the flood of moonbeams; then it contracted itself, swelled up its dark rocky sides, and entered the mountain between two of the buttresses. It terminated high up against the steep rocky side of the summit ridge. Here we had to dismount. We tied our horses in the forest, and, taking to our feet on ground piebald with moonshine and shadows, we began to scale the rocky steep, clambering over stony fragments and trunks of fallen trees, catching hold on bush and jutting rock. Now working our laborious way, then stopping to recover breath for another effort, we succeeded in mounting the summit and taking our stations, some on projecting top rocks, and the more hardy on branches of storm-battered trees before the sun, whose rising we aimed to see, had surmounted the piny top of the Blue Ridge. He soon rose but in a haze, shorn of half his beams, and therefore with much less worshipful glory than when he ascends his mountain throne, full-robed, amidst the pure blue of the ether when no earthborn vapor sullies its transparency.

My first trip, some years ago, was with a party of students only. Then we were disappointed in our hopes by a sudden clouding up of the atmosphere before we reached the place, and we should have made an unprofitable trip had not an unexpected scene afforded us a partial reward for the toils of the ascent. We lodged like Indian hunters not far from the summit, where an overhanging rock affords shelter and a spring trickling through a crevice supplies drink to the weary climber. After we had slept awhile, one of the company startled us with the cry of fire. We saw with surprise, in the direction of the Blue Ridge, a conflagration that cast a lurid glare through the hazy atmosphere. The flame rose and spread every moment, tapering upwards to a point and bending before the night breeze. At first, we conjectured that a great barn was in flames and then that the beautiful village of Lexington was, as it had been once before, wrapped in devouring fire. Whilst we gazed anxiously at the fiery object, it rose higher every moment, and in rising seemed now to grow less at the lower extremity until finally it resembled the last flicker of a dying lamp flame. And then it stood forth, to our joyful surprise—the MOON, half in the wane, reddened and magnified by the misty air beyond what we had ever seen. Its light afforded us an obscure perception of the most prominent objects in the landscape. Shadowy masses of mountains darkened the sight in various directions, and spots of dusky white, glimmering here and there, indicated fields and houses. We perceived just enough to make us eager for a more distinct view; but when the morning came the cloudy confusion of the atmosphere concealed everything, and a rain succeeding put us quickly to scampering down the mountain and sent us home as dirty as pigs, as wet as drowned rats, and with the wings of our fancies completely bedrenched and bedraggled into the bargain. We were cured of scene hunting and gypsying in the wild mountains for that season. But by the next summer my spirit was revived, and I longed for another excursion to the great observatory that was daily standing aloft with its rocky solitudes in the background of our landscape, stimulating the spirit of the students to try what romantic incidents and wide prospects a night's lodging on its high eminence might yield.

So one fair midsummer's day we set off, a dozen of us, full of high enterprise and laden with whatever might be necessary for use and comfort. This time we lodged on the aerial summit of the mountain where we built a fire of logs that illuminated the rocks and trees about our wild encampment and blazed like a beacon fire before the eyes of nearly all Rockbridge. We prepared our coffee, drew forth our bread and cheese, and ate our supper merrily; and for hours we made those gray rocks hear what perhaps they had never heard before, the jests and quips and shouts and laughter of a dozen college youngsters let loose and exulting in the wild freedom of nature.

This time the weather proved eminently favorable. We slept two or three hours and rose before the dawn that we might watch for the opening of the scene. Our fire had sunk to embers; the desolation and death-like stillness of our situation were impressive. The heavens above were perfectly serene; the stars looked down upon us with all their eyes from mansions of the purest blue; but the lower world was enveloped in a dense fog. We seemed to have been separated from the society of the living on the face of the earth and to have ascended to another sphere where we held communion only with the silent orbs and the blue ether that drew our spirits into their heavenly fields. The merriment of the evening was changed into sober thoughtfulness. We spoke little and that with a low voice, and each one seemed disposed to retire from his fellows that he might give his mind to contemplation. Such, at least, was my case. I withdrew to a naked rock that crowned a precipice and, turning my face to the east, waited for the sun, if not with the idolatrous devotion, yet with the deep seriousness of the Persian fire worshippers.

Presently the dawn began to show, at the distance of twelve miles, the dim and wavering outline of the Blue Ridge in the eastern horizon. When the morning light had opened the prospect more distinctly, the level surface of the mist which covered the valley became apparent, and the mountain tops that rose through it in almost every direction looked like islands in a white, silent and placid ocean. I gazed with delighted imagination over this novel and fairy scene, so full of sublimity in itself and, from the sober twilight in which it appeared, so much like the creation of fancy in the visions of a dream. The trees and rocks of the nearest islands began to develop their forms; more distant islands were disclosed to view, various in size and shape, and variously grouped, but all were wild, desolate and still. I felt as if placed in a vast solitude, with lands and seas around me hitherto undiscovered by man.

Whilst I looked with increasing admiration over the twilight scene and was endeavoring to stretch my vision into the dusky regions far away, my attention was suddenly attracted by sparks of dazzling brilliancy shooting through the pines on the Blue Ridge. In the olden time, when Jupiter's thunderbolts were forged in the caverns of Etna, never did such glittering scintillations fly from beneath the giant forge hammers of the Cyclops. It was the sun darting his topmost rays over the mountain and dispersing their sparkling threads through the pure serenity of the atmosphere.

Very soon the fancied isles around me caught the splendid hue of the luminary and shone on their eastern sides like burnished gold. In the west, where they were most thickly strewn over the white sea of mist and where their bright sides alone appeared, I could fancy that they were the islands of the happy (so famous in ancient story), where the spirits of the good reposed in the balmy light of eternal spring. But the pleasing illusion was soon dissipated. The surface of the mist, hitherto lying still, became agitated like a boiling caldron. Everywhere light clouds arose from it and melted away. Then the lower hills of the country began to show their tops as if they were emerging from this troubled sea. After the sun had displayed his full orb of living fire, the vapory commotion increased; and in a little while the features of the low country began to be unveiled. The first audible sound from the living world, the barking of a farmer's dog, arose from a vale beneath and completely broke the enchantment of the twilight scene. When the sun was an hour high, the fog only marked the deep and curvilinear beds of the river.

The prospect of the country around now yielded a pleasure, not inferior in degree, though it differed in kind, from that which I had enjoyed in beholding a scene, rare and beautiful in itself and embellished by mist and twilight with the visionary charms of a creative fancy. The country appeared beneath and around me to the utmost extent of vision. On the diversified surface of the Great Valley, a thousand farms in every variety of situation were distinctly visible—some in the low vales, where winding streams had begun to shine in the glancing sunlight—some presented their yellow harvest fields among the green woods and wavy slopes of hills—and, here and there, others were perched aloft among the primeval forests and antediluvian rocks of the mountains. In the northeast, the less hilly country of Augusta was seen in dim perspective like a large level of bluish green. Stretching along the eastern horizon for many a league, the Blue Ridge mustered a hundred of his lofty heads, among which the Peaks of Otter rose preeminently conspicuous. The valley southwestwardly was in part concealed by the isolated line of Short Hill. But beyond this, at intervals, I caught glimpses of the vale of James River, from the gap where the stream has burst through the Blue Ridge to the place where it has cloven the North Mountain and thence round by the west to the remarkable rent through which it flows between jutting crags in the Jackson Mountain. Here the Clifton forge, though not seen, could be imagined, sounding in the deep ravine with the roaring waters and making the dark cliffs rebellow at every stroke.

On the western side, the scenery differs from that on the eastern. Here it seemed as if all the mountains of Virginia had assembled to display their loftiness and their length. Line after line, ridge behind ridge, peered over one another and crossed the landscape, this way and that way. Here a huge knob swelled up his rotundity; there a peak shot up his rough stony point out of a huddle of inferior eminences, or from the backs of ridges that stretched away far and wide until they faded off in the blue of the atmosphere, and all distinction of form and color was lost in the distance.

When I was able to withdraw my sight from the grand features of the prospect and to look down upon the country near the base of my observatory, I was attracted by the softer beauties of the landscape. The woody hillocks and shady glens had lost every rough and disagreeable feature; the surface looked smooth and green like a meadow and wound its curvatures, dappled with shade and sunlight, so gracefully to the elevated eye that they seemed to realize our dreamy conceptions of fairy land. The little homesteads that spotted the hills and valleys under the mountain, the large farms and country seats farther away, and the bright group of buildings in the village of Lexington relieved the mind from the almost painful sublimity of the distant prospect and prepared us, after hours of delightful contemplation, to descend from our aerial height and to return with gratified feelings to our college and our studies again.

The New Friends in Charleston

When I had concluded my House Mountain story, the brother maintained for a few seconds the attitude of a listener until I remarked that my other visits to the mountain produced nothing new and that my theme was therefore exhausted.

"I am sorry that it is," said he, "for I could listen with interest to much more of the same sort."

Judith, who seemed to be in a state of thoughtful abstraction, now heaved a deep sigh, which roused her; and being conscious that she had sighed, she blushed. And when she felt her cheeks warmed with blushes, she hung down her head in silence.

"Heigh-ho! Judith, what is the matter with you? You pay Mr. Garame a poor compliment for his description of one of the finest landscapes in the world—it seems to have made you sad."

"If I am sad, brother, it is because we may not be able to visit the mountains of Virginia. Mr. Garame will not think me disrespectful when he knows the cause of my sadness."

"Certainly not, Miss Judith," said I with great sincerity, "but I hope that you may still find time to run up to our valley and to look out from our mountain tops."

"Oh, how delightful that would be." She raised her head as she spoke, and her countenance flashed up to more than its wonted animation as she thus continued:

"I love the mountains—I prefer the country to the town—joy springs up in my heart when I look upon the summer hills and valleys, the clear brooks, the green fields, and all the objects and employments that occur in rural life. Most of all I admire scenery like that which you have described, grandeur and beauty spreading to immensity and blending into indescribable labyrinths of variety. There nature feasts the soul with her choicest entertainments; there man leads the happiest life and is inspired with the noblest feelings. The inhabitant of the plain and of the town may be intelligent, virtuous, refined; but the man of the mountains has sources of deep and holy feeling which cannot be found among the artificial structures of a town and the no less artificial forms of city life, which are absent also in great part from the monotonous champaign, especially when stripped of its natural garb and clothed with the petty embellishments of human art. There is beauty even in a scene like this. He who has reared his neat cottage in a grove and can look out upon his fields and flocks in the plain has much to love in his comfortable home. But he has feeble impressions from nature, and through nature draws only faint inspirations from God. But who can look upon the great mountains and not feel his bosom swell with sacred emotions? Who can look up at the towering peak and the beetling crag or look down from them? Or who can see, as you have seen, the sublime ridge that seems to present an insuperable and immovable barrier to ocean and river, cloven from the top to the bottom—yes, snapt asunder by an Almighty hand as you would snap a mouldering twig. Or who can dwell in the valley, fenced on either side by cloud-capped mountains upon whose hoary steeps the old forest shakes his thousand arms in the wind while the cataract roars beneath pine-covered rocks in the dusky ravine, and not feel the movings of the Divinity in his soul? Here are the representatives of the Divine Majesty, the exhibitions of the Universal Spirit. Can a mortal mind contemplate such objects and not feel a high-toned energy infused into it? Must it not catch the lofty impress of these sublime monuments of eternal Power and Godhead? And then the softer beauties of the broad, uneven valley, the round hill top with its sylvan crown, the sweet windling dale with its purling brook and flowery meadow. These seem to me to shed the milder effluences of deity into the soul, to breathe gentleness and love into the heart, to mitigate the fierce passions, and to soothe the wounded spirit. And where both these characters of scenery, the sublime and the beautiful, are combined, as they are among the mountains of Virginia, the people must be deeply imbued with religion and virtue, and their virtues must be a finely tempered mixture of the heroic and the gentle. But," said she, checking herself, "I am running on with my crude notions on a subject that I do not understand; yet still it does seem to me that the people of your country must have a noble character, have they not, Mr. Garame?"

"They certainly have in them the elements of a noble character and need only to be more highly and generally improved by education to become all that you suppose. I think, too, that your theory derives confirmation from the history of the ingenious Greeks of old and of the patriotic Swiss of modern times. Mountaineers are often rude but rarely mean-spirited; and their local attachments are always strong because they dwell among objects strongly characterized and therefore strongly impressed on their minds."

"I am glad to find that my notion of the effect of mountain scenery is not altogether a groundless fancy. I thought while speaking that it seemed reasonable; but then I remembered how often I speak rashly, under the impulse of excited feelings, obtruding my hasty thoughts on others and proving my need of instruction instead of my ability to instruct."

"That is her way," said Eli, smiling. "She is of such excitable stuff that when she hears or sees anything fine, she kindles and flames away like tow in the fire; and often for five minutes she will emit a constant blaze of fancy or feeling, sentiment or philosophy; then she will sink at once into the ashes of humility."

Judith blushed good-naturedly as she said, "Well, brother, I have confessed my weakness to Mr. Garame, and he will have the goodness to pardon my long rant."

"It was not rant, Miss Judith, and needs no apology. I should be very sorry if you conceived it necessary before me to lay any restraint upon the utterance of your thoughts—especially such thoughts. Do me the favor to give them free passage. I love the unstudied, unchecked effusions of the soul in conversation."

She looked up with one of her sweetest smiles and said, "Thank you, Mr. Garame."

"I must do my enthusiastic sister the justice to say that of late she is less often carried out of her usual sobriety by these impulses than formerly. Now it is only something of uncommon merit that has power to tap her spiritual soda fountain; and the jet, although still foamy, is for the most part racy and good."

Here Judith and I at the same time bowed to the speaker and said, "Thank you, sir."

This little scene prepared us for a lighter strain of conversation, and we kept it up with hilarity until the evening. My companions charmed me more and more; their fund of good sense, sprightly wit, and sound knowledge showed no symptoms of exhaustion but continued to supply an increasing flow of thoughts that came with unaffected simplicity and grace from their minds. There was a great resemblance in their mental characteristics as well as in their persons, yet also a difference which every hour became more manifest. The brother had a more ready wit and a superior talent for light conversation, the sister a more lively and profound sensibility to whatever was grand, beautiful, or pathetic—more genius—and, what I could hardly reconcile with the evident enthusiasm of her character, more reflection.

My admiration of these young persons was increased when we happened in conversation to tell our ages; and I learned that Judith would not complete her nineteenth year until the first of June and that Eli was only twenty-two, that is, one year older than myself.

When the twilight came on and we were yet twelve miles from Charleston, the coach stopped to change horses at a country inn. A party of slaves were coming in from the field, and, as often happens, they began to sing with a full voice one of the melodious airs that they have among them. Judith listened with breathless attention as if the strain were new to her. I had heard it before. The same air was repeated to a succession of stanzas destitute of merit, but deriving pathos from the chorus or burden, "Long time ago," which sounded delightful because it was uttered with enthusiasm by many voices joining in symphony from different parts of the neighborhood.

When we were driven off, I remarked to Judith that the air just heard had a sweet and touching simplicity in it.

"Yes," said she with emotion, "it touches both the fancy and the heart; the melody is pleasant in itself, and it makes one think that the people who sing it with such enthusiasm must be happy."

Having spoken these words, she relapsed into meditation and seemed indisposed to further conversation during the evening's ride. We reached Charleston before nine o'clock and obtained excellent accommodations at a hotel.

The next day we spent several hours together viewing the city. After dinner Eli and myself left Judith in her room that we might go to the harbor and inquire for a packet to Norfolk. After some time we found a stout well-built schooner that was to sail in four days. We engaged the cabin for ourselves and the attendance of a half grown black boy attached to the schooner. Then, after strolling about the town, we returned in the evening and found Judith in our private parlor playing the air of the preceding evening on a piano, which I was so unobservant as not to have noticed before or I should have asked her to play. She had arranged the notes on a blank page of the music book before her, which I found to be her own. I was charmed with her style of playing; there was so little appearance of art in it. She struck the keys with such nice tact and in such perfect accordance with the spirit of the piece that she made one forget the player and lose even his self-consciousness in the Lethean tide of music that came stealing over the soul.

When she discovered that we were in the room, she rose with a blush to leave the instrument, saying that we had caught her attempting to learn the Negroes' melody. I asked her to play it again, but she declined with the apology that she must learn it better before she could venture to play it in company; but, at my solicitation, she resumed her seat and not only played several pieces with the delicious artlessness of her art but gratified me also by singing two songs with such "linked sweetness" of melody that one, which was of a pathetic character, drew tears from my eyes and continued to run in streams of sensibility through my nerves during the night.

Our apartments were, as we had requested, in the most private part of the house in a wing designed for families and, as it happened, occupied at this time by none but ourselves. I mention this to ex-

plain an incident that occurred the next evening. When we had all
satisfied ourselves with looking at the public institutions of the city
and had taken our tea, Eli proposed that we should walk the streets
that we might observe the nocturnal customs of the place. I instantly
gave my consent, but Judith, pleading fatigue, declined. And then I
was sorry that I had consented but ashamed to retreat. She locked
the parlor door when we went out, telling us with a playful smile, to
say "open sesame" when we wanted admittance. After we had gotten
to the street, I remembered that my room was left unlocked with
several articles exposed to pilferers. I requested Eli to wait until I
should return and lock the door. I hastened back, ran up stairs, and
had almost reached my room, a few steps from the parlor door, when
my attention was arrested by the notes of the same Negroes' melody
sweetly touched on the piano. The unlocked door, Eli, and all the
world were forgotten in a moment. I was insensibly drawn on tiptoe
quite to the parlor door when a momentary pause in the music allowed me to feel that my heart was palpitating violently. I was beginning to fear that the exquisitely pathetic tones would come no more
when lo!, with the melting tenderness of an angel singing a newly
departed saint to rest, she attuned her voice, as she touched the keys
again, to the same melody. And these are the words of the simple
ballad that she sang:

SALLY OF THE VALLEY

Once I wandered through a valley
  Where waters flow;
There I saw the lovely Sally,
  'Long time ago.'

Trees and banks were full of flowers;
  Soft winds did blow;
Leafy vines made dusky bowers,
  'Long time ago.'

By a rock beneath the mountain,
  She, bending low,
Shed warm tears beside a fountain,
  'Long time ago.'

"Maiden, why so broken hearted?
  Fain would I know."

"Sir, my love and I here parted,
 'Long time ago.'"

"Here he wooed and here he won me,
 Then far must go;
Left his kiss of truth upon me,
 'Long time ago.'

"Soon he sunk beneath the billow,
 When storms did blow;
Then I planted here this willow,
 'Long time ago.'"

"Fare thee well, sweet mourning Sally,
 Keen is thy woe."
So I left the flowery valley,
 'Long time ago.'

Once again I saw the valley,
 Where waters flow;
Then again I looked for Sally,
 'Long time ago.'

By the rock beneath the mountain,
 Saw willow grow
O'er a grave beside the fountain,
 'Long time ago.'

She ceased. I was rivetted to the spot. For minutes I was entranced with the mournful vision of poor Sally's grave under the weeping willow while my nerves yet quivered sympathetically with the heavenly tones that made the simple story of her fate so dolefully affecting. I was roused at last by Eli's voice calling me from the foot of the stairs. I hurried down without thinking of my door. He asked whether I had missed anything out of my room. I simply answered 'No' and walked on, I knew not whither. I spoke not during the most of our walk except when spoken to, and then sometimes I gave irrelevant answers. Eli soon observed my mood and several times looked at me with amazement but made no remark. To prevent unpleasant conjectures, I told him on our return what had so strangely affected my spirits. Whether he inferred anything more than the merit of the ballad and my susceptibility of musical impressions, I know not; probably he ascribed nothing of the effect to the musician as he had not yet passed his novitiate in the mysteries of Cupid. As for myself I did not then reflect on the subject; I was too much absorbed by the emotions produced by the sweet music and the sweeter musician to analyze my feelings and to search out the causes which might be at work in carrying my soul away at such a rate.

At the parlor door we said "open sesame" and were admitted. When I told Judith how I had undesignedly overheard her ballad, she blushed and was a good deal confused at first. Then she began to apologize by saying that the air of the Negro song, chanted sonorously in the calm evening and quiet fields of the country, had taken such possession of her fancy that she could not rest until she had put together a few stanzas according in simplicity of language and sentiment with the simplicity of the air to whose melody they were to serve as a vehicle. We soon stopped her modest apologies by insisting that she should repeat the song, at least for Eli's sake. She did so more sweetly, if possible, than before. That night I dreamed that I visited the flowery valley and saw first, Judith weeping by the fountain side and then, the willow waving its green tresses over Judith's grave.

The Sea Voyage

When I awoke in the morning, I rejoiced to find that my dismal conceptions were but a dream. But I was sad through the whole forenoon and but partially relieved towards the evening by the conversation and cheerful looks of my companions. Pleasant rambles with them about the town, the amusements that we shared after dark, and a good night's sleep had done much to counteract the downward tendency of my spirits. At breakfast time the next morning we were startled by a message from our captain warning us to be on board within two hours because the wind was fair, and he would sail a day sooner than he had intended for fear of a change. We therefore hastened our preparations and were on board by eleven o'clock. According to contract, we took exclusive possession of the cabin and were pleased that no other passengers of any sort were on board. The crew consisted of five men, the servant boy, and the captain.

We set sail immediately. It was one of the most delightful mornings of a Southern spring. Balmy breezes wafted us gently out of the bay whilst from the deck we contemplated the retiring city with its advanced guard of islands and batteries. When these began to sink away in the distance, I had, for the first time, a full view of the ocean spreading its desolate waste before me to the utmost extent of vision and leading the imagination onward still over its vast unfathomable deeps. How different from the diversified scenes of beauty and grandeur in my native highlands, yet even more awfully sublime! It was a scene of such naked simplicity and such outspreading vastness: nothing to divide and relieve the attention, nothing to contemplate but the unvaried immensity of the earth-girding waters. I sat mutely gazing over that liquid desert until it opened to my view the whole canopy of heaven bending down towards the waters. The waters seemed to swell upwards as they spread until all around, skies and waters met and enclosed us in the center of their grand periphery.

Serious impressions of the object before me, thoughts of its fearful might when storms awaken the rage of its billows, thoughts of its gloomy unsearchable abysses, where monsters play among lost treasures and the bones of lost men, all came upon me and sunk my spirits more and more until I was deeply immersed in the melancholy to which I had been tending for the last two days. After I observed how the trees and sand hills of the coast had seemingly slidden away down the western side of the globe and had left us alone in this boundless waste of waters and precariously floating over the dark gulfs of brine, in whose vast receptacle so many dead are hidden till the day of judgment, I became not only sad but terrified. And what made my situation more distressing was that seasickness came upon me with its dismal nausea, itself sufficient to conjure up a fantastic host of goblins from the troubled deeps of the soul.

Eli had left me to arrange some affairs with his sister in the cabin. While my soul was thus sinking to the bottom of the sea, he came up with her and, seeing my melancholy looks, approached me and said with his usual smile of benevolence:

"Now, Mr. Garame, you remind me of the day when I first put out to sea. I kept thinking how wide and how deep is the sea! Yet I have to go all the way over it; and if I should plunge into it some dark, windy night, or a tempest should crack this wooden shell that now bears me up, why then I must sink all the way to the bottom though it were thousands of fathoms down. What made me feel worse, this little sister of mine, who, as you have observed, has a touch of the romantic in her constitution, she sat crying her eyes out. She had an unconquerable fancy to embark with me. She was not afraid! oh! no. She was a bold seafarer enough in her chamber at home, but then when she came into this wide presence chamber of old Ocean himself, her brave little heart quailed before the face of his hoary majesty. However, I must make due allowance for natural sorrow at parting with our father and friends. Judith, cannot you comfort Mr.

Garame by telling him how dismally you felt at first and how, in spite of all your fears, you passed safely over the Atlantic and got well and cheerful before the voyage was ended?"

"Brother," said she, and her voice was like a flageolet breathing soft airs, "I wish that we could cheer Mr. Garame. But what can mere words do for one suffering under two such natural causes of distress: the first awful impression of being out in the sea and the heart-sickening nausea that soon comes to blacken every thought. I know from experience how impossible it is to be cheerful under such circumstances and how little a friend can do to clear the dark current of our feelings."

Here Eli cut her short with the good humored remonstrance:

"Now, Judith, you are paying me a poor compliment on my ability as a comforter, and you are preaching like a Job's comforter to Mr. Garame."

"Nay, brother, I mean not so; I know that you did all that any brother could have done for a distressed sister. You had your own sorrow to bear; yet you forced your countenance to look cheerful for my encouragement, and if your exertions did not succeed in relieving me at once, it was because such a weight of sorrow, aggravated by sickness, could be removed only by degrees. So you removed the load which oppressed my spirits, and so, I trust, we shall succeed in taking off the burden that depresses Mr. Garame. Nay, I think that he will find relief much sooner than I did, for he has two advantages in his case, which did not exist in mine. I was leaving home, kindred and friends on a long voyage. He is returning by a short voyage to his home—his home in the glorious mountains. Mr. Garame, think of that. Then again, I had the heart only of a girl, a timid, foolish girl of the town; he has the heart of a man and the bold spirit of a mountaineer to bear his sufferings."

Here I was thoroughly ashamed of myself and began to feel the mountain spirit rousing up its energies at the life-giving touch of my charming comforter. She concluded in these words:

"So now, brother, I think that I am not as bad as Job's comforters; if not a skilful, I am, however, a well meaning comforter. Am I not, Mr. Garame?"

A sudden impulse had almost made me exclaim, "You are my elixir of life." I had opened my mouth to say it when I perceived the impropriety of so passionate a declaration at this time. With an instantaneous effort I shut it in. But having no substitute ready, I felt confused, lost my self-possession, hung down my head, felt miserably like a fool, and was verging to madness under the mortification of being speechless with confusion when Judith, perceiving my agony, though scarce divining the cause, brought me relief by saying—

"Brother, Mr. Garame has one of the dreadful qualms that overcame me so often, and now I am glad that I have thought of it. I have still in my trunk a phial of the medicine that I took when the fits came on; it did not effect a cure, but it palliated my sufferings. Do you stay and comfort Mr. Garame while I go and search for it."

She started off, but seeming to recollect suddenly that I had been looking down over the side of the vessel as if meditating something desperate, she stopped and, turning round, said half seriously—

"Brother, people sometimes do rash things in a fit of sickness; take care that Mr. Garame's tormenting nausea does not make him leap into the sea."

"No danger, Judith; a plunge to the bottom is not so agreeable to his fancy just now. He has no more relish for a four-mile dip in salt water than I have. But, perhaps, a dive to the sea country would not be so bad an adventure after all, as one is apt to think when he has qualms. Suppose that he should find the Nereides down there combing their wet locks in the green sea meadows among the coral groves, and they should sing him a ditty 'lovely well,' and take him into their shell-caves, and feast him on—let me see—what?"

"Oh! brother," said Judith, interrupting him, "change the subject; you frighten me."

Then she hastened down the companionway.

"Pardon me," said Eli to me, "I meant only to divert you, but probably I have taken the wrong way."

And so he had when he took the way to the bottom of the sea, for I found myself going down again rapidly to the lowest deep of mental dejection. I imagined myself, Judith and all, sunk by a storm in passing Cape Fear, which we must soon approach. What aggravated my sufferings was that the weather had begun to change from fair to cloudy; the wind veered to the southeast and freshened so much as to curl up the waves and make the schooner rock with a quicker and heavier motion. My nausea and mental gloom were consequently growing worse every moment. Eli saw the gathering clouds on my face and said:

"Mr. Garame, resist this sinking of the heart; think of cheerful objects."

"Fain would I, Mr. Bensaddi, but I am constitutionally subject to fits of despondency during which I am the passive and miserable slave of fantasy. Even now, frightful images of distress haunt me. I cannot even shake off the impression that they are ominous of some approaching disaster."

"Oh! think not so," said he again. "Consider that they are the natural effect of a disordered stomach and of your new situation out here in this 'barren sea,' as old Homer calls it."

"Your opinion may have the sanction of reason, but my feelings refuse to be governed by its dictates. They point prophetically to some doleful calamity at hand; they call up a spectral tragedy. Something dark and horrible—I know not what—looms cloudily up to view; it makes me shudder as if it were a real premonition. What can it mean?"

"Nothing, nothing, my friend," said he, moving towards me quickly to let the sailors shift the sails for a different tack of the vessel. "Nothing but the work of fancy operating on the materials of your sickness and melancholy and casting them into misshapen images of misery and disaster."

He had reached the place where I sat on a bench by the side rail and, as he pronounced the last word, was turning round to take his seat with me when he was tripped by a sudden lurch of the vessel and thrown backwards, head foremost, into the sea. He almost brushed me as he fell. Before I could think, he was gone. When I looked, I could see no sign of him but the bubbling of the water where he had sunk.

"A man overboard! Heave to! Down with the boat." These were the orders of the captain, and every preparation was hastily made for the rescue. For my part, my eyes stared with the fixedness of death on the fatal spot as it receded every instant. Soon he rose to the surface but strangling. A bench had been thrown out for him, but he either saw it not or was unable to buffet the waves that separated him from it. The only hope was in the boat; I saw that it was so and felt the rush of a new spirit through my whole man. As the boat was being pushed off, I sprang into it.

"Fast, fast, men. Pull, pull, for God's sake—he is sinking."

My eyes were fixed on him. He struggled convulsively but with a strength that was failing every instant. The rowers strained their nerves to the utmost but all in vain. We were yet ten yards off when I saw his raven locks disappear beneath the wave, and, when we reached the place, not even a bubble marked it. Cruel wave! It had already forgotten its victim.

The boat was turned immediately towards the vessel. I remonstrated.

"It is useless to wait, sir; he will never rise again."

Still I looked back as the boat was dashed through the waves on her return. A shriek smote my ear! I turned with the quickness of instinct. Well did I know whose soul was pierced. *She* was running distractedly over the deck; her tresses fell and streamed in the wind. Her suppliant arms were flung up towards Heaven, then flung down in despair. The frenzy of despair drove her on convulsively—she knew not what she did—against the fatal side rail. She fell over into the sea. Her white robe fluttered as she touched the wave; the wave tossed its ample folds as the briny liquid enfolded her. I cried out, "Oh! mercy!" and became speechless. The steersman urged the rowers; we neared the spot. A vanishing remnant of the robe—that snowy emblem of her purity—was all that could be seen of Judith Bensaddi. The boat was rather too distant to reach her in time. My foot was on the prow; my nerves were strung to a frenetic energy. One heaven-directed spring, and the robe was in my grasp. In my struggle to sustain her, we were both sinking but were rescued just in time. She was carried insensible to her berth in the cabin, where, after some moments, my terrific apprehensions were relieved by signs of resuscitation.

Everything possible was done to complete her restoration and to promote her personal comfort. My presence of mind and vigor of muscle since he, and especially since she, had fallen, seemed almost miraculous. Sickness, melancholy, languor, even consciousness of my own existence, were gone. I had no thought, no feeling, but for Judith's bereavement and Judith's melancholy situation. Poor hapless maiden! Better, so her life had still been preserved, that her consciousness had not returned—at least for that dark night of sorrow, whose thick gloom of clouds and rain gathered over Eli's watery grave just as she began to remember that her brother was lost in the dark stormy sea. Then her breast began to heave convulsively—a sob—a groan—a shriek—the same wild sort of shriek that I had heard in the boat—these were all that she could utter.

In vain did I attempt some words of consolation. She heard me not. External things could make no impression on a soul absorbed in one idea and one emotion. Hours passed away before that one thought and feeling could find utterance in words. Then they came forth only in broken accents during intervals between the more violent paroxysms of grief. Merciful Heaven! Even the distant remembrance almost freezes my blood. Still do I seem to hear that voice, like a mourning dove's, utter its broken notes of woe in terms like these:

"Oh! my brother! Dear, lost brother! Lost in the sea. Oh, my poor brother, drowned in the deep waters! Brother! oh, brother! can you not return? No, never. Too deep—far down in the cold sea. God have mercy on thee, my dear, lost brother! Oh, hapless fate! So sudden! He looked and smiled—he was happy: I went away—they called me—'your brother is lost!' Oh, God of Israel! Pity my lost Eli—so lovely! so kind! so joyful! In a moment he fell, he sunk; they could not save him. Alas for thee, my brother—cold! silent! alone! deep! No friend can find thee there, oh, lost brother! I cannot close thy dear eyes in thy dark briny bed. Thy heart is cold, that heart that loved me so. Oh, my heart will break! Oh, that I had died for thee, beloved Eli! Alas, he hears me not! He hears no more the storms of this dark world—poor brother—in his oozy bed, far, far down beneath the waves. Farewell, lost brother—farewell, forever."

But vainly do I attempt to describe her grief or to give a just conception of her heartrending lamentations.

I will pass briefly over the next stage of her mourning. She began to think of her father's bereavement and to condole for the grief that must afflict his aged breast when he should hear that his only son was lost. Lastly she thought of herself, and then she deplored her sad condition as a lonely and friendless maiden on a foreign shore. Here I made a second attempt to gain her attention, that I might assure her of my friendship and protection. Still, though sometimes her eye seemed to rest upon me, her heart was too deeply buried in grief, her soul too fully possessed with the one idea of her bereavement, to let her recognize my person or remember our late acquaintance. Her eyes, those eyes lately so bright with intelligence and joyful emotions, were now swollen and dimmed with weeping.

I kept anxious watch over her. I was prompt to see and, as far as possible, to supply every want. I had administered a dose of laudanum mixed with a cordial. This ultimately produced a soothing effect, though it was past midnight before she could cease from wailing and lamentation. But exhausted nature, aided by the anodyne, compelled her grief at last to yield to some intervals of repose. She sank first into short slumbers, broken by starts of terror and calls for her lost brother; then she would fall back again into a transient oblivion of her sorrows. Finally she was overcome by a heavy slumber of two hours. When she awoke, the dark, dismal night had passed away, and the morning broke less cloudy and rainy. I watched her anxiously during her sleep and more anxiously on her awaking, fearful lest her slumber should prove to be a respite without relief. For an instant she looked around with a countenance of wild fright. Then, remembering her situation, she began to sob and weep. But to my great satisfaction, she soon became more composed and gave indications of a returning sensibility to present objects. When she looked at me with a countenance expressive of recognition and I drew near to address her, she could only exclaim, "Oh, Mr. Garame," before a new flood of emotions choked her utterance.

"Endeavor to compose yourself, dear Judith," was all that I could say, when I felt a sudden change in myself. Thus far my feelings had been absorbed in hers; my whole attention had been abstracted from self and fixed on the lovely sufferer whose agony of grief was enough to excite a demon's pity. Now, when she was so far relieved as to recognize me and call my name, self-consciousness returned; my existence, as a distinct being, was felt again. Engrossing sympathy yielded to a softer emotion; all the fountains of compassion were opened within me; and for some time we silently shed our tears together.

When I recovered the power of speech, I gave her the most heartfelt assurances of devoted friendship. I exhorted her to rely on me as an affectionate brother; I solemnly promised to treat her as a sister and not to leave her until I had deposited her safely with her friends. I saw with unspeakable satisfaction that she could now listen, that she understood my words, and that she was soothed by them, and, what was particularly gratifying, that her grief, although still poignant, had passed its most alarming stage, and that she no longer suffered the utter despair and prostration of soul which had threatened to destroy her reason, if not her life.

Hoping that she might sleep again, I left the cabin for half an hour, and when I returned, I found her dozing. When she opened her eyes, I asked her to sit up and take some food. She could only swallow a little tea. I then renewed my expressions of condolence and fraternal care. Afterwards I attempted, in the following manner, to direct her mind to the best source of consolation:

"My dear friend, it is natural that you should grieve intensely for the loss of a brother so deserving of all your affection. I, too, have lost in him a friend, whom our few days' acquaintance had taught me to love as one brought up with me from childhood. I cannot comfort myself; how much less can I comfort you? In such a case we are strongly reminded of our dependence on a higher power, who overrules our destiny and ordains both our prosperity and adversity. He has sent this sore affliction upon you, not in cruelty but in love; for when He afflicts, it is in mercy. He wounds to heal and bruises that He may bind up. He designs by the ills of this life to train us for a happier life to come. When He seems prematurely to remove our friends away from us, we should not infer that He does it in wrath to them or to us. We see the good cut off in the midst of their days or suddenly bereft of their dearest friends. Then we should remember that it is not chance nor fate but the Father of mercies who takes them away and that their removal from this world, where sin entices and sorrow afflicts, is no evidence of his having cast them out of his paternal care. He can still behold them with his compassionate eye and reach them with his arm that is not only strong to save, but tender in the guidance of them who fear Him, frail and erring as they may have been. Commit yourself then to His benevolent care. He is your Father and the Father of all whom you love; His tender mercies are over all his works; He calls Himself your Father and teaches you to trust in Him as the God of love. Open your heart now to His consolations. He will heal its pains and mollify the bruises of the contrite spirit. Believe that He has done the best for you and yours and that some day both you and your lost brother will see cause to thank Him for this dispensation.

Such was the tenor of my discourse.

When she heard another speak of the horrible disaster which had since yesterday cut off her communication with the external world, her grief started afresh and threatened a return of her violent paroxysms. I was at first alarmed at the effect of my words and was sorry that I had broached the subject. But as I proceeded, she visibly strove against her feelings and directed her attention to my discourse. When I had concluded, I saw a change in her countenance; its late unmixed expression of anguish was mitigated by perceptible indications of humble submission to the will of Heaven. In a few hours I was satisfied that I had taken the best course when I embraced the earliest opportunity of opening a free communication between our minds on the subject of her grief. She was the sooner drawn off from the first absorbing view of the calamity as a present object and familiarized with the consideration of it as past, irreversible, and, therefore, to be acquiesced in as the will of Heaven. The farther I could put it back in the order of her remembrances by occupying her attention with other objects, the sooner would the keen edge of her sorrow be blunted and consoling thoughts find admission to her heart.

I alone exercised any care over her. The captain and crew showed so little sympathy that I, in the fulness of mine, thought them brutally indifferent as if they considered the drowning of a passenger an event rather to be expected than lamented and the grief of a lovely sister a womanish weakness scarcely deserving pity. I have since learned to make allowance for the circumstance that whilst I had leisure to think incessantly of Judith and her sufferings, they had to busy themselves with their navigation and felt that the "poor girl," as they called her, might be left to my willing and assiduous attentions.

Towards evening Judith could talk with me somewhat freely of her misfortune.

"Oh, my friend," said she at one time, "how kind was it in God to send you along with us on this fatal voyage. Dear, lost brother! if his departed spirit can look back on the affairs of this world, he must feel comforted to think that so kind a friend was provided for his poor bereaved sister. And my good father! bitter enough will be the day when he shall hear that the best comfort of his old age is buried in the ocean, but still more bitter would it be if it had been his lot to hear that his helpless daughter was left alone and friendless on the waves of a foreign shore."

Here a gush of feeling interrupted her speech, but she strove for self command and was soon calmer again. Then, lifting her teary eyes and grief-worn countenance upon me, she continued.

"Mr. Garame, I accept your offered protection—I accept it gratefully; pardon me that I have not expressed my gratitude and my confidence in you sooner. Indeed, my feelings have been too strong for utterance. Now I can say that I feel as much as my bruised heart is capable of feeling. Yes, I do feel that you are truly my friend and will act towards me the part of a brother. Alas! no one else can now show me the kindness of a brother. He that was born my brother and from my childhood endeared himself to me by innumerable kindnesses, my beloved Eli, is now cold and lifeless at the bottom of the sea. Oh! Jehovah, God of Abraham, teach me resignation! Excuse me, dear friend, I cannot refrain. I am a poor bereft thing, a weak creature at best, always needing counsel and guidance, and now more than ever. I commit myself to your care; you will indulge my weaknesses now that I am stricken down and, with my natural infirmity, have to bear a heavy load of sorrow. You will be my guardian, my comforter, and—my brother."

Having said this, she seemed to feel more ease as if she had discharged a portion of her load. She fell back on her couch, sobbed a little and then sank gently to sleep.

As the native vivacity of Judith's feelings made the first tempest of her grief irresistibly violent, so it caused the tempest sooner to spend its force and to settle down into a comparative calm. Never had I seen such agonizing distress, nay, such frantic desperation of grief, as seized her when the lightning stroke of bereavement fell so terribly upon her. By the morning of the third day, however, she could take some nourishment and converse with less frequent spasms of anguish. But the effect on her person of the mental suffering and corporeal exhaustion of the last two days struck a deep impression of sadness upon my heart whenever I looked at her. Grief had, in this short time, driven the rosy flush of health from her cheeks, the sparkling radiance from her eyes, the buoyant elasticity from her members and had left her faded and withered like a scorched blossom of the desert.

What were my feelings when I had leisure to reflect that this lovely drooping flower was now under my sole care! And by what a surprising stroke had Divine Providence driven her for shelter to my honor and benevolence! In herself to me the loveliest, she was made by these affecting circumstances the dearest by far of all earthly beings. My passion, heretofore uncherished in the bud, was thus nourished, expanded, matured, and, at the same time, refined into the tenderest and most unselfish feeling of fraternal affection. If ever my breast was visited by the pure sentiment and seraphic glow of an angel's love, it was now when I looked on that countenance, pale with sorrow—remembering how lately it shone with the light of joyous innocence—and comparing its expression then with its present look, so humbly submissive, yet so keenly sorrowful, so smitten, yet so patient and so holy.

On the evening of this day she began to express regret for the inconvenience and trouble that she would cause me to experience. I replied that if ever in future life I could reflect with unalloyed satisfaction on any of my actions, it would be upon that of restoring her to her friends whatever it might cost me. How feelingly did she look at me and say, "The mourner's gratitude will be a poor reward, but the mourner's Heavenly Friend, in whom you have taught me to trust, will not forget such kindness."

I embraced the occasion to consult her about ulterior movements after we should reach the Chesapeake, asking her to tell me without reserve which course would be most agreeable to her. Whether I should take her to Rockbridge until I could prepare to go with her to London or whether I should take her on straight way to New York or Boston and thence home, leaving deficiencies in my outfit to be supplied by the way.

She meditated a little and then replied that she could now, without scruple, accept my services to any extent that might be necessary but that she was under no necessity of asking me to go all the way to London. Her brother had arranged with a friend of theirs to meet him in Boston, where he had lately settled, and to embark with him there for England. She needed, therefore, to ask no more of my kindness than to go with her to Boston, where that friend would release me from further trouble on her account. She added that as this great extension of my journey would add much to its expense and none to that which she and her brother would have incurred, I would not scruple to use their funds, especially as so unexpected and so large an increase to expenditure might not have been provided for.

"But," said she in conclusion, "though I would not unnecessarily trouble you to go to London, yet if you ever find occasion to visit that city, I claim that you give me and my friends the opportunity of showing that we remember what it is to deal kindly with a stranger in a foreign land."

Whatever vague desire I may have entertained to conduct her on a visit to my native valley, I acquiesced without hesitation in the obvious propriety of the course that she suggested. The same reason that governed her choice of this route made it proper also to proceed without delay from Norfolk to Baltimore by water and thence to Boston through Philadelphia and New York.

VIII

Detention and Separation in Philadelphia

We entered the Chesapeake after a voyage of five days. In Hampton Roads we met a steamboat on her way from Norfolk to Baltimore. As the day was pleasant and the water smooth, we determined to transfer ourselves at once to the more speedy and comfortable vehicle without landing at Norfolk. The boat instantly obeyed our signal; in a few minutes we were snugly bestowed in our new quarters and, with a mighty puffing and splashing, were being dashed through the waters of the "Old Dominion" at the rate of ten miles an hour. The next day we landed in Baltimore, where I asked Judith if her feeble health did not require a day's rest before we proceeded any further. She acknowledged her extreme debility but thought that she could travel in steamboats and desired to go on whilst she was able. So we took passage the same afternoon and proceeded by way of Frenchtown to Philadelphia. We landed at the Chestnut Street wharf the next day at two o'clock and took a hackney coach to convey us to one of the principal hotels of the city. Judith's weakness was now so great—and to me it was alarming—that she admitted her inability to continue our journey until her strength was recruited by a day's rest. A day's rest might have been all if an accident had not prolonged our stay.

The coach had stopped before the door of the hotel. My foot was on the step and my hands were let go to descend when a sudden start of the horses, which were frightened by something unusual, threw me violently on the rough stones of the pavement. I sprang up, unconscious of hurt, and ran after the coach on hearing a scream from Judith. The horses were stopped within ten yards. My feeble companion, with fright depicted on her countenance, inquired as I helped her out if I were not badly hurt.

"No, scarcely at all—yes, I believe I am a little—Ah! my ankle begins to pain me some. My hip seems to be slightly bruised."

We were now in the front parlor; before we reached a seat, I was writhing and limping badly. She looked anxiously into my face.

"Mr. Garame, you are *seriously* hurt."

There was a degree of animation in her look that I had not seen during the week of her mourning. I seated her on the sofa, intending to go instantly and speak for our rooms; but, on turning round, I felt such pangs that I dropped down by her side, put my hand first to my ankle, then to my hip. But intending to quiet her fears, I said, " 'Tis true, I am a good deal hurt—oh! ah!—but no bones are broken—I shall soon get over it—ah! oh!"

I could not suppress these interjections, for at every movement of the wounded muscles, a needle seemed to shoot through the irritated fibres.

What was my surprise to see Judith, whose languor had for several days made her positively unable to walk without assistance, now rise from the sofa, go alone to the barroom adjoining the parlor and, after speaking to the clerk and having two servants called, return and, when the clerk came in, request me to order rooms for us. I told him that the young lady was a friend of mine, in deep distress, and that we wanted private chambers in a retired part of the house with a parlor to ourselves as the lady's situation did not admit of her mingling with strangers. We were accommodated in every particular. When the servant came and announced that our rooms were prepared in the second story, I rose with difficulty and as usual offered Judith my arm. She rose without difficulty and, looking into my face with marks of lively concern in hers, exclaimed: "Oh, Mr. Garame, you cannot go up the stairs without assistance; do, if you please, let this servant call another to assist him in supporting you."

I accepted the aid of the servant on my wounded side but persisted in keeping her on the other. Thus we made our way up the stairs, which, to my pleasing astonishment, Judith mounted, rather giving than receiving support. I wondered and rejoiced at this sudden amendment in my dear charge. From the moment when she saw me writhing with sharp pains, a new vigor was infused into her debilitated frame, new animation was visible in her face, new light beamed from her eyes. And from this moment, while she officiated with the tenderest care as my nurse, her health and spirits continued to return with a rapidity which was not only surprising, but at first unaccountable and the more so because my sufferings were a new affliction to her. She sympathized keenly with every twinge of pain that she saw me endure, kept anxious watch for the minutest occasion to serve me, and where she could not relieve, to share the suffering. But this pungent anxiety on my account was doubtless the cause of the happy change in her own condition; it effectually diverted her mind from the depressing contemplation of her late disaster, gave a new turn to the current of her feelings, started new trains of thought, and put the terrible accident that afflicted her far back in the series of recent facts and interesting experiences. Had my sufferings been of a more appalling character, they might have aggravated her malady, but they were just sufficient to excite the languishing powers of nature without exhausting them. Thus she soon recovered the elasticity of her mind so far that she was able in some degree to control her grief by the exercise of reason and conscience. And this she did, for she told me a few days afterwards that she deemed it ungrateful and rebellious towards God to persist willfully in grieving for any loss that He saw good to inflict upon us. Therefore, although she could not avoid mourning for the loss of her dear brother, she felt in duty bound to reconcile herself as soon as possible to the Divine Will and to subdue a grief which could serve no good end, except so far as it was involuntary, and which would, if wilfully indulged, unfit her for the duties of life and the enjoyment of the blessing yet left to her. One end of grief might be, she thought, to exercise us in subduing it. This might be one of the appointed trials of our piety towards our Heavenly Father, a salutary discipline to fit us for serving Him in all circumstances, whether of prosperity or adversity. In these rational and devout sentiments I fully concurred with her. But it is time to resume the thread of my narrative.

I was scarcely disposed on the sofa in our parlor before a surgeon (the most eminent in the city as I afterwards learned) was ushered in by a servant and, without preamble or introduction, ordered the servant to "strip that foot." Judith had just finished the operation of pillowing it softly on a stool. As she rose from her reclining posture, she whispered to me that the clerk had sent for the surgeon; then she told the maid in waiting to lead the way into her chamber.

The surgeon, whose abrupt order had surprised and for a moment irritated me, glanced at my ankle and pronounced it badly sprained. In the same breath he asked, "Have you any other hurt?"

"Yes, on my hip."

"Strip his hip, servant—quickly."

He gave it a hasty look and a touch.

"It is only a bruise; rub it with liniment and apply a flake of raw cotton. Put a bread poultice to your ankle."

"How long shall I be confined, doctor?"

"That will depend on your care and on circumstances. Do not tread on that foot. Drink no stimulants, eat sparingly, and take a Seidlitz powder or two daily. Good day, sir."

He spoke and was gone.

The next morning after breakfast he called again—asked just three questions, stayed just two minutes, and was off instantly after uttering these words:

"Continue the same application till the swelling and soreness abate. Nurse your ankle until it is well, a week or more if necessary; if it gets worse send for me. My hat, boy! Your servant, sir."

I saw him no more, but I did see that he was full of business and had no need of complaisance.

Judith, my sweet nurse, was present when he enjoined on me a week's confinement or more. I saw a little cloud of sadness flit over her countenance when she heard it. I could easily conjecture why this detention should be unpleasant to her, especially when I remembered what Eli had said about the necessity of a speedy prosecution of their journey. But as to myself, shall I confess it? The prospect of delay foisted a secret joy into my heart in spite of bruised flesh and an aching joint—in spite, too, of my biting conscience, which bade me wish for a speedy return of Judith to her friends, whatever delight I might take in her company. But when I looked upon my dear companion whose eyes of reviving brightness were now directed towards me, how could I help longing for a continuance of our intercourse? But if the desire was itself unconquerable, it did not subdue my conscientious feeling so as to prevent my acting in accordance with my duty on this occasion. I asked my dear charge what was to be done now. Would she wait until I should be able to travel, or would she write to her Boston friend that he might come and meet her here? She answered that she ought to write and make known her situation without delay.

"Then," said she, "having done my duty, I can wait patiently, whether it be the will of Providence that you shall carry me on further after your recovery or that my cousin shall be able to come and release you from the necessity."

She retired to her room and wrote the letter. When she came with it into the parlor and rang the bell for a servant to have it carried to the post office, the marks of recent tears were upon her face. And when the servant closed the door, on going out with the missive that would probably in a few days bring her a new protector, she turned with drooping head and staggered to a chair. No wonder that she was deeply affected, for the writing of that letter "renewed the sad remembrance of her fate." But, oh! the weakness of human nature—at least of my human nature. For I—yes, even I—so lately the purely disinterested, the simply fraternal lover, now felt the wish that a part of her emotion, even the greater part, might be on account of her approaching separation from me *myself*. How was my love descending from its angelic height and settling upon the low grounds of human selfishness! In truth, at this moment, when I contemplated the loss of her society, my passion began to be ambitious of conquest and jealous of interference. I coveted all the affection of that dear heart; and any suspicion that it throbbed for others and chiefly for them, whilst every sight and every thought of her raised the strongest pulsations in my heart, produced in me an irritability and sensitiveness of feeling, new, painful, earthly, and humiliating to think upon. Not only how selfish but how inconsistent had my love become. It had been produced, nourished and refined in a great measure by her various manifestations of a heart, rich in every tender, virtuous and amiable affection; and now my full grown or overgrown passion, after being so born and bred, demanded that for its gratification she should feel a less dutiful affection for others and that, in order to satisfy its cravings, she should make herself less worthy of being loved. Still, however, if I had been sure that love for me was seated on the throne of her heart, I might have allowed other affections to occupy a high but still a subordinate place. But whilst the precedency was unsettled, I was jealous of all possible rivals; even filial love was not pleasing in my sight.

Whilst the letter was speeding its way and we waited for the result and for my convalescence, our days were spent almost exclusively in each other's society. Happy days they were to me—transcendently happy I may call them, notwithstanding the cloud shadows that often flitted across their summer brightness. I allude not to corporeal sufferings; for under the balmy care of the sweetest nurse in the world, my bruises were soon mollified, and my wrenched ankle ceased to pain me. Yet it was a week before I durst attempt the passage from parlor to bed chamber and contrariwise without the help of the servant who attended upon me. But too fleeting seemed the quarter of a moon which brought my dear companion the answer from her cousin that he would follow in two or three days and requesting her kind friend to stay with her until he should arrive. That 'kind friend' needed no persuasion to detain him, nor would he have left her one day before necessity required, even if he had had the wings of a dove to fly away.

Meanwhile I saw with delight how Judith's grief yielded daily to sober cheerfulness and how returning health was continually restoring the vernal bloom to her cheeks and the starry radiance to her eyes. Though still a deep mourner, she soon began to show occasionally, in placid smiles, the budding promise of a new springtime of the heart. When I saw the first of these renovated smiles illumine once more the beauties of her countenance, what a rushing tide of joy flowed through my heart!

Every day increased my admiration of this extraordinary maiden. I had seen her in the days of her joyous vivacity, drinking the pleasures of bountiful nature from a thousand springs, every sparkling feature and buoyant motion expressing the gaiety of an innocent heart.

Then, all in a moment, I had seen her riven with a thunderbolt of misfortune and hurled into the lowest deep of affliction. And now I saw her rising again to the light of consolation and walking in the mellow shade of patient resignation and dawning cheerfulness. In this diversity of situation, extreme and intermediate, every feeling of her heart and every trait of her character seemed to be developed. And whatever light shades of human infirmity might be discerned, such a character of intellectual brightness, moral purity, and unsophisticated amiability of temper, all becomingly set forth with such personal beauty, had never before realized itself to my perception. Whether my fancy contributed to adorn this lovely being or not, the vision was to my heart so perfectly enchanting that I was rapt (if I may so express it without profaneness) up to the third heaven of love. Whether others have been so entranced by the sweet passion, I cannot say; probably few—for few indeed have been placed in such peculiar circumstances—but this I know, that I could not possibly love a mortal being—no, not angel—more. My heart was full.

To avoid all expression of my love until Judith should be with her friend, as a delicate regard to her feelings required, became at last impossible. Whilst I abstained from verbal declarations of more than fraternal kindness, tokens of my deeper passion began to steal from me every hour that I spent in her company. If the reader has felt the strong workings of the tender passion and observed their effects, then the reader knows that there are a hundred signs of love more expressive than words, signs, which they whose hearts are tenderly attached, but not yet conclusively affianced instinctively, give and instinctively understand. Many of these are too delicate in their nature and pertain too exclusively to the mysteries of the passion to be intelligible to the uninitiated. Not until one's heart is illuminated by nature's love torch can one read the language of love spoken by the eyes—the tender meaning that plays about the lips, the sentiments delicately suggested by certain undesigned postures and inadvertant motions, or by certain tremors, certain touches of the hand, the interesting significancy of certain accents, tones and stammerings of the voice, flushings and blanchings of the cheek—all expressive. And the more so, because, to be felt by the one party, they must spring undesignedly from the feelings of the other. They are nature's language and therefore inimitable by the feigning pretender, who, attempting to act without feeling, is almost sure to be exposed to the instinctive sagacity of real passion.

Such signs I could no more repress than I could have stayed the eruption of a volcano. I detected them springing involuntarily forth in every form and on every occasion. They were understood—that I saw; signs of reciprocity were not wanting. They broke through the guarded modesty of Judith's heart; they could not escape the vigilant sagacity of mine. My satisfaction would have been complete, my joy unbounded, had these auspicious tokens come alone. But they came attended with others of such sinister omen as to baffle my judgement and to becloud my hope. Tokens of pain attached themselves to her tokens of love. When she appeared to apprehend in me the symptoms of more than a brother's affection, nature, speaking back from her heart and flashing through every avenue of expression, told me that my love was both pleasant and painful to her soul. Whenever something in my voice and manner indicated the ardor of my feelings, the tremulous joy that sprang forth to her telltale countenance was in a moment saddened by a twinge of anguish, as I have seen on a rainy day the blooming meadow of my native vale, when the flashing beam of sunlight that disclosed its flowery beauties, was suddenly extinguished again by the shadow of the rain cloud.

A remarkable instance of the kind took place on the fifth morning after the letter had been sent. We had just finished our private breakfast and Judith was asking if my ankle were not in a painful position on the stool where I still kept it during most of the day, when a servant brought up a newspaper with the landlord's compliments and suggestion that we might find something in it particularly interesting to ourselves. On glancing over the columns, I found an article taken from a Norfolk paper and headed "Affecting Incident at Sea." I soon discovered that it was our captain's account of poor Eli's fate and of Judith's fall and rescue. He had done full justice to my agency in the affair but stated as a fact a conjecture of his own, that Judith and I (but only the initials of our names were given) were betrothed in marriage.

Judith, perceiving my agitation, asked with great concern whether I had found any bad news.

"Nothing new to us. It is the captain's story of our misfortune. You will have to read for yourself. One of the circumstances mentioned by the captain is a mistake; you may pardon that as all the rest is correct."

She took the paper with a trembling hand and retired into her room, which, like mine, opened into the parlor. Presently I heard her half-suppressed sobs; then she was silent during a few moments. Then, as if moved by a sudden impulse, she started up with the exclamation, "My preserver, and I knew it not! I might have gone home without knowing my chief obligation to him."

She was hastening towards the open door but stopped where I could see that she was still reading. Soon she again returned to her seat, where I could not see her, and sat in profound silence for a quarter of an hour. It may be readily supposed that Judith was not sensible of the part that I had acted in rescuing her from the sea, if indeed she could remember that she fell into it; and she was not likely to be informed unless I had told her myself, which my sense of delicacy forbade, though I was not at all displeased that she should learn it in such time and way as she did. Nor was I sorry for the mistake about our betrothal because it might obviate disagreeable remarks about our secluded intimacy in the hotel; and, moreover, it might assist me in judging how the idea of such a relation would affect her. But it placed her in a very embarrassing situation, impelled as she was by gratitude to rush in and make her acknowledgements, yet restrained by the fear that I might give the wrong interpretation to the warm expression of her feelings.

Finally, she again rose from her seat and came into the parlor, slowly and stealthily, hanging down her head as if ashamed. My heart palpitated, and I felt confused, not knowing how I should receive her. So I seemed not to be aware of her approach and kept my eyes on the floor as if engaged in meditation. She stood a minute at the end of the sofa opposite to that which I occupied with my lame foot on the stool. I looked up towards her at last; she had her eyes fixed on me with a look of indescribable tenderness and sadness. Her eyes met mine, and the mutual glance of feeling overcame her; she put her handkerchief to her face with both hands and dropped to her seat on the sofa, exclaiming, "Oh, my preserver!" and burst into tears.

"Thank God, my dear Judith, that I was able to preserve so precious a life."

She recovered sufficiently after a few moments to say, "I can never compensate you, my friend; but I am not sorry to lie under obligation to such a benefactor—one more than a common friend—a brother who risked his own life to save mine—yes, a kind, good brother—alas! alas! the only being on earth whom I can now call brother, and him only by courtesy. But I will cleave to the privilege; I will try to show that I am not unworthy to be your sister and shall always claim to be so considered."

I spoke some kind words in reply, and while I spoke happened somehow or other to move a little nigher to her end of the sofa, and, taking the hand that she had dropped while the other still held the handkerchief to her face, I drew it slightly. Her body obeyed the gentle attraction, and her head, with the handkerchief still over the eyes, dropped upon my shoulder but had not rested there before she suddenly drew back and gave me a glance of heart-piercing love and anguish. Her glowing cheek was suddenly blanched; and, with an interjection expressive of keen suffering, she rose, hastened to her room, and threw herself on a chair, moaning and sobbing till she so far conquered her emotion as to become perfectly silent.

I was at a loss. The shrinking delicacy of her feelings and the doleful remembrances so lately recalled to mind did not solve the phenomena; there was a visible pang unaccounted for—a shooting pang —that could in one instant drive back the warm current of love in a freezing eddy to the heart. What could be the matter? Of all the suppositions that I could think of, one only carried an air of probability—she must be affianced to another. The conception was torture to my soul. I dwelt upon it until I was persuaded of its truth. "Her promise to another and her love for me will account for the struggle in her heart," said I to myself. Then, before I was aware, a heavy groan broke forth and started me out of my reverie.

Judith also started up at the sound and came with an agitated look, exclaiming, "Oh, Mr. Garame! pardon my rudeness. I left you as if I were offended. No, no, it was not that. I could not suspect—I did not imagine—that my preserver, my brother, meant anything wrong or offensive—oh, no!—it was pure friendship and brotherly kindness— I knew it was. Something else came to mind—but—"

Here she stopped abruptly and appeared much embarrassed as if she had some painful communication to make but felt a delicacy or reluctance to make it.

I assured her that I did not suspect her of being offended and that my distress had a different origin, a painful thought suggested by the appearance of some secret cause of pain in her mind. Here I was on the point of declaring all my heart, but feeling unprepared and deeming it improper at this time, I stopped short and became embarrassed in my turn. She relieved me with the ready tact, of which she had before given me striking examples.

"Well, brother," said she, with all the cheerfulness that she could muster, "now, as our mutual confidence is restored, let us drop these delicate matters and resume our book. I will read first; then you may take your turn."

So we occupied ourselves with *Specimens of American Poetry* and our comments on the passages read. By dinner time our minds were restored to their usual calmness.

That night, after mature reflection on my pillow, I resolved to defer my declaration no longer than until another occasion should arise when I would make it without abruptness. I sighed to unburden my heart and to solve the mystery of her painful love for me. I was persuaded also that she would gladly accept relief from the embarrassment of understanding and being known to understand my feelings, yet unauthorized to admit, without a breach of delicacy, that she did understand them. The mystery of the pangs which embittered her love for me did not continue so to torture me as they had done. My fond heart began to flatter itself that all might arise from the black fountain of her recent grief, together with her virgin diffidence in the secluded company of one so new to her acquaintance. This more comfortable view of the case presented itself in the loneliness of my bed chamber after a gratifying review of the manifest tokens that she had given me, involuntarily, of her devoted affection. And under the persuasion that if she were not at liberty to accept my love, she would not have left me to go so far in ignorance of the fact. Still I longed to be rid of suspense and of a fearful apprehension, certainly not without cause, that my hopes might still be sadly disappointed.

The next morning I found my ankle so much better that after the servant had helped me into the parlor and breakfast was over I sent him to order me a crutch, which came at dinner time; and to my joy I found that with care I might safely hobble about the room upon it.

When the servants had cleared our table and left us alone after dinner, we began to speak of the probability of our speedy separation. This afforded the occasion that I waited for to introduce the avowal of my passion. I omit the series of remarks by which I gradually prepared her for the declaration. I apologised for broaching so delicate a subject before the arrival of her friend. I alleged my unrestrainable affection and my fearful doubts besides the painful embarrassment which I inflicted on her by involuntarily signifying the passion which I had not explicitly declared. I further alleged the near approach and probably suddenness of the separation, when the shortness of the time, the hurry of preparation and the distress of parting would render such an explanation intolerably painful whatever the result might be. Finally, I avowed my passion in all its fulness and offered her my hand with the expression of my perfect assurance that my life could in no way be so happily spent as in the closest and most endearing connection with her.

"But," said I in conclusion, "I am not so rude as to ask of you at this time any answer or explanation of your feelings if the slightest reason would incline you to defer it. Be assured, however, that if you should now or hereafter tell me of some impediment to our union, be it whatsoever it may, grieved as I shall be that the fondest desire of my heart cannot be gratified, I shall cling with but the closer attachment to the admitted relation of brother and sister and will love you as my dearest friend if I may not love you as the partner of my bosom."

Thus I brought my speech to a successful conclusion, although at the commencement and through the greater part of it I had hesitated and stammered so much as to feel doubtful of a safe deliverance.

She was again sitting at one end of the sofa while I sat at the other with my crutch between us. When she discovered the drift of my discourse, she first hung down her head. Then beginning to tremble, she turned and leaned over the back of the sofa to steady her nerves while I could see the alternations of blushing and paleness upon her cheek. Then she put her handkerchief to her face, and, when I had concluded, I saw the tears streaming from underneath the handkerchief; and when these had ceased to stream, sob after sob started from her full breast. But she soon evinced the desire to compose herself. She wiped her eyes, changed her position, swallowed her sobs, and gradually sank with bended head into the posture of silent meditation. I waited anxiously during fifteen minutes till she lifted her head from its declined posture, and, turning herself towards me, she began with downcast eyes and with a voice low and plaintive, gathering strength as it proceeded but still sweet as the sweetest tones that summer wind ever stole from Eolian harp:

"Mr. Garame, you have acted kindly to tell me your feelings before the parting hour. I have seen the involuntary signs of your tender affection for me; they placed me in a situation of painful delicacy. I could not conceal that I understood you nor speak as if I did. You have now but added one more to the many proofs before given of your honorable affection and tender regard for my feelings. I will at once confess what I suppose that I have heretofore betrayed—that your love is not disagreeable to me nor met with a cold return in my heart. No, my dear preserver; on the first day of our acquaintance I felt a new and strange sort of pleasure in your company. Then I thought not of love; I expected soon to see you no more. And though I was sensible of a strong reluctance at the thought of parting with you, I did not suspect that a new passion had sprung up in my heart. What followed—you know. Oh! how could my bruised and desolate heart do otherwise than love such a friend? Since I have recovered sufficient composure to reflect on my feelings and have observed the evidence of yours, I have become conscious of a sister's devoted affection and within these three days of more. I need not affect to conceal it—I can go all lengths with you in affection. There is no want of love to make me happy in the most intimate connexion with you; nor am I debarred by any engagement or impediment of any sort so far as *my* feelings or circumstances are concerned. Yet there is one thing which you have not heard—an important fact; it may be fatal."

Here she paused to struggle with her feelings. Presently she continued while pale dread sat brooding upon my heart. "I have lately reproached myself for not telling you sooner. But before my calamity I thought it unnecessary. During the agony of my grief, I could think of no such matters, and, since I have recovered the power of reflection and have seen occasion to tell you, I have waited for an opportunity of doing it without abruptness. Now the opportunity has occurred. Oh my friend! Prepare to hear a disclosure which must pain your affectionate heart. You have looked upon me as a suitable companion for life. When you know all, you may think differently. You are a sincere Christian; will you not shudder at the thought of marrying a Jewess?"

Never was intelligence more surprising. My fearful and busy imagination had created a dozen impediments, such as a prior engagement, a father's refusal, or even a plague spot of infamy upon the family but had never caught an inkling of the reality, which now struck me like an electric shock.

"A Jewess! you a Jewess?" said I with a start and an emphasis that conveyed more than was meant. Her eyes were upon me, and, when she saw and heard the effect of her disclosure, a new gush of feeling came and overpowered her.

"Oh," said she in a tone of sudden grief, "my fears were true!" Then she rose in confusion to leave me while the tear drops began to fall. Now my former feelings, like refluent waves which the dash of a tornado had displaced, came rushing tumultuously back again, and I exclaimed, "My dear Judith, do not leave me now. I am surprised but not changed. If you will not let me hope, tell me so at once. But why should a mere name blast my dearest prospects and sever those whom affection united?"

She fell back on her seat, almost choked with emotion, and sobbed out, "I love you none the less for that name. It is not *my* heart that such a circumstance will change. But I am afraid that my being a Jewess will canker your love for me."

"Oh no, no," said I quickly.

She continued in a calmer strain: "My heart is yours; the difference in our national descent and religious education shall not prevent me from giving you my hand if, on full consideration, you and your friends think that these things will not prove fatal to your happiness. Some of my kindred have married Christians; my father has told me that if I should meet with a Christian whose temper and character were suitable to mine, he would not refuse to own him for a son-in-law. I am no bigot. Though educated in the religion of my fathers, I have learned to respect the Christian religion. I have perused the New Testament and love its excellent precepts of benevolence and purity; and, though I do not profess the Christian faith, I could easily live in concord with one who professes it as mildly and sincerely as you do. But I am aware of the prejudices which many entertain against my nation and what a horror they would feel at so intimate a connection with an Israelite. I know, too, that a sincere Christian may feel conscientious difficulties in such a case. I do not know what feelings and sentiments you may have entertained on this subject; the case is probably new to you and therefore demands serious and mature consideration before you proceed further. It would kill my poor heart to find, when too late, that I had caused—" Here she became so deeply affected that she had to break off and retire to her chamber.

I also got up and with my crutch hobbled to my room in deep agitation, delighted yet troubled. My lameness and perturbation of mind effectually precluded all regular thinking while I was on foot although my mental machinery was driven with an impetus that disposed me to bodily action at the same time. I lay down on the bed that I might compose myself and obey the injunction to consider well this new feature of my love case. And somewhat after this manner did my mind work at the task of sapient reflection:

"Reflect! She tells me to reflect whether I can press that dear affectionate heart to my bosom! Yes, that heart! What sobriety of reflection is mingled there with the light of genius and the living fires of sensibility! She loves me with all that heart, sweet child of sorrow! How candidly has she told me that she is a Jewess though she expected to make me loathe her by the intelligence—and that too at the very moment when she confessed her love! True, I have never liked the character of the Jews, either ancient or modern, but she has charms enough to put all such prejudices to flight. And why should I object to marry a daughter of Abraham, the friend of God, and the father of all believers? Were not the prophets and the apostles and the son of God himself Israelites? And am I to feel degraded or mismatched when I marry a kinswoman of theirs? But were the Jews never so vile or loathsome as a people, my Judith has sufficient personal merits to redeem her from all objection and to cover all her people's sins. Has not the Creator stamped on her lovely person the evident marks of his favor and delight? How divinely sweet has he fashioned her? What a pure and lovely spirit has he breathed into the beauteous structure! Those eyes beaming tenderness! That mouth, so rosy-lipped and so eloquent—every smile a young Cupid—every word flavored with ambrosial melody! Such a soul in such a body! Formed and compounded to lead captive every sense and every faculty of the soul! And I am to question whether I can live happily with her! Have I not been with her a month in pleasure and in suffering and found her equally amiable, equally engaging, whether I ascended with her to the ethereal heights of joy or descended with her to the Stygian caves of sorrow? If a month—or is it a month? No, scarcely three weeks; but such a specimen of all experiences may give assurance for a lifetime. But, says an objector, she is not a Christian. But in spirit and feeling she is a far better Christian than nine-tenths of those who make the loudest professions. She loves the rules and the spirit of the Christian religion, and I have no doubt that she only needs to be placed in Christian society and under Christian influence to be soon persuaded to believe fully in Jesus of Nazareth. Oh, then what a happy life could we live in some sweet vale of my native land! I see plainly that all is safe. Shall I then bid her go for a Jewess and break her heart with mourning her slighted love or bestow her unrivalled charms on another? No, by all that is precious, I cannot, I will not. Even now she is weeping for the perturbation that she gave my spirits. I have reflected; I am prepared to give her the result and to ease her dear heart at once."

With this conclusion firmly grasped, though reached through a confused mixture of arguments and feelings, I got up and returned to the parlor. Not finding Judith there, I became restless and limped and stumbled about the room, full to overflowing of my sage meditations and impatient to deliver the result to my beloved Israelite. When she heard me hobbling about and striking against stool and chair under the impulse of my boiling thoughts, she came in with a countenance of half-subdued anxiety and said: "Well, my dear friend, I have allowed you a short time to compose yourself after the shock that I gave you and to consider the consequences of a marriage with one who turns out to be not so unobjectionable as you supposed. But you must have a much longer time to settle upon a final conclusion."

"No, my dear Judith, I have had time enough; the thought of giving you up is distraction to my soul. I see no impediment in what you have told me to our loving and blessing each other for life. When you discovered to me what I had never conjectured or imagined, the suddenness of it startled me a little; but the fact itself cannot shake my love for you. It cannot mar my delight in you; and I can now most freely offer you my hand again with a heart untouched by fear and altogether devoted to your happiness."

"I have," said she, "the most perfect confidence in your sincerity, but the case as it now stands is quite new to you; it is but half an hour since you first conceived the possibility of your ever marrying a Jewess. I cannot with a good conscience bind you by an absolute promise so soon; I must give you time and opportunity to deliberate coolly on the subject and to consult your friends at home. As to myself, I have heretofore considered whether I might honestly and safely give my hand to one against whom no objection could lie except our difference in one point of religious belief. My mind has been made up. If he, after full consideration, can freely and conscientiously make me his companion for life, then I can accept his offer if our affections are united. I am authorized by my father and prepared by reflection, as well as by feeling, to give my beloved friend and preserver all the satisfaction which the most solemn pledge can afford. This I will now do, and I rejoice that I can do it without fear, without hesitation, and with all my heart."

So saying, she rose and advanced to where I stood leaning on the back of a chair, and, putting first her right hand in mine, she then with queenly grace and dignity, yet with all virgin modesty, addressed me in these words: "Here, my dearest friend, I give you the disposal of my hand that you may accept or decline it finally after you have considered the whole case in the presence of your kindred. You will then come to the conclusion whether you can safely do what your heart desires. Write to me then. If you confirm our engagement, I shall rejoice as much as gratified love can make me. If you annul it, as you have the right to do, I shall grieve for the result; but I shall not blame you for exercising your liberty and consulting your happiness instead of destroying it, and then mine with it, by an unsuitable marriage. You will at all events be gratefully remembered and unceasingly beloved as my friend and preserver. Thus I commit myself to your disposal. And now as my mind is deliberately made up and unchangeably settled, I hazard nothing when I call upon my God and yours, the God of Abraham, as I solemnly do, to witness the sincerity of the vow that I have made."

She then let go my hand and seemed about to retire. My first emotion, when she concluded, was deep reverence inspired by her language and manner. Next, when I looked upon her lovely face and considered her now as my affianced spouse, I could not resist the impulse to clasp her to my bosom. "My love!" said I, as she began to retire. I advanced a step and opened my arms. She looked at me with angelic sweetness, mingled with shrinking diffidence; and as she uttered these words, "Excuse me now, dear friend," she drew back and returned to her chamber, but without closing the door. She would not indicate the slightest fear—she did not feel it—for well did she know that I held that sanctuary of hers as inviolable as if it were the consecrated abode of a divinity.

The painful embarrassment of our late position was now over. The satisfaction that she meant to give me by her solemn pledge I felt in all its fulness. We had settled our engagement on terms which left me nothing to wish for and left her apparently very little to fear. At least she had acted towards me with such a conscientious and self-denying generosity as might convince me, if I had not been convinced before, that a heart of such rare and amiable virtues could never make me unhappy.

Now the few remaining days that we spent at the hotel flew away in all the delights of innocent affection, restrained without being diminished by my dear companion's maidenly reserve, combined with the most winning evidence of her confiding love. But ah! too soon were these happy days brought to an end! Only four suns were suffered to shine upon our plighted love before a servant entered our parlor to announce that Mr. Von Caleb, my Judith's cousin, and another gentleman with him had arrived. We told him to show them up as soon as they were ready. I retired to my chamber that I might not disturb the first feelings of the interview. When they came in, I soon heard the sound of mingled weeping and rejoicing. I was made to hear also that the companion of Mr. Von Caleb was a Jewish acquaintance picked up at New York, who, as he had just arrived from London, brought intelligence that Judith's father and other relations were all well.

After the salutations and first inquiries were over, I opened my door and joined the company. Judith introduced me first to her cousin, Von Caleb, and then to her friend, Mr. Levi. I noticed that she did not emphasize the word "friend." Mr. Von Caleb shook my hand affectionately and at once thanked me fervently for my kindness to Judith. He was a middle-aged man, with a stout well built person and open pleasant countenance. But friend Levi was a small, old, shrivelled, sharp-visaged man, with little gray eyes deeply sunk under projecting shaggy eyebrows. His head was bald on the crown, but this defect was amply made up by a gray frizzled beard, which filled up all the spaces under the chin and jawbones about the neck as if it were a cravat. He gripped my hand tightly and with a squeaking voice, broken frequently into huskiness, uttered some friendly words; but I did not like either the looks or the manners of friend Levi. Nowhere and at no time would I have liked him. Here, just at this time, I was most disagreeably affected to behold, in living reality before me, such a representative of the Jews according to my former habitual notion of them. The disagreeable impression was, however, effaced for the time by a glance at my lovely Judith and the open, benevolent face of her cousin. These were enough to sweeten anyone's imagination of the Jews.

After a few minutes' conversation I got myself down to the barroom that I might give the friends opportunity for a more private conference. In a short time Mr. Levi came down also, and, seeing me alone in one corner of the room, he took a seat beside me. After some questions on his part about poor Eli's fate, I began from a natural curiosity to make some inquiries about Judith's father and family. I found the little man so communicative that he soon told me more than I had asked to know. Soon, too, he discovered to me that his darling theme was money; for start him on any track whatsoever, and he would speedily arrive at this goal of all his thoughts and affections. To this propensity I was indebted for a piece of information which had now become more interesting to me than the little miser was aware of. The following specimen of his part of the conversation will convey the same information to the reader and at the same time show the turn of the speaker's thoughts and expressions. I should remark also that he spoke English with a German accent, betraying the land of his birth.

"Is Judy's father very old, you ask—why, no, not so very; his hair is gray like mine, that's all. He walks on 'Change like a young man; and when he goes to his bank and counts the monies, he can see as sharp as anybody—sure he can. Is Nathan Bensaddi a banker, do you ask? Why, yes, sure he is; everybody in London knows that. He owns one of the greatest banks in London, I know—sure I do—for I have been his agent to collect money. Ah, he has the monies—sure; yes, money, money. Oh, so much money! That is not all—sure it is not. He lives in a big, fine house on the street called Piccadilly. I have been in it. I have eat dinner there on feast days. Yes, the feast of Purim, and then I saw with my own blessed eyes what fine things he had in his house. Why, sure, his table was covered all over with plate. Yes, gold plate and silver plate—silver this and silver that—gold here and gold there—this, that and the other, all gold and silver. Ah, sure, you would think it was Solomon's house. Rich, you say? Yes, sure, that he is; and I have not told you all. Isaac Von Caleb told me last night that Nathan Bensaddi has mortgages on a great sugar estate in the West Indies, on an island they call Saint Kish, or Kitts, or something like that. Yes, and he told me that Nathan would soon have the land and the slaves and the sugar and the coffee and the spices and all—sure. Yes, and that Eli was gone to see about it when he got drowned. Yes, and he told me too that Judy had a great fortune of her own besides. I knew that before—sure I did. Yes, I know how she got it too—sure I do. Old Simon Mordecai, her uncle by the mother's side, was so pleased with her nursing him in his long sickness when he had no wife nor child to do anything for him—and he was so cross and snappish, nobody could please him—but Judy pleased him— sure she did. And when his will was opened, there was Judy left heiress of all Simon's three percent stocks. Yes, sure, a hundred thousand pounds. Ah! who would not nurse a sick man, if he was crabbed, for such good pay? Did it out of kindness you say? Why, yes—sure she did. She is the kindest thing in the world. I have heard her friends say so. She is too kind. She gives away too much money. Ah, Judy is a good girl—so rich. And sure, yes, she'll have the half of Nathan's fortune, too, when he dies now that Eli is drowned; and she has only one sister, Rachel, older than Judy. And she is married to a Christian—hang him; I don't mean you—but I hope Judy won't marry a Gentile."

By this time my squeaking friend had fallen into a half soliloquizing mood as if an idea had struck him and drawn off his attention from me. A servant now entered and brought me a request to walk up to the parlor. I arose immediately to go, and, while adjusting my crutch, I observed that friend Levi's chin had dropped meditatively upon his breast while his tongue played incessantly, though his voice had sunk to a husky murmur. I heard only these words more, "Judy will be rich, rich—ah, so rich! Now, sure, if my boy Joseph—." I was by this time out of hearing and hobbling towards the parlor with brand new ideas blazing before my imagination. I had conjectured that Judith's family could not be poor, but neither Eli nor Judith had ever given me a hint from which I could infer great riches. In fact

Judith had seemed to me rather too reserved on this point, especially since our matrimonial engagement; for, both before and since, I had let her understand that my parents were not rich and that my inheritance would be small. I had hitherto in my dream of happiness with Judith indulged no splendid fancies; my modest aspirations were limited to a snug cottage by a fountain side in some green vale where forest trees bordering a meadow would yield "in summer, shade—in winter, fire."

But now, as if touched by a magician's wand, the picture changed and presented me, instead of this humble scene, an elegant mansion seated upon a hill commanding a view of the Great Valley and its mountain boundaries, with a fine library, not without paintings and other specimens of the fine arts, and windows looking out on all sides—here upon a park—there upon meadows in the vales around —and yonder upon fields on hillsides. And here and there on white cottages sending up wreaths of smoke from the firesides of happy tenants, a tribute grateful to the hearts of the proprietor and his lady. This new picture was completed just as I entered the parlor and saw Judith conversing with her cousin. She, after all, was herself the sweetest vision of my heart, and the lovely reality dissipated the illusions of a dreaming fancy.

On seeing me, she rose blushing and retired to her chamber. Mr. Von Caleb also arose from his seat and, again taking me by the hand, expressed his approbation of our matrimonial scheme of which Judith had just informed him. After we were seated, he continued in these words, lowering his voice that Judith might not hear:

"God must have designed this union of two such good hearts, or he would not have brought you so closely together by such an extraordinary dispensation of His providence. Now, after he has bound your affections together by so many ties, I would think it an impious resistance to his will to throw any hindrance in the way of your marriage. I could wish that you were both of the same religion; but still, if *you* are willing to take a daughter of Abraham for your wife, I do not see why you may not both agree in worshiping the God of Abraham. And if you serve him as father Abraham did, He will bless you though you may not have the same belief on some points. One thing

I feel sure of, that Judith will never willingly disturb you on matters of conscience. I have known her from a child. Father Abraham never had a lovelier daughter; her temper is the sweetest and kindest in the world; her discretion is extraordinary for so young a person; it was so remarked a year ago when I left London; and she has an uncommon turn for improving by experience. I heard a poet of her acquaintance say, 'She is like the busy bee, gathering the honey of wisdom from every blossom of experience in the pathway of her life.' And now I must do what she has just enjoined upon me, that is, tell you all her faults, without favor or partiality, as if upon oath. First and foremost then, they say she has too much feeling, or sensibility as they call it. This not only makes her suffer too much for the sufferings of others, but it lays her open to the impositions of beggars and rogues of all sorts. I don't mean that beggars are all rogues; but some of them, knowing the tenderness of her heart, impose on her by falsehood or exaggerated stories of their distresses and make her give them more than they deserve. This is only an excess of goodness, and I think that experience and hard rubs in this scuffling world will teach her more prudence in this particular, and in this only has she seemed to lack discretion. So much for her first fault; now for the second. Let me see. What is it? Yes, they call her an enthusiast because, I suppose, she takes fits of high feeling sometimes and talks a little wildly like a prophetess. I have heard her two or three times in these fits; I thought she talked very beautifully if she did go out of the common way. She will get over this too, I think, as she grows older and as she finds by mixing more with mankind how much low selfishness and rascality there is among them. This will give her less poetical views of human life and make the world seem less fit to kindle enthusiasm and more as it is, a scuffle field for the base passions and interests of men. That is my view of it after twenty years experience, for so long I have been trying my hand amongst my fellow men. The more I have had to do with them, the less confidence I have in the greater part of them. But I am forgetting Judith's faults. I have told you two; next comes the third, but I believe I have forgotten it. I thought she had three notable ones. Little human weaknesses she has like other people, but I had a third with a name to it that she told me not to forget.

Oh yes, she is *romantic*; that is what they call it. She is, indeed, too romantic in some of her notions. She doesn't like fashionable society and city amusements. She is too fond of climbing the lonesome mountains, and of standing on a rock by the seaside, and looking at the waves when the wind dashes them against the shore. And when other people go in summertime to the wells at Bath or Cheltenham to drink the waters and dance in the splendid saloons, she loves to steal out into the country with a companion or two, where she can wander among green valleys and gather flowers along the sides of brooks, or sit on a sod with her book and read under a shady tree where a spring bubbles out of the ground. And I verily believe that she would rather go out and eat a cottage dinner with plain country folks than attend the richest city feast with its gay company of lords and ladies, its gold and silver wares, and all its wines and comfits, its ice creams and syllabubs. Yet I have seen her dine at home with a great company when her father made a feast; then she could enjoy it and behave herself with the finest lady of them all. So I think she will some day get over her romantic notions, too, and make you a good sober housewife.

"And now that I have done her bidding and told you all that I know of her faults, I will tell you another thing that she has not authorized me to tell. It is right that you should know it; and I understand that she has not told you, for she has just expressed to me how much she was gratified that you offered to marry her without knowing or seeming to care whether she was rich or poor. Well, if you set no value on riches and are satisfied to have Judith alone, still I hope that you will not throw her large fortune into the sea. You will find it right convenient to have her three thousand pounds a year when the business of love has been settled and the business of housekeeping comes on. Then her rich father, if no misfortune happens, will be able to give her a great deal more. But, my friend, if you find, after a trial, that a great fortune is good for nothing and more plague than profit, why then, you may just give it to me and be done with it. So much for that. One thing more, and then I shall be through. I am sorry to tell you that I am so straitened for time that I cannot give you another day with Judith unless you go with us to Boston. I was ready to embark and just waiting for poor Eli when I got Judith's letter. I have important business in London that cannot be put off, and there are papers in Eli's trunk that must go directly to England; they relate to a great plantation in St. Kitts that is in suit between the owner and my cousin Bensaddi, who has a mortgage on it. What say you, my friend, will you part with Judith tonight, or will you go with us to Boston?"

Gladly would I have gone to Boston or any other place with Judith, but an obstacle lay before me which would have been removed in a moment if Judith or cousin Von Caleb had known or even suspected its existence. But strange as it may seem, just now when my charmer's newly discovered wealth came fresh and glittering into view, I felt a most swelling repugnance to a disclosure of my beggarly account of an empty purse although I knew that she would esteem it a great favor in me to accept any thing from her hands. She had put her purse into my hands at Norfolk and requested me to defray all our expenses out of it, but I told her that I would not consent to defray more than her own; and when I was lamed at the hotel, I returned the purse, telling her that she had better keep it now until we left the hotel. So I had given no sign that my funds were low. Now on counting, I found that I had scarcely a sufficiency to carry me home. I had to choose, therefore, whether to accept a supply from her who had given herself and her all to me or to go home straight way. I chose to go home straight way. Why such reluctance now to put my poverty in glaring contrast with her riches? Was it a just feeling of self-respect? Or was it pride a little spiced with envy? Or a compound of all these? However this may be, the feeling seemed natural. The fact may serve to illustrate the various workings of the human heart. Yet the discovery of my Judith's wealth was unquestionably pleasing to my heart—highly pleasing. Was this also natural, that a purely disinterested lover should rejoice at finding the gifts of Mammon attached to one who had been loved and sought solely for the qualities of her mind and person? What sayest thou, reader? Would not such a discovery have *gladdened* thy heart? Thou art human—so am I. Happy is he who can content himself in his poverty. Contentment is better than riches; but let the poor man, happy in virtuous poverty, find a gold mine in his barren field, and in a moment his heretofore contented heart will swell beyond the confines of his poverty; and the loss of his gold mine would make him sit down and weep. But to resume my story. After a moment's consideration, I told Mr. Von Caleb that I too was under a necessity (and was I not?) to return home speedily; and, as I hoped ere long to follow Judith across the ocean, I felt the less difficulty at parting with her now because a quick return home to make my preparations would enable me the sooner to set off on my voyage.

"Well, then," said he, raising his voice, "our boat will go tomorrow morning at six. As this will be your last evening together for some time, I will leave you to yourselves. You will not be sorry for that, I suppose? I shall be out awhile on some business with Mr. Levi. He will not interrupt you, for we are after *money*." He smiled as he spoke the last words.

"Then," said I, "as you go at six in the morning, I may as well take the Lancaster stage that goes at three o'clock."

"So then we have settled it," said Mr. Von Caleb. "Good-bye, till supper time."

He went out with his usual heavy tread; and, when he had shut the door behind him, I heard Judith's door open gently on her side of the parlor. I had risen and was standing about the middle of the floor without my crutch, which I no longer needed. I turned and met her eyes with mine. What a look she gave me of commingled love and sorrow! I approached the chair on which she leaned. She looked up again into my face. I saw the rising moisture of her eyes as she said, "This night, then, we must part." The last word was stifled under a wave of emotion. I opened my arms, she fell upon my bosom, and for the first time we felt each other's embrace. Oh, Elysian moment! It was the seal of our betrothal and the pure delight of love. Several minutes elapsed before we could utter a word. We had seated ourselves on chairs, and we continued to sit with drooping heads until we recovered the power of conversation.

After some exchanges of sentiment on the prospect of separation, I took occasion to allude to what I had just heard of the wealth of herself and family. "Then he told you that too? Well I am glad that you did not know it sooner."

"Since I have heard it at last, dear Judith, I will tell you that it gives me the satisfaction to know that you can afford to take a poor husband."

"Poor in pelf he may be," said she promptly, "but I know the wealth of his mind. That is the highest of all endowments, and in comparison with that gold and silver are but dross. If such earthy dower as I can bring be of any consequence, I rejoice in it for this, that you can the better afford to take me for a wife. Such wealth as I have is nothing to be proud of, for millions of it would argue no personal worth but only good fortune. I have hitherto found my worldly goods rather an obstacle to my happiness; for while they brought me numerous suitors, they brought with these applicants for my favor the painful suspicion that my fortune, not myself, was the object of pursuit. Therefore, I could love none of them because, however sincere their professions might be, they could not give the proof of real affection that my heart required. Often did I wish that I could appear divested of accidental circumstances and just as I was in myself, an honest, simple maiden; and then might I find some congenial soul whom I could freely love and who would love me heartily for myself alone. I wished on another account to form an attachment in this way. My friends call me romantic, and I confess a fault which they would not impute to me without evidence. I am conscious indeed of a warm and, I suppose, a romantic attachment to the country—London bred as I am. Particularly do I love mountain scenery and would most delight to spend my days among the sublime and beautiful works of nature and a virtuous rural population such as are found in your country. With my strong predilection for such a life, how could I expect to form a happy alliance in London, where all or nearly all are bred to relish artificial objects and manners and to covet wealth as the means of artificial splendor and the pompous show of fashionable life. I could not entrust my heart to any where the prospect of finding a congenial spirit was so hopeless. In the days of my sorest affliction, God was pleased to show me a heart in all respects agreeable to my desires and to give me the love of that heart under circumstances that banished all possibility of suspecting its sincerity. He has bound us together by the strongest ties of sympathy in all that makes prosperity joyful and calamity grievous. But I forget that there is one root of bitterness planted in the garden of our affections."

"Forget it, dear Judith, forever; it shall never spring up to trouble us."

After a little further conversation, the servants brought in our tea, and we sent an invitation to Judith's friends to join us. Mr. Von Caleb came. After tea I went out for half an hour to enter my name at the stage office and to give Judith and her friend the opportunity of completing their arrangements. On my return from the stage office near the hotel, I found Mr. Von Caleb in the barroom. He shook my hand affectionately and told me that he would let me and Judith spend the remainder of the evening alone; so, with another friendly shake of the hand, he bade me farewell.

When I entered the parlor, I found Judith sitting pensively on the sofa. We were both sad almost to death. We first arranged that I should write to her at farthest by Mr. Levi, who was to embark at New York on the first of June. I might write to her as soon as I reached home and then the oftener the better, she said, were it only to let her know of my welfare. I promised not to be hasty in my final determination about our engagement, for so she again required although a sigh escaped her when she made the requirement. If I ratified the engagement, she would be happy to see me in London as soon as I pleased, but I must understand that she could not put off her mourning weeds for a bridal dress until she had given a full year's sorrow to her dear lost Eli. So that if an early visit to London should not suit my convenience, she would not impute the delay to alienation of heart. If I annulled the engagement, I must still consider her as my grateful, devoted friend, who would rejoice at any opportunity of showing her gratitude for my disinterested kindness and care. Her voice faltered when she spoke of the contingency that I might decline the marriage; yet her conscientious judgment on this point wavered not, painful as the expression of it evidently was. She made the self-denying sacrifice of her own feelings to give me every advantage for the security of my happiness. Many expressions of tenderness did she utter and of ardent gratitude and unalterable friendship whatever I might do with our connubial engagement. I wondered—in fact, I was not well pleased—at her repeated allusions to the possibility of my discarding her, an act as remote from my thoughts at that time as Heaven is from Tartarus. But she had evidently reflected much upon the causes that might operate a change in my views. As to her own part in our correspondence, she promised to write as soon as she landed in England and then wait for a letter from me before she wrote again.

Having in these and other particulars come to a full understanding with each other, we had leisure to feel how distressingly near was the dreaded moment of separation. Two or three hours more, and we *must* part. What were our feelings? Oh, hours of sorrow and delight! How did we snatch every fleeting moment to fill higher and to mingle deeper the cup of our youthful love! We clung to each other's embrace; our tears mingled as they fell; our hearts answered throb for throb. How could we part? The clock struck eleven. "Adieu"—but she stammered in the attempt to utter it.

"Not yet, not yet; I cannot leave you." One more hour passed away—the last hour—it flew with eagles' wings as it shed down upon us all the delicious luxury of innocent sweetest affection saddened—the full relish of the bittersweet of love—the fiery rapture of joy, flooded with grief yet bursting through the flood.

Propriety admitted of no longer delay. The clock sounded the hour of midnight, long and loud, with clang after clang. Clang after clang struck on our hearts the knell of the last blissful hour; then all was still again except our beating hearts. Our time was come; yes, the last moment of our realized union with its unutterable sensations; the separation must now begin and widen and widen till lands and seas should intervene, and time and chance should cast all their changes and their hazards between us and possibly open a gulf impassably broad and deep, across which our now blended hearts could never commune again. Once more she meant to say "Adieu," but the word died on her lips. I caught the expiring accent as I pressed my lips to hers; the balmy sweetness remains to this day. We retired to our respective chambers like criminals going to execution so deadly was the sadness of that parting.

Could I sleep? Not a wink. The sensations of the evening kept thrilling in my nerves; unconquerable musings on the past and the future ran perpetually through my mind. I seemed to have lived an age within the last three weeks. To go back alone to the home and the landscapes of my boyhood, though less than a month before it was the object of my fondest desire, seemed now like going into the shades of death; for whilst I would be returning to my hills again, my Judith would be on her way to cross the wide ocean and would soon be far hidden from my sight among the myriads of London. But I imagined myself following her course, traversing the seas, pressing her again to my bosom, yes, to my "heart of hearts" in the dear character of wife, and bringing her back to bless my sylvan days in the green valleys of Virginia. This was the new age of gold that was rising to my mental vision, arrayed by fancy in all the charms of happy love and pastoral scenery.

IX

The Student's Return

Fifteen minutes before three o'clock, my waking dreams were interrupted by the servant, who announced that the stage coach would soon be at the door. I got up, dressed myself in a hurry, and wrote another adieu to my love, which, although but five lines in length, was sufficient to carry me away again into the fairy land of dreams. There I sat with my elbow on the table and my head on my hand till the servant, supposing me asleep, jogged me. I started up, hastened down to the bar, and called for my bill, which the clerk had, rather strangely I thought, declined to furnish until now. When he gave it to me, I found the surgeon's and all as I had requested, made out in full, but unexpectedly paid by Mr. Von Caleb according to a receipt appended. With the bill the clerk also handed me two other papers. The one was a sealed packet directed to myself and the other a receipt for me to sign, acknowledging that my bill was presented with the receipt as aforesaid and that a packet was given me, directed as aforesaid, and sealed with a seal having the word "Fidelity" for its motto. "Who wrote this?" I asked. "Mr. Von Caleb," answered the clerk, who added that Mr. V. was a very particular man in doing business. "Yes," said I, "he seems to know how to guard against tricks upon travellers."

I had scarcely signed the receipt before I was summoned to take my seat in the coach. I handed the clerk my billetdoux, thrust the papers into my pocket, and hastened out. On taking my seat I looked up at Judith's window—it was lighted—her sadly declining form was distinctly shadowed forth upon it, with the head resting on the hand as if she were looking down upon me. "Shade of my beloved," said I in my full heart, "shade of my beloved, fare thee well, fare thee well." The whip cracked, the wheels rattled over the pavement, and I no more saw even the shade of my beloved. "Now we are parted indeed," said my heart, aching and not ceasing to ache.

I was driven rapidly to Lancaster, heavy with grief and watching yet unable to rest from the spontaneous workings of the imagination. The dear image floated continually in the fields of mental vision; the music of that voice still sweetly chimed upon fancy's ear; those eyes, whose look could never be forgotten, shed incessant love-beams into my soul; and that pure, soft heart—I felt it beating yet responsively to mine.

I spoke not to my fellow passengers. I heard not their conversation. Time and space were flying past as the vehicle crushed the pebbles of the road and the flintstones sparkled under the armed hoofs of the horses; but I marked not the flight of time or space; my spirit was away with Judith, first in the parlor, next in the steamboat, watching the teardrops as they fell from her eyes and the palpitations of that affectionate heart. And my thoughts, like spiritual messengers, seemed to penetrate into the recesses of that throbbing breast and to find my own image cherished as a nursling there. Thus I enjoyed a realizing sense of the fact that although time and space might separate our bodies, our souls could still melt and mingle into one.

At the breakfast house I took the opportunity to open the sealed packet that I received at the bar. Under the envelope I found two sealed billets; the one was superscribed in Judith's handwriting and contained something hard. I opened the other first to have it out of the way. I read as follows:

Mr. Garame,

Pardon me for using a little art to do you an act of justice which you might have declined otherwise to accept but which, as agent for my cousin Nathan Bensaddi, I could not in good conscience neglect, nor would he be satisfied to learn that it was omitted. Your kindness to his daughter has put you to considerable expense and trouble. The enclosed note of one hundred dollars may reimburse the expense; but for the trouble, which you would count as nothing and for the generous kindheartedness, which we count above all price, I know not what compensation we can make you except you conclude to take my sweet, young cousin her-

self. However that may be, I pray the God of Israel to reward your goodness with every blessing.
  Farewell, kind friend,

                                        Isaac Von Caleb.

This was all quite agreeable. Agreeable in matter because delicately agreeable in manner. I thought I saw my Judith's delicate tact
in the management of this little affair. The other note was surprisingly interesting.

> Two o'clock. How can I sleep when the sound of the wheels that are to
> carry you away will soon be heard in the street? My cousin, Von Caleb,
> sends me word that he is awake and will take care that you receive what-
> ever communication I may yet have to make. This only I would repeat to
> my dear friend: in your happy valley think of your Judith, but be prudent
> and destroy not your happiness and consequently hers by obeying your
> desire at the expense of your judgment and conscience. If, after reflection,
> you cannot marry a Jewess—yet I know that you love one—always love
> her. Yes, my heart tells me that you will. Write at all events before June—
> as a friend if nothing more. The enclosed memorial was brought from
> England by cousin Von Caleb and put into his trunk when he left Boston.
> He had forgotten it until after he went to bed. He has sent it to me, ask-
> ing what I would do with it. I give it to my beloved preserver, knowing
> that he will value it as a keepsake and value it the more if he should
> never again see—Oh, that painful thought! let it die in silence. Farewell,
> once more, dear friend, farewell, farewell.
>
>   J.B.

The last words of this note were blotted with tears. With trembling hands and a beating heart, I unwrapped the memorial, wonder-
ing what it could be that under its wrappings felt roundish and hard
like a coin but considerably larger. Think of my exultation when I
discovered it to be an elegantly wrought golden locketcase, which
opened with a spring and exhibited to my eyes a perfect miniature
likeness of my own Judith! Oh, that sweet face! That well formed
bust! Whilst I leaned over and devoured this picture with my eyes, I
was called to breakfast. "Breakfast indeed!" said my heart. "Who
could leave such a feast of the soul to put coarse viands into his
stomach? Let the body wait for its earthy nutriment until the spirit
is satisfied with this celestial nectar and ambrosia." So I gazed upon

the lovely portrait—kissed it—then gazed—then kissed it again, alternately, until the stagedriver's signal roused me. I put the dear jewel into my pocket and resumed my place in the coach. Away we went with whirling wheels, which left behind them a train of dust ground from the stones of the pavement. At the rate of eight miles an hour was I carried homewards but away from the place where I had parted with Judith. Nine times, according to my conjecture, did I read my Judith's note and nine times steal a look at her portrait before we stopped for dinner at Lancaster. I dined without appetite and continued my journey towards Harrisburg. About ten o'clock at night we reached the sleeping house. I went supperless to bed and, after tossing about till midnight, fell into a troubled sleep. At Lancaster I had suspended my beautiful locket case by a ribbon about my neck and put it into my bosom directly against my heart. I was wakened out of my unquiet sleep by some unusual sensation. I felt for what was uppermost in my thoughts, the golden treasure of my bosom and behold! I found it drawn out and lying at the full length of the ribbon towards the front side of the bed. I knew instantly that some rogue had attempted to filch it and had failed only from my ready wakefulness. I suspected a fellow passenger who slept in the room with me. I had that afternoon detected him eyeing my jewel once when I drew it out to take a sly look. I thought then that he coveted my treasure and had the look of a rogue. For safety, therefore, I locked it up in the very bottom of my trunk, hard as I felt the self-denial to be when I deprived myself of the opportunity to look at my Judith's likeness some ten or twelve times a day.

By three o'clock the next morning I was again on my way. At Harrisburg I ate a little breakfast; then, crossing the Susquehanna, I reached Carlyle early in the afternoon. Here my strength and spirits began to fail so greatly that I doubted my ability to pursue the journey without a day's rest. The extraordinary scenes in which I had been engaged during three weeks had kept me in a state of constant excitement. Ten days confinement in Philadelphia had impaired my health, and now two days of violent emotion, watchfulness, and loss of appetite had exhausted me. Such a protracted strain upon the nervous system, followed by loss of appetite, want of sleep and fatigue of travelling, was more than human nature could bear without a distressful prostration of both corporeal and mental powers. In the case of one who, like myself, is constitutionally subject to fits of melancholy, the necessary consequence would be a state of deep mental dejection accompanied with sombre and dispiriting views on all subjects. I cannot otherwise account for a change which, on this second day of my journey, began to come over my spirit.

I frequently read my dear Judith's note, at first in the morning with the same unmixed pleasure as on the preceding day, but in the afternoon the word "Jewess" began to grate a little on my feelings and to suggest some thoughts, transient and obscure, yet rather unpleasant, amounting to no more than a general impression that my happiness in love would have been complete if, with all its positively agreeable circumstances, this unfortunate one of my beloved's Judaism had not been mingled.

In the neighborhood of Carlyle, I recognized clearly the features of the Great Valley, my native land, with which, previous to the last few months, all the affections and pleasures of my life had been associated. Here, though with less sublimity of mountain and less variety of low ground, were the parallel ridges and the wide interval of rich slopes with their limestone rocks and rivulets, all which reminded me strongly of the objects of my boyish delight. This effect of scenery, to revive old habits of thought and feeling, was increased on the third day when I felt partially refreshed after some hours of sound sleep. I had pursued my journey notwithstanding my exhaustion; better probably had it been for me if my impatience to reach home had permitted me to stop and recruit my wasted strength. However, on the third day I saw the country assuming more and more the appearance of my native land; then more and more did my thoughts revert to former days—days of calm delight in study, or cheerful amusement in rambling over hill and dale, fishing in deep shady pool, or gathering flowers on meadow sides or wild mountain steeps.

With the revival of old and fixed habits of mind, my new delirium of passion began to abate. Not that I thought Judith less beautiful or less worthy, but now when the placid current of old thoughts and

feelings was started afresh, the new torrent of amorous passion began naturally to exhaust itself. Judith, all charming as she was, no
longer engrossed all my powers of thought and feeling. Her lovely
presence, with all its affecting circumstances, our parting with its
unutterable emotions of delight and sorrow, had raised within me a
turbid and overwhelming tempest of feeling, which had so far abated
under the influences just mentioned that calm reason could now begin to shoot some rays of its light through the troubled atmosphere
of the mind. Yet the mental fluctuations that followed ought perhaps
to be attributed as much to the disease of low spirits as to the efforts
of reason to sway the violence of passion. I shall not stop to phi-
losophise but proceed with my story.

Whatever the cause might be, it so happened that on the third day
of my travels the word "Jewess" in the dear note so often read began
to strike positively disagreeable impressions upon my mind. Whilst I
would be musing on my lovely Judith and seeing her with fancy's eye
arrayed in all her charms, that troublesome word "Jewess" would
come with some ugly thought behind it and dissipate, as with a
wizard's spell, the fascinating colors of the vision.

On the fourth day, when I entered Virginia, the souring tendency
of my thoughts increased. More frequently would that detestable
word return and trouble the sweet current of my feelings. "Jewess,"
"Jewess," would I say to myself and that, too, in spite of myself.
"Am I really in love with the daughter of a Jew? Am I to connect myself with that accursed race?" Every successive day would such villainous thoughts rush in more obtrusively. When I looked at the
mountains on either side of the way and at the everchanging views
occurring along the road and recognized the likeness of my dear
homestead in many a wood-crowned hill and rocky vale, I would
think of my youthful delights and the long-familiar faces of those
whom I loved. Then, gliding from the past to the future, my heart
would take the amiable Judith to the home and society of my former
days and imagine what new pleasures she would bring with her and
with what new charms she would invest my future dwelling place in
this lovely land. Then, uncalled for, would the same and other loathsome ideas come in like imps of Satan and thrust their ugly visages

into the very foreground of the picture. "Jewess," "Jewess," would I repeat, as if by some instigation of the arch fiend. Yes, a Jewess is to be my wife. My children are to be half-blooded Jews. My neighbors are to point at her as we pass by and say, "That is the Jewess." When we go to church—*we*, do I say? Perhaps she will not go to church but be wishing for her rabbi and her synagogue. But suppose that in compliance with my desire, she does go to church; then every eye is upon her—whispers go round, "The Jewess has come to church! Do you know whether she is likely to be converted?" and so on. Then the minister preaches at her and deals out anathemas against the unbelieving Jews—and I am to be reproached, and to reproach myself, for the inconsistency of professing Christianity and yet marrying an unbelieving Jewess and making her the mistress and the mother of my family. Oh, how can I do it?

I groaned with horror at these reflections, unable to banish them as baseless fancies, and vexed with myself for admitting them. But every day they crowded harder into my mind, assuming at each return more grim and appalling aspects. In vain did I muster facts and affections against them. Judith's personal charms, Judith's amiable temper, extraordinary intelligence, admirable genius, exquisite accomplishments, fascinating manners—our congenial tastes, our mutual love, her generous pledge to me, my assurances to her—all that had filled and captivated my soul for weeks—all were brought forward on the side of love, and admitted on the other side to be true—yet could not all these considerations banish the hateful accompaniments of that cursed word, "Jewess!" Still would it come and fetch its goblin retinue of conscientious scruples and ingrained prejudices.

Sometimes, indeed, my love was victorious and beat this haggard crew out of the field. Judith would rise in all her charms before my imagination; memory would tell the affecting story of our grief-born union of hearts; reason would demonstrate her inestimable worth; impassioned fancy would adorn her, as nature had adorned her, with the hues and lineaments of angelic loveliness, and my heart would be feeding on the delicious vision. But then, my black bile beginning to work, all of a sudden, like the harpies of old and quite as abominable as those monsters, a new flight of black vulturine thoughts would descend upon the banquet of my soul and change the zest into nausea by their defilements. "Jewess," "Jewess," would I again mutter like a demoniac. "A Jewish wife must make me miserable. When I teach my children the doctrines of Christianity, their Jewish mother will be a hindrance to their faith and a grief to mine. I must either omit the worship of God in my family or be disturbed in my devotions by the thought that when I utter the Saviour's name and express my reliance on his mediation, the partner of my bosom, whether she kneel like a hypocrite or sit like an infidel, will in her heart attach the title of impostor to that venerable name." Then would my heart rise up with disgust against the whole race of unbelieving Jews, ancient and modern. Then in rapid succession would texts of Scripture, facts in history, passages in books of travels, and all that I had read or heard that was dishonorable to the Jews rise up in my memory and fill me with detestation of the very name of Jew. "The Jews! The stiff-necked, hardhearted race," would I mutter bitterly, "who provoked the patience of God until He, by his prophets, cursed and banned them out of his mercy and from the pale of human society and made them a hissing and a curse among all nations. Did they not, like furious demons, cry out 'Crucify him, crucify him?' And how many acts of fiendish malignity and loathsome baseness have they committed? They are hated by all nations, by Christian, Musselman, Pagan—'by saint, by savage, and by sage'—all concur in executing the Divine curse upon them. And I am to marry one of them? Oh, why was so beautiful, so amiable a creature born of the accursed race? The miserly knavish race! The scorn and the detestation of travellers in Poland and wheresoever strangers are exposed to their knavish tricks and unprincipled exactions! Faugh! The squalid occupants of suburbs and streets where a decent passenger is nauseated by their filth! The bearded vendors of old clothes! The malignant Shylocks of the money market! Their very name has become a term for villainy and extortion. 'Jew' signifies miser and rogue. Yet these people I must take into my bosom for my wife's sake and call them cousin!"

Such was often the train of my reflections, especially when the evil spirit of melancholy diffused his bile over my thoughts. Judith herself was always lovely to my soul; the black demon could not dim the lustre of her beauty nor stain the purity of her character except by incorporating her with the mass of her nation so as to obscure the merits that shone out from her charming individuality. But the one fact, personal to her, her Judaical education, combined with prejudices against her people, harassed me from day to day and crossed the path of my love with an omen too sinister and too obviously real to be any longer regarded as a mere freak of the brain originating in melancholy.

The contest of antagonist principles began at last to assume a degree of regularity after the misty turbulence of my feelings had measurably subsided. But the violence of the mental strife rather increased as the opposing principles began more distinctly to array themselves for the contest. I will not call it a contest between love and reason, for there was evidently much reason on the side of love; but in the ranks of the other side there was not only a host of prejudices but something besides of giant force and of ghastly aspect.

The agony of the struggle was temporarily abated by the appearance of my beloved Rockbridge. When I entered its confines, I hailed with delight the grim aspect of the Jump Mountain as he reared his black and shaggy brow over the border of the landscape. Not less did the great Hogback please my eye when I saw him, the next in order, bend up his swelling ridge bristled with pines. But most joyfully did I behold the rising majesty of the House Mountain, as it gradually stood forth in solitary grandeur and exposed to view its double ridge and huge buttresses like a palace built for the king of the giants. Again were my homefelt pleasures more vividly restored when I crossed the high swell of Timberridge in the middle of the Great Valley and saw far away in the southern horizon the dim Peaks of Otter shooting their points deeply into the vault of Heaven. Next, the familiar scenes near my father's cottage shed their sweet influence upon my heart, from verdant hill and from meadow brook, stealing its way long the dale beneath the covert of its willows. When the cedar cliffs by the river showed me the pathway to the dear nook where I drew my infant breath, I sprang from the coach, threaded each well-known turn by rock and tree, saw in all its rural quietude the home of childhood, bounded into the house, heard the cry of joyful surprise, flung myself first on one breast, then on another, of parents, sisters and friends, and received with delight the enthusiastic greetings of the servants, whose sooty faces were enlightened by the shining white of their teeth and the not less shining whites of their glad eyes. Now for awhile I felt as simply happy as I had been when

> In rustic boyhood, free from care,
> I hooked the trout and chased the hare.

But soon I relapsed into my distressing meditations. When the first gale of delight on arriving at home had blown over, I remembered my matrimonial engagement with a Jewess, and the remembrance struck a damp on my feelings. "Now," thought I, "comes my sorest trial. I must tell my parents and friends that I am about to fetch a Jewish wife into their circle, and how it will shock them! How they will wonder and grieve!" I had walked out to look over my old playgrounds and my favorite bank for summer fishing and reading beneath the shade of a broad elm, when these painful thoughts occurred. To banish them I returned to the house and busied myself with conversation. I was not yet delivered from my tormentors when my sister Elizabeth asked me for the key of my trunk that she might dispose of my apparel. Then I remembered the dear portrait, which I had not taken out and, in the confusion of my thoughts, seldom even remembered since it was put away. Fearing that it might be found and bring on a premature discovery, I hastened upstairs alone, took it out, opened the case, and again felt the witching charm of those lovely features to such a degree that all doubts and fears vanished like ghosts before the rosy-fingered beams of Aurora. "I will write tomorrow," said I as I closed the case and locked it up in my drawer. On going to bed I looked at it again and felt doubly assured that the soul which beamed through those eyes could never make a husband unhappy. "I will write tomorrow," said I again, "and inform her of my safe arrival and of my unalterable determination to fulfil our engagement." I went to bed and mused sweetly on my Judith until my waking thoughts faded away into the purple twilight of dreams. Then Judith herself appeared in a green meadow of fairy land, gathering sweet flowers, her form invested with the airy lightness of a sylph and colored with the rainbow tints of a blessed spirit.

The next morning I slept so long and soundly that when I awoke I heard the family at breakfast. I dressed myself and hurried down to join them. After breakfast we went into the parlor, where I was pleasantly engaged during the forenoon in conversation with the family and some friends who called to see me.

Towards noon my father alluded incidentally to the sale of a horse, which he had lately made to a traveller. I asked some question which led him to give us an amusing account of the transaction, amusing to all the rest, and it would have been equally to me if my unsuspecting parent had not used an expression which I had often heard and often used myself but which now had gall and wormwood in it to my feelings.

"He tried to *Jew* me," said my father.

"Was it that little bald, sharp-faced man that I saw with you at the post office?" asked my sister.

"Yes," said my father, "with small gray eyes and a shrill voice."

"Perhaps he *was* a Jew," added my sister.

"Possibly enough," said my father, "his knavish looks would at least become a Jew. He tried first to impose on me by undervaluing the horse and then by passing uncurrent money upon me, protesting that it was current. If he was not a rogue of a Jew, he was a Jew of a rogue."

These unusually bitter expressions of my father went like daggers' points to my heart. But my kindred most undesignedly condemned me to still keener thoughts. My good mother spoke up and said:

"It is a happy circumstance that we have no Jews among us in the Valley. I should hate to have any thing to do with them."

My mother's face exhibited her anti-Jewish disgust as she spoke.

"They are not *all* so bad," said my father in extenuation, and I thanked him in my heart for the sentiment. But my mother drove the dagger up to the hilt when she replied: "Good or bad, a Jew is a Jew, and I should hate to have any of them about me."

This was too much for my feelings. I rose hastily and went out to conceal my agony. Doleful indeed were my dumps. "They will never consent," said I as I rushed away from the house with as much hurrying impetuousity as if I were stung by a swarm of hornets. "Perhaps they never ought to consent" was the next reflection. The whole train of my evil thoughts returned, headed this time by the squeaking miser Levi, so like my father's horse buyer. I hurried wildly on till I found myself on the brow of a precipice by the river side. I was not prepared for a lover's leap into the stream below; therefore I stopped and, seating myself on a rock, leaned my head upon my knees and in that meditative posture sank deeper and deeper into the black sea of my reflections. Here I was found by a Negro boy sent to tell me that dinner was ready. After swallowing what I supposed might conceal my want of appetite, I remembered that Judith's portrait had hitherto operated as a charm, either to keep off the black demons or to exorcise them if they had possession. Inspired with eager hope, I rose from table and went hastily upstairs for the portrait. I found my table drawer unlocked as I had inadvertently left it in the morning. I hastily searched the drawer, and lo! The portrait was gone! My talisman was gone! Instead of the hoped-for relief, additional miseries came upon me; the dun clouds of despair boiled up more thickly and fearfully in the horizon of my soul. Who could have taken my jewel? I could not conjecture, and I durst not inquire because inquiry would end in a disclosure of my love engagement with a Jewess—a secret, which, in my present state of mind, I could not bear to reveal.

After some days my conscience smote me for withholding so important a communication from my parents, who had a right to know my matrimonial scheme and who were best qualified to teach me by their cool and experienced judgment how to distinguish the dictates of sober reason from the illusions of passion and the suggestions of prejudice. Freely could I tell them all but the one fact, that although my Judith was the best and the most beautiful of maidens and wealthy withal, yet she was that most disagreeable thing—a Jewess. Oh misery! How often, when the story was on the point of my tongue, did I shudder and draw back at the thought of telling that. But *that* was the critical point of the case; to withhold that would be to evade the gist of the difficulty.

Days and weeks rolled on but gave no return of brightness to my soul, no decisive result to my agonising reflections. I moped and mused and pined away. My friends observed my melancholy air and haggard looks. They ascribed all to returning consumption and often took counsel about the means of cure. Alas! they little dreamed that the malady was consuming the heart and not the lungs.

Thus I drooped and hesitated until the month of May was three-fourths gone. I had not written even the friendly letter which my Judith had so earnestly requested. What a beast was I! Now the time was come when I *must* decide the matrimonial question, either by action or by procrastination. I must now write to my lovely Jewess or forfeit all claim even to her friendly regard. I had promised to write my decision *at the latest* by the sharp-visaged miser Levi, who would embark at New York on the first day of June. Often did I sit down with pen in hand resolved to write something. But what could I write? That I was well? No. That I had decided to marry her? No. That I had consulted my friends? No, not even that. That I was tormented with doubts and fears and yet unable to decide? Yes, but why write a fact which could only distress her? Better not write at all; the failure of the promised letter might be imputed to accident. But on second thought this appeared unfeasible, for she had reason to expect several letters, and all could hardly fail. One other course remained: I might, if I pleased, say to her, "Forget me, lovely Judith." In a misanthropic mood, when every thought was dark and bitter, I twice sat down in desperate resolve to end the strife by writing her a letter of dismissal. But ere the fatal sentence, "I have decided not to marry you, my Judith," could be finished, I seemed to hear thunders roll at a distance and to see the lightning flash of my tutelary angel as he descended at this awful moment; and then a monitory voice within me would whisper, "Cast not that pearl away!" Then I could not—for my life I durst not—wilfully cast that pearl away.

The eve of the last day had arrived when I must write to secure the stipulated conveyance. To defer my answer beyond the next day would be, in effect, to discard my beloved Jewess. The sun of the evening had set in the deepest gloom of a cloudy atmosphere; my soul was gloomy as the shadow of death. My powers of mind and body were almost prostrated by long and deep melancholy, now reaching the acme of a doleful hypochrondria. I sat in my room; my candle burned dimly with its knobbed, unsnuffed wick. I leaned over the back of my chair with my elbow behind it and my temple supported with the palm of my hand; my eyes were half closed and scarcely sensible of the glimmering light in the room. Horrid spectres now for the first time flitted across the fields of my imagination and disappeared. Then they reappeared, bloody and fierce; they stopped and gloated and grinned at me until I almost fainted with terror. I was verging on absolute madness. Suddenly I heard a low tapping at the door. I started up, shuddering with dread; for I conceived that murderers were coming with daggers to stab me. "Who is there?" I cried, with a scarcely audible voice. "Me, massa Willie," was the answer. I felt instant relief when I recognised the voice of old Hannah, my nurse in infancy, who always had for me a mother's affection. She opened the door softly and completed my restoration to sober sense by the sight of her honest face. "Massa Willie, I don't want to 'sturb you now when you got so poorly again. I jist came to ax you if that slut Poll that Massa hired last Christmas didn't take this curious piece o'money, or whatever it is, from you. I thought it must be your'n, for I know it ain't none o' her'n. See, here it is," said she, coming forward and holding up what I saw instantly to be my locket case—my talisman! As the famished tiger on the boa constrictor springs upon his prey, so did I spring forward and clutch my jewel; and when I had it in my grasp, I lifted both hands aloft and cried, "Thank God, thank God, I have her once more." Then I said quickly, "Go down now, aunt Hannah, I wish to be alone." She was amazed, as well she might be, but retired promptly, saying as she went, "That can't be money, no how, that makes Massa Willie so glad." I hastily locked the door after her, already sensible of a new spirit within me; then, taking my seat at the table, I snuffed the candle and pressed the locket spring. The lid flew up and again presented to my longing eyes that sweet enrapturing face. The picture restored with magical force and rapidity the lovely traits, corporeal and mental, of the dear original now so nearly abandoned. I looked and looked; the beauteous image seemed to acquire animation as I gazed upon it and to rise before the imagination into the living fulness and reality of Judith's lovely self. Yes, now my Judith was herself again. Melancholy, with all his imps of darkness, vanished at her presence. Again I felt the impression of those love-darting eyes, again heard in my soul the soft melody that flowed from those sweet lips. Memory awoke and presented in pristine freshness, and with enchanting effect, all the affecting images of the past: the journey to Charleston, our stay there with the piano and the songs of heart-melting pathos; then the disaster at sea, the throes of her grief, and the sympathy of our souls; then our sojourn in Philadelphia, the maturity and the embarrassments of our love—the purity, the self-control and the intensity of her affection; lastly, the parting hour, its keen sorrows and thrilling delights, with all that made them keen and thrilling. I saw and felt them all again. After this revival of former emotions in my soul, could I then give up my Judith? No, no; the dominion and the wealth of the world were a boon too poor to buy her out of my arms. I would have dared the stormy deeps of every sea; I would have crossed frozen Alps and torrid Sahara; I would have braved the shadow of death and gone down, like Orpheus for Eurydice, to the dusky mansions of departed spirits and would have deemed myself well rewarded to win so lovely a creature at last. The clouds were now dispersed that had so long obscured the bright prospects before me. The word "Jewess" no longer drew after it the gloomy conceptions of fear and of a diseased imagination; it was now associated only with Judith's self, with the radiance of her beauty, the unalloyed sweetness of her temper, the unsullied purity of her principles, and all the attractive qualities of her mind. Even my religious scruples, heretofore aggravated by melancholy, now gave way again to the conviction that Judith already so esteemed Christianity and was so nearly persuaded of its truth as only to await the influences and the occasion that our marriage would present to believe and to profess the whole. What then had I to fear? Nothing. Such was my conclusion within two hours after her portrait had begun its reviving influence upon my heart. Some of the reasonings which led to this comfortable conclusion may have been the logic of reanimated passion. Whether it were so or not, my understanding then accorded its approval to the desire of the heart.

I hesitated no longer but wrote the chief part of the letter that night, declaring my undiminished love and my fixed resolution to go and claim her hand as soon as she would permit me. I apologised for my delay by acknowledging the diseased state of my mind and the gloomy views that succeeded and produced a long struggle. I expressed my intention to visit her in London before the expiration of the year but said that I would await an answer from her, that I might, if she gave permission, go unprepared to consummate our union before the next spring, which was the time that she had appointed as the earliest period of our nuptials.

Having written thus much, I went to bed, leaving what remained to be filled up in the morning after a consultation with my parents. The next morning I *did* state the case to my parents, but with fear and trembling. Not that I expected opposition from them after they should hear all, but I scarcely hoped for their full approval. Nevertheless, although they were shocked, as I expected them to be, at the Judaism of my betrothed; yet after I had given them a full history of our acquaintance and exerted my eloquence in depicting her excellencies, not forgetting the symptoms of her inclination for Christianity nor the fact so generally agreeable to parents, that she was very rich, I had the satisfaction to hear them yield their approval and advise me to write immediately. They saw the hand of Divine Providence in the circumstances and were persuaded that my happiness would be less hazarded by consummating the marriage than by doing violence to my feelings and plunging again into the deeps of melancholy.

So I finished my letter and directed it under cover to Simon Levi at New York. It went by that day's mail and would in due course reach New York on the 30th of May.

But one expression which the gray-eyed miser had dropped about his "boy Joseph" gave me a suspicion that if he knew the state of affairs between me and Judith, he might suppress my letter with the view of getting Judith's fortune into his own family. Therefore, to avoid the possibility of failure in this way, I wrote a second letter, directed to Judith's self in London, to go by the usual mode of conveyance in the New York packets. This I put into the post office four days after the other. Thus, if the one should fail, I might rely upon the success of the other. I met with an immediate reward for my late fidelity; for when I put the second letter into the office, I found one there from Judith, short and written very hastily on her landing at Liverpool. She apologised for its brevity, saying that a swift sailing packet was to sail immediately for New York and that she had time only to tell me of her prosperous voyage, good health and unchanged heart. She concluded with the promise of writing fully on the receipt of my first letter, which she hoped to receive within a fortnight after her arrival at home.

The expression of this hope gave me a severe pang of self-reproach. "Wretched procrastinator that I am!" said I, "how sadly disappointed she must be!" But I had done my duty at last.

Now the months seemed ages until I should receive her answer. I began to make preparations for my expected voyage and became weekly more impatient for the summons of my betrothed. I watched the growing and the waning moons, and "chid the lazy lagging foot of time." The delightful summer of our mountains seemed interminably long, for it shed its flowers and matured its foliage but brought me no answer. I had set four months as the utmost limit to which even fear could postpone the return of an answer. Three months I thought sufficient; I was by that time prepared for the voyage and went to the post office every mail day expecting to find the desired summons to depart. Every mail day I went disheartened away but still indulging the hope that the next mail would not disappoint me. Thus, the fourth month passed over my impatient spirit, but to the end of it no letter came. I saw the leaves of autumn put on the bright hues of approaching decay, making the forest glorious to all eyes but mine. Still no letter came. Impatience was converted into fearful anxiety. I saw the leaves of autumn fade and then fly, withered and sere, before the northern blast until the forest looked sad beneath the gathering storms of winter. Sad and sadder grew my heart, for not a word from Judith reached my longing eyes. Winter shed his snows over mountain and valley; Christmas came, and New Year came when days are shortest and dreariest in the outdoor world, but hearts are merry by firesides. But my heart was more dreary than the dead earth and the leaden face of a cloudy sky. The winter began to yield to the benign power of the ascending sun; nature began to revive under the genial influence, but not so my desolate heart. Early flowers looked out on sunny banks; meadows drank new verdure from the joyful streams that gushed out of showery hills and bounded through the valleys. Now came the anniversary of the journey to Charleston, then of the sea voyage, then of the love pledges and the parting hour. The star of my hopes had faded into utter darkness; my letters were never to be answered; what could be the matter?

Whilst I had been able to cherish a lingering remnant of hope, that slow passages or accidental detention by sea or land, had only delayed the answer, I clung to that and waited for the result before I would take any other step. But when five and then six months had passed away, my characteristic hesitancy on such occasions again operated to make me postpone any decisive movement to solve the mystery of my disappointment. One of two things I might do: write again and repeatedly or go myself to London. To write again presupposed that either both my letters or her answer had failed to reach their destination. But not only was I discouraged by the fact that such failures had become very rare, but there was this further difficulty, that by writing again I could gain no explanation in less than three months, a delay which my impatient heart could not resolve to incur. I concluded at last to renew my preparations for a voyage, but various difficulties (and in my desponding state of mind molehills swelled to mountains) caused delay until the opening of the spring. I was then completing my arrangements and expected soon to depart when an unfortunate accident gave another turn to my feelings.

I have, since my college days, been passionately fond of botany and have never failed, when the mild sunshine and early flowers invite the lovers of nature abroad, to make frequent excursions about the warm dells and romantic cliffs of my homestead. One day, late in March, when the sun shone sweetly and my heart was troubled with gloomy thoughts, I took a farewell stroll about the rocky steeps of the vicinity, expecting in two or three days to leave them in search of my lost bride. I was clambering along the side of a steep cliff, washed at base by the river now swollen and muddy from late rains. Happening to espy on the brow of the cliff above me a flower of rare species and of attractive form and colors, I started eagerly to reach it by climbing the precipice. But, in my haste, I slipped and fell back almost into the river. I saved myself only by catching hold of a sapling as I slid and rolled. My bodily hurt was small, but my sick heart received a fatal wound. My precious locket case, which I still wore in my bosom, fell out, was caught by a stub as I descended, and the ribon being broken, the case rolled down and plunged into the angry flood, out of sight and out of reach. "Oh, mercy!" I exclaimed. "She is gone! she is gone!" Vainly did I go to the water's edge and gaze wistfully at the turbid current as if I expected it to restore my talisman, my Judith. The reader knows me well enough by this time to anticipate the consequence. Despair began to flap her raven wings over me and dismal phantoms to haunt my imagination.

Hitherto I had refused to entertain a suspicion of Judith's fidelity. When such a thought occurred, one look at her portrait was sufficient to dispel it. I was perplexed, discouraged, and sad enough at the long delay and ultimate failure of an answer to my letters; but, rather than think her false, I would suppose that the letters had been lost on the way or that death had snatched her beyond the reach of my arms. Now I began to fear that she had repented of her engagement, that her return home to her kindred and friends had affected her as the same circumstance had for weeks affected me, with the restoration of habitual feelings first and then less pleasing views of the brief episode of our love adventure. My suspicion, once allowed to take root and nurtured by a brooding melancholy, grew apace into a dark and bitter jealousy. In a few days I could even say in the bitterness of my soul, "Why should I go to see her? Or why write a third time? Shall I allow her to show myself or my third letter to her cockney beaux of which she told me that she had crowds, that they may laugh at the uncouth simplicity of a mountain bumpkin of Virginia, who by his services at a critical period, when her grief was deep and her heart unguarded, had made a transient impression on her, but whom, in her cooler moments, she could not think of marrying though she felt obliged to him for his kindness and had, under the impulse of gratitude, given him more encouragement than prudence allowed?

Shall I expose myself to such treatment as this? No, verily I will not!"

These suggestions of the melancholy demon were sometimes resisted by my better feelings, but never subdued so that I could resolve again to prosecute my ill-fated love. I still indulged, from time to time, my bitter surmisings of Judith's falsehood although my conscience often whispered that they were unjust. What inconsistencies will not a wretched man perpetrate in the bitterness of his soul!

Finally, I resolved that as the case seemed to be desperate, I would strive to forget that I had ever loved Judith Bensaddi. I was impelled to some decisive course by the dread of a settled melancholy and imbecile moping, or of downright madness, for life. Once conclusively resolved, I was as prompt and energetic in execution as I was indecisive and procrastinating in cases of doubtful deliberation.

"Perhaps," said I to myself, "it is a merciful interposition of Providence that has thwarted an affection which might have planted a thorn in my breast for life. A Christian is forbidden to marry an infidel, and the prohibition is a wise one. Now for study and learning and the glorious achievements of professional exertion."

My studies had been much interrupted by consumption first, then by love and melancholy. During a year I had made little progress; now I betook myself with renewed zeal to my books. But many a time and oft, while leaning over my learned author on the table, did I start out of a reverie and find that my soul had unconsciously strayed into the regions of love and drank sweeter waters at the fountain of Venus than Helicon had ever yielded to poet or philosopher. But, by persevering efforts, I conquered this propensity to revive scenes and emotions, which, however delightful once, were fleeting as a dream, and, like a dream, should be forgotten.

An Unexpected Letter

By the end of the ensuing summer, my mind had recovered its usual tone and steady habits, and I had just finished the preparatory studies of my profession when an incident occurred which again raised my feelings to a tempest and formed the closing scene of my story.

Going by the post office one forenoon, I was called to receive a letter which had arrived by the last mail. I turned in, expecting nothing unusual; when lo! it was a ship létter with the London postmark. I instantly recognised upon it the handwriting of Judith Bensaddi! Good Heavens! what a volcanic stirring and heaving, what a rekindling and burning of irrepressible fires did I feel immediately within me. The flame of love had been smothered by despair; but the fuel was unconsumed and the fire smouldering in secret. The first breath of hope was sufficient to reawaken its dormant energies.

I hurried out of the town on my way home, intending, as soon as I reached a private place, to tear open the mystery at once. But when I found a suitable place, I could not summon the resolution to break the seal. Hope shed reviving rays upon my soul, and I longed to realize its promise. But fear drew up a cloud from the Stygian lake that threatened to overwhelm and extinguish forever the last star in my heaven of love. Hitherto, the evidence that Judith had changed her mind was purely negative; I had received no communication from her, that was all. Now I was to learn from herself the certainty of what I might still hope or of what I had long feared. The question that had cost me so much excruciating conjecture was now to be solved; I was to know in a moment whether the lovely Judith might yet be mine or whether the gulf between us was now fixed and impassable. When I put my thumbnail to the seal and felt that I was about to read the doom of a love whose renovated power now ruled my soul, "terror took hold on me and trembling which made all bones to shake." I could not break the seal. I staggered homewards under my load of fearful anxiety. Several times I stopped and said, "Now!" but I could not; every nerve in my body quivered. When I got home I stole unobserved into my room and locked the door. "Here," said I, "is the place, and now is the time." Still I hesitated; I sat; I lay down on the bed; I got up and paced the room. It would not do; my heart quailed and shrunk from the dread revelation. "I cannot do it here," said I. "I must go to the woods and rocks." To the woods and rocks about the farm I went. For hours I wandered from shade to shade and from rock to rock in deep and agitated thought, often forgetting where I was or what was the matter. Often I took out the letter from my pocket, looked at it, one while examining the superscription, another while the seal; and then, returning it to my pocket with a groan, I wandered again like the evil spirit, "seeking rest and finding none." It may seem strange that I should voluntarily undergo this lengthened agony of suspense when I could end it in a moment. But I durst not end it. What man could dare, if he might, unseal the book of his final destiny? He would rather live in the uncertainty of a trembling hope than hazard the withering blast of a remediless despair.

Towards evening I found myself by the riverside in a solitary nook to which I was wont to resort when in a musing mood. It was a snug corner, with the river in front and high cliffs, topped with cedars, curving round the other sides. Three or four trees spread their umbrageous tops overhead, and beneath, a small fountain drew its silvery thread of cool water from the inner angle to the river between turfy banks and mossy stones. Here I had often meditated on my love, and here I resolved at all events to know its issue. I threw myself down upon a sweet grassy bank near the river that ran murmuring by. Here a tuft of the goldenrod waved its yellow plumes in the breeze; at the base of the cliff, near my seat, the wild aster was opening its purple-fringed eyes, seemingly to watch the dog star in his nightly rounds. Elsewhere the atmosphere was glowing with summer heat; here all was cool, dusky and still. Again I took the letter from my pocket, and again I trembled all over like an aspen leaf. But my resolution was taken. "Now it *must* be done." My thumbnail was again applied, and with a convulsive jerk I tore off the seal. With trembling hands I unfolded the closely written sheet, and with palpitating heart I read as follows:

London, July 10th, 1820

My Beloved Friend:

With you it is impossible for me to be ceremonious. I have experienced too much of your kindness and, I may add, of your love to suspect you of unkind neglect or to think of you with any other feeling than gratitude and friendship. I wrote you a few hasty lines from Liverpool by a packet that was about to sail immediately after our landing. I will now give you the outlines of my sad history since I left Philadelphia.

The night when we parted! I yet weep at the remembrance of it. Had I then anticipated our long, long separation, my grief would have turned to distraction. Our journey to Boston was speedy and would have been pleasant if any thing could have given pleasure so shortly after that parting hour. Two days afterwards I took ship with my cousin. The ship and the sea revived all my griefs, for they brought affectingly to mind the horrible day when I lost the dearest of brothers and found all a brother's kindness in you. The voyage, as I wrote before, was prosperous, and on the thirty-fifth day after our separation I was in the arms of my dear father. Cousin Von Caleb had written him notice of our calamity from Boston on the day when he received my letter, so that before our arrival my afflicted parent had learned his irreparable loss. Now he seemed equally divided between joy for his recovered daughter and grief for his lost son.

I related to him as well as my feelings would allow the circumstances of the disaster and the history of my acquaintance with you from the first day to the last, omitting at first the affair of our love. I told him how you had saved my life at the hazard of your own and how you had thenceforth nursed me in my desperate grief, cherished me as a sister, and taken me far out of your way to restore me to my friends until your care of me occasioned the severe hurt that confined you in Philadelphia. "Now blessed be that good young stranger," said my father with tears in his eyes. "How can we reward him for his goodness to my poor destitute child? I owe him for your life; yes, twice—for without him you would first have perished in the water and then in your grief. We must do something—yes, a great deal, to show our gratitude. I trust that you showed yourself grateful, daughter—did you?" "Yes, father, your daughter endeavored to show that she could love such a kind protector and such an honorable, worthy gentleman." So I went on, until I had told him all. "He shall have you, Judith; he deserves to have you; he is the very man to make you happy." Then was the joy of my love complete.

I hoped in a fortnight or sooner to receive a friendly letter, telling me of your safe return if nothing more. The fortnight seemed very long; and when a month passed without bringing me a letter, it seemed to have been a year. "But I am sure of one by Mr. Levi," said I; and so I endeavored to comfort myself. I could hardly wait until he should come, and when at last I was told that he was arrived and actually in the house, I ran breathless with joy and demanded my letter. "None," said he, "I went to the post office the first of June and found none for you." "None?" said I. "No, sure, not one." I remember nothing more until I found myself in bed and the physician by my side.

Still, though stricken down, I was not in despair. "Some accident has disappointed me," said I, "the letter may have miscarried, or he may choose to come and give me a joyful surprise by bearing his own tidings. I shall hear or see before long." But another month passed—so long!—yet no tidings. We heard of a New York packet ship wrecked on the coast of Ireland, the letter bag lost and some passengers, but your name was not among them. On this chance of your letter being lost, I fed my declining hope. But long months of fruitless expectation compelled me at last to conclude that you had found the scheme of our union unpropitious to your hopes of happiness and that your kind compassion would not suffer you to tell me so. I had promised not to blame you; I did not, but my heart bled, nevertheless—ah, many a weary day and weary night. I fled from the crowded city to hide my grief and, if possible to relieve it, among the lakes and mountains of Cumberland. They reminded me of the delightful scenery which you had described, where you made me hope to live, communing with nature and with the dear friend whose heart seemed purposely formed to sympathize with mine. But I must not pain that dear friend with the recital of my sorrows.

Long was the time before I could give you up with dutiful resignation. I imagined various reasons for your long silence and sometimes renewed my hope on the ground of some vain supposition. Sometimes again I feared that you were dead, and then I mourned for you as for my brother. But I was relieved of this painful apprehension two months ago. A friend of my father's has some lands in the mountains of Virginia. When he went to see them, my father requested him to visit your village and inquire after you. He learned that you were alive and well. Then I knew that you had abandoned our engagement and that longer hope was vain if not sinful. Often had I dreamed both asleep and awake of rural felicity with you, my comforter in sorrow and my chosen companion for life. But when I found that all was a dream and that I must resign my heart to widowhood, I resisted the fondness of a love that could only make me miserable. Hard was it to bring so sweet and so cherished a passion within the bounds of moderation. Often would it invite the fond illusion that your difficulties might yet be removed and that your love for me was yet sufficient to bring you over the waters in search of your Judith. But one long year and months of another passed away, during which all the winds of Heaven had blown without wafting to me even a sigh from my friend. How then could the faintest illusion of hope remain, or ever dawn, upon the darkness of my soul? "No," thought I, "that dearly remembered night of our parting made me feel the last throbs that I shall ever feel of a heart that will be dear to me until this poor heart of mine shall throb no more." When this second summer came and my last day of hope was gone, I fled again to the woods and the lakes and there, after many a prayer and many a struggle, subdued my heart to a merely kind and grate-ful remembrance of you. So at least I thought; but what mean these fre-quent returns of my pen to the passionate expressions of tenderness which flow spontaneously from my heart and which, after repeated trials, I find will flow and mingle with the simple narrative that I meant to give? And what mean the tears and sobs which almost disable me from writ-ing? May the gracious Redeemer, who knows what human frailties are, enable me to be faithful! My friend! oh my friend! I must not, I dare not, love you now as I formerly loved you. When my heart abandoned itself to widowhood and I sought consolation from the Most High among shades and rocks and waters, where, as well as in His word, the Divine Spirit dwells, I happened to meet a stranger on a visit to the same retreats, one who, in mind and person, in tastes and principles resembles you, my dear friend, and who for that reason interested me in my desolate state. His company and conversation last year soothed and instructed me, but *then* my heart was beyond the reach of his love. A friendly acquaintance was all that occurred between us until this summer when I returned in my despair to the woods and lakes, where I unexpectedly met with him again. He sought my company; I was pleased with his; he saw that I was a mourner, and he comforted me. He had learned that I was a Jewess, and he labored faithfully and eloquently for my conversion to Christianity. By the blessing of God he succeeded in removing all my remaining doubts and difficulties respecting the Christian faith. I was almost persuaded when I parted with you, but I would not suggest hopes on that subject until I should be fully persuaded. Now my faith in Jesus of Nazareth is my chief consolation; and the eloquent and pious friend who won me finally to Christ has also gained so much of my esteem and affection that I have, after much hesitation, accepted his offer, and we are betrothed. Now, my dear preserver, hear the last request of one whom you once tenderly loved and whom no changes can release from her obligations to you. Should you ever find that I or my friends can do you any sort of service, I intreat you, by the remembrance of our voyage together and by all the love that you may still bear me, to let us know it. Call on me or, if death should have taken me away, on my father or my sister for all the assistance that you may need. The half of my fortune I can easily spare and would rejoice to impart to a friend whose disinterested kindness and essential service to me I can never repay; but I shall thank Heaven if an opportunity be given me to prove that I am, and will ever be, your grateful and devoted friend,

Judith Bensaddi.

Before I had finished reading, my eyes grew dim. Self-reproach for my unjust suspicions and my fatal procrastination wrung my heart. The knell of departed hope boomed on my ears as if the gentle murmur of the river had swollen to the roar of a cataract. I fell back and lay in a stupor of astonishment at my late blindness of heart and at the unrolled scroll of my hapless destiny. I was for some time prostrated, soul and body, at the astounding revelation. When I recovered strength to rise, the sun was shooting his rays horizontally from mountain top to mountain top! The turtle dove, from her withered tree in the field, was cooing forth her evening lamentation. Shades almost as gloomy as my soul were thickening around me. Frantic with grief, I called to the dark-frowning rocks and to the waters that were rolling by to pity me. I made the echoes respond to the name of my loved and lost Judith. Once my perturbed imagination pictured her looking down on me from the cedars of the cliff and illuminating my dark retreat with the love-inspiring radiance of her countenance; then her fairy image seemed to be floating off in the air and to beckon its sorrowful adieu as it faded away and was lost in the gloom of descending night.

And now, farewell, sweet Judith Bensaddi! Time may soothe my anguish and mitigate my passion to the soft feeling of a mourner's love, but death only can dim the bright image of feminine loveliness which my soul has caught from thee. Henceforth thou art my heart's model of what is sweet and pure in woman. Others I may see fair and affectionate, virtuous and holy; but none can take thy place. I am wedded to remembered beauty. Alas! all but the memory of thy charms is lost to me; once more and forever, farewell, farewell, sweet Judith Bensaddi!

SECLUSAVAL

Or

the Sequel to the Tale

of Judith Bensaddi

A Young Lawyer in the Gold Country

When I wrote the former part of my story, I expected never again to hear of Judith Bensaddi. Her residence was in England, mine in the Appalachian mountains, among which, or at least within sight of their blue summits, I expected to spend my days. Whatever fortune might betide either of us, it seemed improbable that any intelligence of the one should ever reach the other. Heaven seemed to have ordained that our future experience should have nothing in common except the sad remembrance of our disappointed love, which we might each in our far distant homes continue to cherish in secret and I at least would cherish, in loneliness and sorrow, to the last hour of life. But the way of man is not in himself. The power that rules our destiny had ordained that I should visit London and there receive most affecting intelligence of Judith. What I heard, what followed to agitate and perplex me still more, and what the issue was I shall now proceed to relate after premising a brief recapitulation of my former story in order to refresh the reader's memory.

I was studying law when symptoms of consumption drove me from my native Rockbridge to spend a winter in South Carolina. In the spring I set out with renovated health to return home by way of Charleston and the sea to Norfolk. In the stage I found Eli Bensaddi of London and his lovely sister, Judith, going by the same route towards Boston. We travelled in company, mutually pleased to have met and I somewhat more than pleased with the beautiful, black-eyed sister.

On the first day of our voyage, poor Eli fell overboard and was lost. Judith, in her first paroxysm of grief, also fell into the sea and was saved by my leaping into the water as she sank. I took charge of the lovely mourner and was conducting her to a friend of hers in Boston when my ankle was so sprained in Philadelphia that we were detained ten days until her cousin Von Caleb came from Boston to take her home.

Meantime, my love for this pure and amiable young lady grew so intense that I declared myself and offered her marriage. She frankly confessed that our love was mutual but, to my great surprise, informed me that she was a Jewess. And because I had not known and considered this fact, she would accept my offer of marriage only upon the condition that after my return home I should deliberately and freely ratify the engagement.

From her cousin Von Caleb and a miserly Jew named Levi I first learned that her father was a wealthy banker and that an uncle had devised her an independent fortune of three thousand pounds a year.

Judith and I parted with deep sorrow. On my return, a fit of despondency came on me and presented my intended marriage with a Jewess in gloomy colors. After a severe and protracted struggle of opposite principles, I was able to decide in favor of the marriage through the influence of Judith's miniature, which she had given me. I wrote two letters, the one to go by the miser Levi from New York as had been arranged in Philadelphia, the other to go by the usual means of conveyance. The former was probably suppressed by the designing miser, who desired Judith to marry his son; the latter must have been accidentally lost by the way. I waited in vain for an answer till the next spring when I prepared for a voyage to London that I might solve the mystery but was deterred from going by the loss of Judith's portrait. This unfortunate accident threw me into another fit of mental gloom and unfortunately put an end to all hope and all exertion to secure the lovely prize of my heart. I rashly concluded that my innocent Judith was false.

The ensuing August I was surprised by the receipt of a letter from her, giving me the history of her disappointment and despair at my long silence—her struggle with hopeless love for me, her conversion to Christianity through the persuasive eloquence of an amiable young gentleman, whom she had met with among the lakes in the north of England, and her final consent to marry the gentleman, to whom she was indebted for her Christian hope and consolation.

This letter filled me with grief, with self-reproach, and with unutterable despair. Such was the unhappy conclusion for the time and, as I then thought, forever, of my love adventure with the beautiful, the accomplished, and the pure-hearted Judith Bensaddi.

All that I could now do was to love without hope and to mourn without consolation for my lost bride until time and some other engaging pursuit should distil their mitigating balm into my deeply wounded heart.

Now I would fain hear no more of my lost one, that I might ever think of her as my own lovely bride snatched by some evil fate from my arms between the betrothal and the nuptials. I abhorred the conception that she lived on this earth as the happy or the unhappy wife of another man. Whenever I found the train of my thoughts leading towards this painful conception, I shuddered and broke off the train, saying with King Lear in the tragedy, "Ah, that way madness lies."

My only hope of relief from paralyzing melancholy was to engage promptly and assiduously in the practice of my profession. My preparation was thorough and complete. Experience had now taught me the evil effects of indecision and melancholy. Dearly had I paid for the indulgence of these native tendencies of my mind. I was reduced to such a state that I must rally or perish. I summoned all my remaining energies to the rescue. I resolved to make the weak points of my character the objects of constant watchfulness and of strenuous efforts at moral improvement. With the Divine blessing I succeeded in overcoming them, not wholly nor at once (for vices of character are not cast off by a single effort), but to such a degree from time to time as to encourage persevering exertions and to furnish a salutary example for the imitation of other young men.

My circumstances required a field of action more wide and promising than my native Rockbridge. I determined to try my fortune among the gathering population and stirring pursuits of the Carolinian gold country.

The day before I left the home of my youth I took a farewell ramble over the loved scenes of the vicinage. Among other spots of peculiar interest, I visited the one by the riverside where I had so unfortunately dropped my Judith's miniature. I searched once more if peradventure I might find the golden locket case, for the portrait I presumed to have been blotted out forever by the envious water. To my joyful surprise I found the elegant case lodged in a crevice of the rock above the level of the river now shrunken by the drought of summer. Eagerly I pressed the spring—the lid flew up—and so did my heart when I beheld the unsullied likeness of my Judith, whose lovely self appeared once more to look upon me. The picture had been preserved by a glass cover sealed hermetically to the raised edge of the case. I conceived I know not what vague hope from this unexpected discovery. Heretofore, this picture had operated with talismanic power to revive my love and to brighten my matrimonial prospects. But now, when Judith was spell-bound by solemn vows to another, what potency could there be in this or any other charm to disenchant my lost bride and bring her again within the reach of my arms? I could not tell; but nevertheless, the recovery of the miniature diffused a new warmth and an obscure glimmer of something like hope through my soul.

Again I hung the precious jewel in my bosom and ceased not to wear it for years afterwards. A thousand times did I open the case and feel anew the fascinating beauty of that countenance; as often did those dark eyes of love seem to give me an inspiring look of encouragement. But when I would close the case and look around at the realities of my situation, all my sweet visions fled and left me to utter solitude of heart.

I reached the gold country in time to attend the fall terms of the courts. I was so fortunate as to obtain immediate employment, first in a criminal case and then in a civil one; and each time, I happened to make such a creditable effort that I sprang at once into reputation and a lucrative practice. Whatever portion of my first success might be attributed to good fortune, I strove with all my energies to sustain and to elevate the reputation so happily acquired. I labored night and day to extend my knowledge of the law and to prepare myself thoroughly upon every case put into my hands. I knew full well that with ordinary talents such diligence would ensure success and that no degree of natural talents could give me ultimate success without laborious application.

So lucrative was my practice that within six months I found myself in possession of more than a thousand dollars of clear gain; and,
what was of more value, my heart was relieved from melancholy; my
soul was prompt to resolve and vigorous to pursue the course resolved upon. Such were the happy effects of diligence in an honorable vocation.

Speculation in gold mines began to rage, but I felt no inclination to
deviate from the safe road of my profession into the hazardous experiment of gold mining. I was too full of law to think of gold in any
shape but that of fees. Avarice was not my passion—chicanery I dis-
dained—but the fair rewards of professional ability I sought and felt
justified in seeking. Yet was I incidentally involved in the gross
earthy process of digging for gold.

A poor man had employed my agency to recover a meager tract of
land, out of which he had been defrauded by a speculator. But success in his suit was likely to make him poorer than before; for the
soil would not repay the labor of cultivation, and the failure of the
speculator in some mining experiments upon it made the tract un-
salable as gold land. At last my poor client came and besought me to
give him eight hundred dollars for his eight hundred acres of barren
hills and vales. More out of pity than the hope of gain, I paid the man
his price and sent him rejoicing with his family to the rich lands of
the west. For this charitable purchase I was ridiculed by the knowing
ones and had to hear sundry unfavorable auguries respecting my
prospects of future wealth.

However, I was not discouraged but immediately employed an
honest man acquainted with the business to search my barren free-
hold for the precious metal. In a few days I turned the laugh against
the knowing ones by the discovery of a rich deposit of gold in a little
valley which had not been scrutinized by the speculator. It was the
most productive mine yet discovered in the country. Besides the fine
grains usually met with, lumps of gold weighing often an ounce and
sometimes a pound were picked out of the gravel. My clear profits
from this source amounted to about a thousand dollars a month.

Now my attention was drawn to the mineralogy of gold mines. I
began to study the subject at intervals by way of relaxation from the

arduous labors of my profession. I examined the localities of the mines, noticed the character of the minerals among which the gold was found, observed the conformation of the hills and valleys, and marked how the layers of rock were disposed. In this new pursuit I derived an unforeseen advantage from my college studies. In the course of my education I had gone through the mathematical and physical sciences, more with the view of gaining the honors of scholarship than with any hope of practical benefit in future life. How often do young men mistake their true interest when they neglect, as unprofitable, any part of those studies which the wisdom of ages has prescribed as necessary to a good education! My knowledge of chemistry, mineralogy, and geology—imperfect as it was—enabled me to pursue the study of gold mines with facility and success. In less than a year I had acquired considerable skill as a gold finder.

A gentleman of my acquaintance was involved in a lawsuit about a valuable gold mine in Georgia. I accepted his offer of a liberal fee to manage the case for him and consequently had to make a visit to the newly discovered gold region of Georgia. This was about six months after I had commenced the study of mines. I embraced the opportunity of improving my knowledge of the subject by examining the Georgia mines. The suit was not tried until the succeeding spring when I went a second time to the same country and succeeded in obtaining a verdict in favor of my client and thereby an additional fee of one thousand dollars for myself. But this was only a small part of my good fortune in Georgia.

On my return homewards, wishing to see the hill country, I was skirting the Cherokee border by an unfrequented route when my attention was arrested by indications of gold. A torrent filled by extraordinary rains had lately torn up the ground in a ravine and exposed the rocks at the base of a mountain. After a diligent examination, although I discovered no mine, I was strongly persuaded that gold might be found about that locality. I went to the owner of the land in the open country below and found him disposed to sell but so disgusted with mining speculations, by reason of his ill success in digging on this very land, that he refused an offer of partnership. I bought the tract and immediately hired men to dig for gold. In a few days a rich and extensive vein of gold was discovered on the mountain side where I had observed the favorable indications. A professed mineralogist examined it and certified to its great value. The agent of an English company immediately offered me fifty thousand dollars for my discovery. I refused to sell until further exploration should more completely test the value of the property.

Thus, by a lucky accident in the first instance and by a fortunate exercise of scientific skill in the second, I found myself become a wealthy man within twenty months after I had left my native land, a poor young lawyer, to seek my fortune in the gold country.

Had I been less fortunate in my speculations, I might have continued to pursue the hazardous game of mining. But my extraordinary success itself alarmed me; after two such brilliant prizes, I could not hope for another. I might rather expect to find myself the next time on the descending side of Fortune's wheel. I resolved to quit the pursuit at once before the spirit of adventure should grow into a habit and lead me, as it leads most of its slaves, to misfortune, debt, and imprisonment. For the better security against temptation, I resolved also to sell the mines which I had discovered as soon as I could get a fair price for them. My prudent resolutions on this subject were aided by the influence of another scheme more congenial with my natural temper than delving in gravel and quartz rocks after the miser's god. What this new attraction was I shall proceed to unfold in the next chapter.

The Vale of Seclusa

During the first nine months of my residence in Carolina, I toiled incessantly at my profession until my health was seriously injured. After the discovery of my Carolina gold mine, I diverted myself occasionally with mineralogical studies, but they were not sufficient to reinvigorate my overwrought system. When the summer heats became oppressive, I laid aside all my studies that I might take a few weeks vacation in the mountains. Often had I looked with desire towards the great Blue Ridge of this country, whose magnificent summits cut their waving outline in the western sky. In Virginia this range of mountains is broken to let the rivers pass through from the Allegheny to the sea; here it casts off the rivers from both its sides and compels them to seek a passage from its impenetrable flanks by winding and tearing through other mountains of less stern and massive solidity.

To this sublime wilderness I directed my course, with the intention of exploring its deepest recesses and its most eminent summits. My good horse soon carried me out of the realms of anxious gold-seekers to the forest wilds where the herdsman and the hunters dwell in solitary huts and breathe the free spirit of the mountains. About the sources of the Catawba, the Broad and the Saluda rivers, I found the most gashed, craggy, and savage region that I had ever seen. It was the very sort of country that I would have chosen to visit, consisting of ancient, steep, forest-covered mountains, rent, rugged, and grim with deep ravines, or dissevered by rich valleys of less horrid aspect—all watered with perennial streams, clear as crystal—here hidden beneath impenetrable thickets of evergreens, there leaping over precipices in splashing cascades, or gurgling through loose rocks in damp mossy ravines, or purling over gravelly beds in the rich low grounds of wider vales and eddying here and there under crumbling banks and bare tree roots in deep bluish trout pools.

With delight I threaded the valleys, crossed the ridges and mounted the tall peaks, catching every hour some new aspect of Nature's wild magnificence. Sometimes I lodged in dwellings of hewn logs in the wider valleys where civilization had begun to make inroads upon the savage wilderness. At other times I partook of the hunter's fare in his smoky hut of round logs in the deeper recesses of this rugged land. One while I wrought my solitary way along horse paths in dusky glens or up and down the mountain sides; then again my journey was through pathless wilds and to desolate summits where the deer ranges and the wolf makes his den.

In the course of these laborious rambles my attention was attracted by a remarkably high summit, or knob, a few miles south of the main Blue Ridge. The whole region about it was distinguished by the cragginess of its mountains, and the richness of its vales. I resolved to scale this conspicuous observatory. A pleasant valley led up to its base where the valley contracted itself and was parted into two deep, narrow ravines; the one on the left seemed to be impassable to my horse, so I took the one on the right, which led me up by the northeastern side of the great knob, where it expanded into a beautiful vale sufficiently large for a moderate-sized farm. Near the head of this lonely vale I found a practicable way to the top of the mountain. The sides of this great eminence consisted in part of almost perpendicular precipices, supporting broad terraces of ground so gently sloping that arable fields might be formed upon them. The top was capped by a flat rock elevated upon high natural walls that gave it the appearance of a vast, half-ruined castle.

The view was immense. On the side of the Pine Ridge nothing was visible but huge mountain masses with deep rents between them; but on the east and south I could overlook the craggy-sided mountains of the vicinity and see the pleasant hill country next beyond them; and over the hills again, I could discern at a great distance the lower champaign stealing out of sight under the blue veil of the atmosphere.

After I had looked awhile over the distant regions, I cast down my eyes and was smitten with admiration at the romantic beauties of a valley that lay under the southern side of the mountain. It was enclosed on every side by mountains of great height and every diversity of form and aspect. The sides of these mountains were deeply cut with wild narrow glens, one of which lay directly under my feet beneath a perpendicular precipice a hundred fathoms deep. These glens all converged towards the centre of the valley. From their dark, shady recesses, streamlets flowed out, and, uniting their cool pellucid waters, they formed a brook, which passed out of the valley by the deep contracted ravine that I had avoided as impassable.

The main valley was more than two miles long and at the broadest part not less than a mile and a half in width; but the outline was so irregular that its shape is nameless and indescribable. The surface was as irregular as the outline. Low-grounds nearly flat, dales of various width and curvature, hills of every shape, round topped, flat topped and ridgy, smooth or rocky, all gave an infinite diversity to the surface. The valley looked like a terrestrial paradise. Nature luxuriated in all possible wildness, richness and variety, requiring only the hand of man to prune and dress its profusion, to make it outvie all the pastoral beauties of Arcadia in the golden age.

When I descended, I entered the valley by the uppermost and longest glen, which led its murmuring streamlet from the main Blue Ridge. I had no sooner plunged into its dusky solitude than I lost sight of all the sunshiny world. The lofty treetops formed so dense a screen that the few straggling sunbeams which penetrated to the moist ground were not recognised as daylight, but looked like glowworms or fallen stars amidst the surrounding gloom.

Not a sound was heard for some time but the soft purling of the brook among the mossy stones or the occasional chirp of birds in the lofty boughs over head. After I had proceeded some distance towards the main valley, I heard the splashing of a waterfall. The sound appeared to rise from a deep cavern. I soon discovered that the brook fell into a chasm a hundred and fifty feet in depth and then flowed out between precipices of limestone into the main valley. There was a romantic wildness about this cascade, in some respects exceeding anything that I had ever seen. The water fell into a deep shady pool, where I could discern scores of trout enjoying themselves.

When I got into the main valley, I followed a blind cow path, which led me a winding way by hill and dale, one while in the dusky shades of the forest, another while through native lawns and shrubbery, until I found myself at the base of a flat-topped hill that projected from the foot of the great knob on the upper side of the deep glen which I had seen under my feet from the mountaintop. This hill was about midway between the upper and lower extremities of the valley, and I knew from its position that it would afford me the best general view of the landscape that could be had from any point within the valley itself. I ascended its gently sloping side and from its brow had a near and delightful view of the dales and hills and glens and mountain sides. I gazed in a sort of ecstasy over the charming landscape. Never had a place so captivated my fancy. The scenery was so various and so rich, so wild, so sweet, so majestic; the place was so shut up from the bustling and contentious world that it seemed to have been made for a hiding place from the storms of life. Yet was it not so completely cut off from the haunts of men as to wear the aspect of a prison; for on looking through the ravine that let out the waters, I caught a glimpse of the open country of hills and valleys at a distance.

"Here," I exclaimed in a transport of admiration, "here is the place where in all the world a lover of nature, of retirement and of books, might find the most delightful retreat; and yonder is the loophole through which he might still look forth upon the outer world of insatiate passions and self-tormenting hearts. So sweet a nook shall not be nameless; I call it 'The Vale of Seclusa,' or in one word, 'Seclusaval.' This flat-topped hill, which opens at once all the beauties of the landscape but essentially the romantic glens on every side, is the hill of Glenview; and yon lofty mountainhead, which frowns so haughtily over this nearest glen, through which I look up at his sublime crags, is Craggyhead. I thank his grim majesty for giving me the first sight of this lovely Seclusaval, which, if Divine Providence grant the wish of my heart, I will purchase and improve and make the retirement and the resting place of my future days. Oh! had it pleased God that *she*, the lost one of my heart, should enjoy with me the rural beauty and quietude of an abode so perfectly agreeable to her taste. The world might be searched in vain for a place where we could have spent our lives together so happily as in this beautiful and romantic valley."

These last reflections saddened me, and thus I experienced that delight may be the immediate cause of sadness by suggesting some painful reminiscence. I looked again silently over the thousand beauties of Seclusaval; I drew from my bosom the portrait of my lost Judith; those eyes of love seemed again to beam into my soul; and then I sat down to weep, under an overpowering sense of loneliness and desolation, amidst the thousand beauties of Seclusaval. At length I closed the locket case and returned it into my bosom. The shadows of evening had covered the valley and were following the sunlight up the pine-covered precipices of the mountain. I led my horse down the hill and directed my course to a solitary hut near the lower end of the valley. Here a hunter had pitched his habitation, cleared a field in the rich low-grounds of the valley, and seemed practically at least to be "monarch of all he surveyed"; for it must have been a rare thing for any stranger to visit this secluded valley. I went nevertheless with confidence to seek a lodging in the "poor man's nest." On approaching I was met by three fierce mastiffs that forbade my entrance without leave of the family "first had and obtained." The man came out and, after calling off his dogs, invited me to enter. I stepped in, saluted the wife, and took my seat on a three-legged stool. After some introductory account of myself, I asked the favor of a night's lodging. It was granted, of course, but with more appearance of coldness and suspicion than is usual among mountaineers. It behooved me to make myself more decidedly welcome.

I had no sooner been seated in the character of a guest than the dogs came in and smelt at me as if to try my quality. Finding the scent of the woods upon me, they wagged their tails; and when I patted their heads they gave me the friendly salutation of tongue and paw—licking my hand and leaping upon my breast, all of which I took very kindly and thus secured the good will of their master. When I first entered the house, I saw four or five children run and hide themselves under the bed and then slyly peep at me. When I had done with the dogs, I called a little fellow coaxingly who had ventured to put his head out of the hiding place. But at first they all drew back and seemed frightened at my invitation. Finally, however, I got the boldest one to venture near me. I patted his frizzly pate and took the dirty urchin upon my knee, after which I soon had the whole swarm upon me. Thus I won the mother's heart. I assumed an easy familiar manner with the whole family and took everything as if I had been accustomed to such accommodations. Consequently I was soon treated, not as a guest merely, but as a friend. The good woman did her best to show me kindness. She prepared me an excellent treat of johnnycake, venison, and onions. She could have treated me also with new milk, but she was not disposed to put me off with such homely fare. She burnt some coffee berries to cinder, tied them in a linen rag, pounded them on the hearth-stone with the axe, put the pulverized charcoal into water, and boiled the mixture in a skillet. She then poured the black bitter liquid into her queensware bowl with blue flowers pictured on it, and putting in a little milk and maple sugar, handed me the finished product of her kindness. The water was irretrievably spoiled by the process, but what of that? Should I not drink the well meant gift? Certainly I should and did with the firmness of resolution and fixedness of muscle which the occasion required. And let me say unto thee, gentle reader, that shouldst thou ever be placed in like circumstances, then drink thou also, yea, drink heartily, for the giver's sake. Think not that thou canst ever show good breeding by turning up thy nose at the poor woman's fare; nay, on the contrary, thou wouldst but show thyself impolite, ungenerous and every way ill-bred to scorn the kind hospitalities of the poor. Therefore, should the draught be never so bitter, drink it even to the dregs rather than mortify thy kind entertainer. Away with silly pride and contemptible affectation. Remember that in a few years thou wilt be as poor as thy neighbors. Death will soon bring down thy pomp and thy circumstance and put an end to thy affected airs of superiority. But I will not tire thee with my homily.

From Larkin Strone, the hunter, I learned that Seclusaval was in the midst of an extensive tract of mountain lands owned by Major Mudge, an old gentleman who resided at the distance of thirty miles in the country below. The next morning, after a farther exploration of the valley, I made my way out with some difficulty by the ravine and went straightway to Major Mudge, confirmed in my resolution to attempt the purchase. I found him eager to sell; for being an indulgent father, and having several sons brought up to no useful occupation, he was greatly embarrassed to pay the expenses of their prodigality. The demands of their creditors, and of his own, were just now so pressing that he offered at once to sell me his thirty thousand acres of mountain lands for the small sum of five thousand dollars. The price was very low; for notwithstanding the ruggedness of the country, the tract contained several thousand acres of rich valleys and arable mountain sides. Seclusaval alone was in my estimation worth the whole price. I therefore accepted his offer without hesitation, and, proceeding home immediately, I raised a sufficient sum from the profits of my gold mine to make the first payment and to commence a system of improvements on my new acquisition. I was peculiarly fortunate in obtaining an agent to manage my intended improvements.

Seven years before, Major Mudge had brought from England an intelligent and judicious gardener whose name was Baylor. This man had conducted the improvements on Mudge's estate with a union of taste and economy that pleased me exceedingly. He operated on the plan of following and assisting Nature instead of attempting, by dint of labor and expense, to force upon the place a set of features and embellishments inconsistent with the design of Nature herself. Hence the garden, the park, and the other grounds of Major Mudge's estate were all beautiful because every operation of art was conformable to the genius of the place.

Major Mudge, for an obvious reason, was glad to transfer Baylor to my service, and Baylor, knowing the old gentleman's pecuniary embarrassments, readily accepted my offer of employment. When he saw my valley, he was delighted with its appearance and rejoiced in the task of assisting its natural beauties with the touches of art. He not only understood at a glance my theory of improvement but suggested several things that I had not thought of, but which, on hearing his observations, I heartily approved. The primary operations were to be directed to the following objects: namely, first to open a farm and build mills in the valley three miles below Seclusaval; secondly, to convert the rich low-grounds from the ravine of Seclusa up to Glen-view into a meadow—retaining, however, many of the fine trees, ei-ther singly or in clumps; thirdly, to convert the beautifully sloping sides of Glenview into a garden, retaining here also a number of the fine trees, shrubs and vines; and lastly, to beautify the remaining hills and dales of Seclusaval by removing unsightly trees and clean-ing the surface so that grass could flourish in these native parks. My faithful agent went promptly to work whilst I returned home and re-sumed my professional avocations.

I did not revisit my wild barony until December when I was on my way to Georgia. Seclusaval was already assuming the appearance of a park. Whatever was unpleasant to the eye was disappearing from the noble woods; sweet lawns, winding and branching in various ways, not only gave variety to the landscape but opened to the eye, as one passed through time, the most delightful views of trees, hills and mountains on every side. The plough and the spade were preparing the soil for the grass of the meadow and the vines and shrubbery of the garden.

Baylor now suggested a sort of improvement that I had never thought of; this was to cover the lowest grounds of Seclusaval with the waters of an artificial lake. I was pleased with the idea of a lake but hesitated to incur the expense until he informed me that he had taken all the levels and measurements and had carefully estimated the cost, which was surprisingly small. He showed me first a narrow cleft in the ravine where a dam could be easily built of the loose rocks near the spot. Supposing the dam to be twenty-eight feet high, the water would be thrown back a mile and a half to the foot of Glen-view. He then traced for me the exact boundaries of the lake. On the meadow side the outline would wind beautifully with divers sinuosi-ties. On the opposite side, the water would lave the bases of the hills, some with sloping, some with precipitous sides. At one place, half a mile below Glenview, a little bay would run a furlong up a dale be-tween gently swelling hills; at another place, near the lower end of the lake, a narrow glen with steep rocky sides would conduct the lake water to a spring head, deeply hidden in the flank of the moun-tain, where the atmosphere was ever cool and dusky between tall crags and densely interwoven tree tops. At the broadest part of the lake, the water would spread out to the breadth of a hundred rods, but generally the shores would be from fifteen to thirty rods asunder. The fountains that would supply the lake being cool, clear and perennial, the lake would consequently never become stagnant and would not only be at once beautiful and salubrious but would moreover yield both pleasure and profit as a fish pond; thousands of trout and other fish could live and fatten in its pellucid waters.

By the time that Baylor had shown me all these things, I became enthusiastic. "Mr. Baylor," said I, "I thank you for this delightful scheme of improvement. Go to work, and by the next summer let me see the lake of Seclusaval reflect every object around it, from the green meadow banks up to the cliffs of old Craggyhead." "It shall be done, sir," was the prompt reply.

My income from my gold mine and from my law practice was sufficient now, I thought, to justify incipient measures for the erection of a permanent dwelling on Glenview. I resolved to build a stone cottage on the brow of the hill where some fine trees of majestic stature overtopped a dense thicket of undergrowth, embowered and festooned with a profusion of wild vines. Baylor had already commenced pruning this tangled wilderness, which needed only his skilful hand to convert it into a labyrinth of umbrageous walks and rustic arbors, romantically sweet, "for whispering lovers made." My fancy was pleased at the thought, but a twinge of sadness came over me when I reflected that all the charms of this lovely place would be in a great measure wasted on the lone heart of a bachelor who had lost his bride and could never love again. Nevertheless, I ordered stone cutters to be employed and materials of all sorts to be prepared for a neat, rural mansion. What better could I do? If I was lonely, I needed the more to seek pleasure and consolation from all the sources yet open to my desolate heart.

I did not again visit Seclusaval until the next spring when I was returning from Georgia after the discovery of my second gold mine. I found the improvements going on to my heart's content. Tenants had been settled in several rich vales besides Seclusa. The mills and the farm near them were in a state of great forwardness. A passable carriage road was made from the older settlements below to the mills and thence through the ravine into Seclusaval. The dam and area of the lake were prepared for the waters, which began to fill their destined bed as soon as the massive wall of the dam was closed by casting earth upon its upper side to stop the crevices. I marked with interest the hourly growth of the lake. In three days it was full and began to shed its superabundant waters in a pretty cascade over the dam while the glassy expanse above reflected the budding woods on the margin and the hoary steeps of Craggyhead. I launched a rude boat on the calm waters and circumnavigated the sweetly indented borders of the lake. I was delighted with the scenery on every side but most interested with the romantic wildness of the dusky glen now filled with water between its craggy sides. When I entered its narrow channel, it looked like some infernal river, with its dark, still waters pent up between frowning precipices and the sombre foliage of the pine and the hemlock that stretched their branches over the chasm. This stygian recess was the more impressive to the imagination from the circumstance that while we let our boat lie still on the water and held our peace, not a sound was heard unless it were the low murmur of the foliage in the breeze and the soft gurgling of the fountain, which at the head of the glen poured its little contribution into the lake through loose rocks coated with moss. But no sooner did we speak or strike the oar upon the boat, than a dozen echoes awoke and multiplied the sound as if we had roused a troop of angry spirits to mock us from rock and tree. Hence I gave this the name of the Echoing Glen.

When we returned to the open lake, a light breeze came up through the ravine. Hoisting sail, we were soon wafted to the foot of Glenview, where the garden had already begun to look beautiful and gave promise of becoming in another year a paradise of delights.

The recent discovery of my Georgia mine determined me to enlarge my plan of improvements. I ordered the foundation of my cottage to be laid immediately, on a larger scale than I had intended, and pretty cottages to be erected for my steward and other tenants. Among the rest, a shepherd's cot was to be set in a romantic place at the foot of a precipice on the opposite side of the valley, for I designed

to give little of my beautiful grounds to the plough but to make Seclusaval a pastoral scene, where flocks and herds might graze the
lawns and mountain sides and the sound of the shepherd's pipe
mingle with the song of birds and the chime of waterfalls to animate
the beauties of the landscape. The natural loveliness of my valley inspired me with ambition to make Seclusa the most charming of all
the ten thousand vales embosomed in the Appalachian mountains.

III

The Voyage to London

The purchase of my lands and the improvement of Seclusaval involved me in so much expense that I was under the necessity of selling one of my gold mines. For reasons formerly explained, I resolved to sell them both and to renounce all future connection with mining speculations. Immediately on my return from Georgia, after my fortunate discovery there, I sold my Carolina mine for thirty thousand dollars. I could have obtained a higher price if it had been set to sale a few months sooner, for it was becoming less productive than it had been although it still yielded a large profit.

My supply of cash was now sufficient to complete my scheme of improvements and to leave me still a considerable surplus. I had before made arrangements to transfer my residence to a village about twenty-five miles from Seclusaval. Here I took up my abode now that I might be near my beautiful valley. I preferred this new place of residence also on account of its agreeable society. Several families from the low country had left their estates and settled in the neighborhood. The scenery was pleasant and the climate salubrious, and the nucleus of an intelligent and refined society was thus formed; and around this attractive centre new families from below were yearly gathering. Literary institutions would naturally arise among such a people. An academy for boys had been founded and put into successful operation. But an attempt to raise funds for a female seminary had failed. The subscriptions were insufficient to erect the necessary buildings. The cause of the failure was an obstinate dispute about the location of the seminary, some desiring to place it in the village beside the academy, while others insisted that it should be located near a country church lately erected at the distance of four miles from the village. The contest became so warm that the whole scheme was abandoned. Thus it often happens, that a dispute about some incidental and subordinate matters defeats the most important enterprises.

On my settlement at the village, I found several persons regretting the failure of so useful an undertaking. Now the question occurred to me whether I was not morally bound to contribute, out of my abundance, to an object of such great and manifest utility. I was a bachelor, indeed, and never expected to have a daughter to be educated, but that circumstance seemed to increase my obligation to aid literary institutions inasmuch as my exemption from the burden of a family afforded me the more abundant means to become a public benefactor. I was a member of the society of mankind and, no less than others, dependent for my welfare upon the intelligence and the good morals of the people. Divine Providence had given me extraordinary success. For what end? Not surely that I might consume this affluent store on personal gratifications. And then I considered what an amount of blessings would flow from a well endowed seminary for females, what expansion of intellect, what refinement of sentiment, what elevation of character, what new sources of happiness to the individuals educated, and, through them, to society and to posterity. The more I contemplated the object, the more did the feeling of obligation grow upon me. Finally, I thought of Judith Bensaddi, how much more charming, how much more useful she was, by reason of her excellent education. I drew forth her miniature by the golden chain to which I had attached it and caught fresh inspiration from the sweet picture of my beloved. "I have lost her," said I, "but she shall be my good genius on this occasion. I had thought of subscribing a moderate sum for the seminary; now, for her sake, I will make myself responsible for the undertaking. With the blessing of Heaven I will be the founder of a seminary and will make up all deficiencies in the contribution of others. The institution shall be complete in every thing necessary to the good education of females."

Such was the conclusion of my meditations. I instantly set to work. I headed a subscription with two thousand dollars, which I bound myself to pay upon the condition that double the sum was raised by others. I called meetings of the people and addressed them earnestly on the subject. In a week my condition was complied with, and six thousand dollars were secured for the seminary. The location at the country church was named in the paper and was preferred by me on account both of the beauty of the situation and its shorter distance from Seclusa. It was in the valley that led up to my intended home. Seven gentlemen were nominated as trustees, of whom I refused to be one because I was soon to be absent on a long peregrination and because I was a young bachelor. A plan of the building was soon agreed on and contracts made for the erection of it without delay. I told the trustees to adopt a liberal scale of building and if they fell short of funds to consider me responsible for half the deficiency. Thus I had put a most benevolent enterprise into operation; and I felt a pleasure in reflecting on this good deed, a pleasure in some respects more heartfelt and consoling than all the gratification that I had experienced from the treasures of my gold mines or the delightful scenery of Seclusaval. It was a pleasure which, if less exhilarating at the moment, was felt to be of such durable stuff that time could not wear it away, nor could misfortune poison its sweetness.

Before I had engaged in this labor of love, circumstances had directed my thoughts to the subject of a voyage to London. I desired to sell my Georgia gold mine and to invest the proceeds in some productive stock. I was advised to sell in England, where speculation in gold and silver mines had risen almost to a mania. Mining companies had agents abroad, exploring America from Chile to Carolina in search of mines. In London I could sell under all the advantages of competition among the buyers. Though I had received constantly increasing offers for the purchase, yet none came up to what I considered a fair price.

Continued explorations had laid open the extent of the vein along the hillside and proved the richness of the ore. Several mineralogists had examined it; two of these were agents of the Londoners, and all gave me satisfactory attestations of the value of the mine. These and all other needful documents being provided, I gave notice to the agents that I would sell the mine at auction in London about the first of August.

When I was prepared to set off, I made a parting visit to Seclusaval on the first day of June. My beautiful valley was putting on still new charms. A hundred varieties of trees, vines, shrubs, and flowering plants were blooming in the garden and about the margin of the lake. The meadow was green with its first crop of grass. Birds were merry in every grove. The cottage on Glenview was rising in beauty, and carpenters were busily constructing other cottages in pleasant situations. Baylor, my faithful steward, now recommended another improvement, which I adopted instantly. He had ascertained that the spring which flowed out of Craggyhead through the glen that opened by the side of Glenview had its source at so high an elevation that it might be conducted in pipes to my cottage for family use and the overplus made to water the garden on the hill side.

"It is an excellent notion," said I, "and I will order you a set of iron pipes in Philadelphia. Meantime, have the ditch made and the pipes laid in the course of the following winter." "It shall be done, sir," was the answer to this and all my orders to my worthy Baylor.

Having given directions about the various improvements to be made in my mountainous barony, I rode on horseback to the nearest stage road and then travelled rapidly to New York, where I embarked for Liverpool in a packet ship on the fifteenth of June.

The thought of my going to London, where, as I supposed, my beloved Judith dwelt, kept her dear image more constantly and more vividly present to my mind than it had been during the two last years of my busy and enterprising life. The renewed habit of meditating on this dear lost one gave a strange susceptibility to my fancy. Often when I obtained but an imperfect view of some young lady of her size and somewhat like features, I conceived that it was Judith herself, and my heart fluttered as if the notion were not imaginary.

A notable instance of this sort occurred when our ship was leaving the harbor of New York. We met in the narrows a French ship from Bordeaux. The day was fine, and the passengers were on deck admiring the scenery of the noble bay. The near approach of the vessels turned the attention of each party on the other. I was immediately struck with the appearance of a lady on the French ship. She was dressed in mourning. Her form and stature first, then her black locks and dark eyes, as they seemed to me, reminded me of Judith Bensaddi. Her eyes seemed to be directed towards me individually. The more I looked at her, the more did I think her like my Judith. I was so fascinated by this apparition that I forgot to use the telescope in my hand until the vessels were full twenty rods apart. When I directed the instrument towards this interesting object, I could get but a momentary glance of her features; but that glance put me in a tremor, for I saw those lovely dark eyes still fixed upon me, and the whole face was to my conception the face of my lost one. So persuaded was I for some minutes that it could be only she that I would have returned instantly to the city if an opportunity had been given me. But before the pilot left us in his boat, I had reasoned myself into doubt, as I soon after did into utter disbelief, of the truth of my impression. "How can I believe," said I to myself, "that Judith of London, married no doubt and settled in her native country, should be just now landing at New York in a French ship from Bordeaux?" Thus I soon got rid of the agitation produced by the strange lady. By the end of the voyage I ceased to think of the circumstance.

On my arrival in London, I applied myself instantly to the business on which I had come. I called on the officers of several mining companies and exhibited my documents. I advertised the sale of my gold mine in three of the principal journals. My papers and statements were authenticated by two agents and an American gentleman of science who had seen the mine and knew my character. Thus I was able to give purchasers the most ample assurance that all was right. Bidders manifested a high spirit of competition and ran up the price to the unexpected sum of twenty-five thousand pounds sterling, equivalent to one hundred and twenty thousand dollars.

Having thus successfully concluded my chief business, I spent a few days in making purchases of books, scientific apparatus, and various other articles for myself or for the female academy. I was then prepared to leave London for Paris.

But how could I stay a month in London and not even inquire for my lost Judith? Yet I did so, though I did it with an aching heart. But, although I felt the most anxious curiosity to know her present state, I dreaded to learn it. And although I longed most intensely to see her lovely face once more, yet I shrunk from an interview with one so beloved, when the sight of her and the living look of those eyes that had awakened unquenchable love in my heart could only pain me now and might affect me beyond the power of self-control. To see her as the wife of another was intolerable; I could not encounter the shock of feeling that such an interview must produce. Nor could I believe that she would meet me now without the most distressing emotions.

Still, when I found myself on the eve of departure, and no remnant of business served to divert my thoughts from the tender theme, my heart began to smite me sorely for having been so long in London and at last intending to go away, never to return, without even a word of inquiry after Judith Bensaddi. She would not have treated me with such cruel neglect had she known that I was so near her dwelling place. I was aware too that I must feel exceedingly unhappy if I left my ardent curiosity unsatisfied and learned nothing of her when I could so easily gain intelligence. I therefore resolved to call at her father's house in Piccadilly and, having obtained whatever intelligence I deemed interesting, to hasten away from a place that contained an object so painfully dear to my heart.

I had brought with me a memorandum which Judith gave me in Philadelphia, containing an exact description of the situation and appearance of her father's house. Guided by this I found the house without difficulty. Just as I had satisfied myself that there was no mistake and was approaching the door, I was startled by seeing a young gentleman come out with an elegantly dressed lady of Judith's size. A cold shudder ran through my nerves when I conceived that this might be Judith and her husband. But I was soon relieved by a sight of the lady's blue eyes and light hair. When they had gone, I stepped up to the door and, to my astonishment, read upon the knocker the name, not of Nathan Bensaddi but of Sir David Monteith. Yet this must be the very house described in the memorandum, remarkable in its appearance, and one of the most magnificent on this splendid street.

Presently I knocked and was admitted into the hall. From the porter I learned that Sir David Monteith had occupied the house but a few months and that the previous occupant was a Jew named Bensaddi as well as the porter could remember. I sent in my card to Sir David, requesting the favor of a brief interview. After I had waited ten minutes, I was ushered into a parlor, where I met a brawny red-haired gentleman, who bowed with haughty coldness and stood before me as if to signify "What is your business, sir?" I took the hint and instantly inquired, "Have I the honor to speak to Sir David Monteith?" "You have," and another cold bow. "I came to this house, sir, expecting to find it occupied by Mr. Bensaddi, the banker. I desired to see some of his family with whom I became acquainted two or three years ago in America. Being a stranger in the city, I would take it as a favor if you would give me such information of him or his family as might enable me to find them."

The cold haughtiness of Sir David relaxed immediately; he saw that I was not a designing nor an idle intruder. He asked me politely to be seated and began to tell me several things in answer to my inquiries until he gave me the intelligence, of which the following statement expresses the substance.

"I will with pleasure give what information I possess respecting Mr. Bensaddi and his family. It is a mournful story. I never knew any of his family, but I was personally acquainted with him in his character of banker. About two years ago I had some claims on him, and hearing at Edinburgh, where I then lived, some alarming accounts of his losses, I hastened to London to see him. He had lost heavy sums by failures of houses indebted to him, but he so well satisfied me of his safety that I not only left what I had before in his hands but increased the deposit to a considerable amount. No banker in the kingdom had more of the public confidence, both in respect to his personal uprightness and his sound condition as a banker. He seemed to have completely recovered from the shock, when, about a year ago, I was astonished to learn of his sudden and total bankruptcy. This catastrophe was brought about by one of the most artfully contrived frauds of two as nefarious villains as ever deserved a halter. The one of these was old Levi, a Jew, whom he had imprudently trusted too far as an agent and lately as a small partner in the bank. This old villain combined with the other, who was no less than the son-in-law of Bensaddi himself. His name is Brannigan—he is an Irishman—a smooth-tongued hypocrite, who imposed on Miss Bensaddi by the most lamb-like airs until he made her his wife. After he had drawn what he could from Bensaddi in the way of dowry and was admitted as a partner in the bank, he joined Levi. And by embezzlement and other villainous manoeuvres, which have never been fully unfolded, they got most of Bensaddi's funds into their clutches and then left him to meet all the demands of the creditors. So vast was the sum which they embezzled that on settlement the remaining assets were found sufficient to pay the honest creditors only twelve shillings in the pound. Now Bensaddi's amiable daughter came forward and did an act which deserves to be engraven forever on brass and marble. She had a large fortune left her by an uncle. This, I presume, she retained in her own hands by the marriage settlement; for, although she was neither legally nor morally bound to pay her father's debts, yet she promptly came forward and, at the expense of her whole fortune, paid up all just claims to the uttermost farthing, saying that she would rather labor for her daily bread than see her father's creditors go unpaid. She separated from her villainous husband, I infer— yet I do not know the particulars. However, when I came here to reside about four months ago, I heard with sorrow that she had gone in bad health to the south of France along with her father whose health was also very low; and about two months ago I was grieved to learn that after burying her unfortunate parent she died of a broken heart and was laid by her father's side."

Here my feelings overcame me, and I exclaimed, "Dead! Did you say that Judith Bensaddi is dead?"

"You mean Mrs. Brannigan, I presume. I grieve to say that she is unquestionably in her grave. I saw the fact announced in the papers."

When the baronet thus solemnly confirmed the doleful intelligence, I groaned; I gasped for breath; my eyes grew dim; my ears tingled; and I was sinking into a swoon when Sir David, observing my situation, sprang up and brought a glass of water, some of which he sprinkled on my face, and the rest he gave me to drink. This timely application revived me, and I gradually recovered the faculty of speech. I then felt it incumbent on me to explain the cause of my deep emotion at the news of my Judith's sad fate. I gave him, therefore, a succinct account of my acquaintance with her, including the chief incidents of our mournful love story. He was so interested by the narrative that he called in his lady and a beautiful blue-eyed daughter of eighteen, and after presenting me to them and explaining the object of my call at the house, he requested me to repeat my story to them. I did so and went more fully into the particulars. I spoke with a natural pathos, prompted by my feelings, and so affected the ladies that they wept at my story and continued to shed tears for several minutes after I had concluded. This sympathy on their part unsealed the fountains of my own tears, and I uttered my lamentations with a freedom which nothing but the tears of my auditors could have justified in a stranger like myself. After our feelings had subsided a little, I rose to take my leave, but they pressed me to stay and spend the evening with them.

I stayed several hours. Lady Monteith added some particulars that she had heard respecting the Bensaddi family and their misfortunes —all going to confirm my belief that the hapless Judith had married an arch-deceiver and had sunk to the grave in the flower of her youth brokenhearted. "There at last," said I to Lady M., "her many sorrows have come to an end—all lovely as she was in the beauties and the virtues of the earth, she is lovelier now when arrayed in the unfading charms of a glorified spirit. It is selfishness, therefore, in me to complain of a dispensation of Heaven which has taken her from a world that was not worthy of her and has left me only this memorial of her lovely features." On saying these words, I took out the miniature from my bosom and, slipping the golden chain over my head, put the open picture in Lady Monteith's hand. She expressed her admiration of the countenance and handed the case to her daughter, who looked steadfastly at the portrait for a minute. Then, lifting her eyes glistening with tears, she said to me, "How unfortunate that one so lovely should have been deceived into a fatal marriage and thus taken from a gentleman who could appreciate her beauty and virtue and would have made her happy. How unfortunate!" I felt that this was not a fashionable compliment but the unstudied effusion of a sympathetic heart, and I loved the beautiful speaker for the interest she took in my ill-fated love and its more ill-fated object.

When I expressed a desire to copy the article in the newspaper which announced my Judith's melancholy death, a search was instantly made among Sir David's files, and, the paper being produced, I read as follows:

"Died, at the village of Clairfont, in the South of France, on the 20th of last month (April), Nathan Bensaddi, late banker of London, and on the 30th the same month his daughter, the unhappy wife of Patrick Brannigan. She had gone with her father to seek health and retirement for him and for herself from unpropitious skies and more unpropitious connexions. But bright suns and kind strangers could neither restore their bodies to health nor their hearts to enjoyment. They have found repose in the grave. This notice is sent by a surviving friend that all who yet care for a once flourishing, but now ruined, family may know the sad fate of the father and the daughter who trusted and were betrayed."

I felt so melancholy after reading this notice that I took leave of the worthy baronet and his family although kindly invited to become their guest during as many days as I might choose to remain in London. I could stay no longer in a city where such distressing intelligence came upon me and where all was strange and now gloomy to my imagination. I hurried over to Paris, where I spent a fortnight and endeavored to divert my melancholy thoughts by looking at the gay sights of that metropolis of pleasure. But I had come in vain; unless it were that I purchased some books and other articles for my retreat in Seclusaval, to which I designed now to confine myself as soon as I could make the necessary preparations. From Paris I went to the south into the districts where wine and silk are cultivated. Here I engaged four Protestant families to come over and settle on my estate. My object was to employ them in the culture of the vine and the mulberry in a warm sandy valley of my estate, a place thought to be excellently adapted to these productions. I visited Clairfont and with difficulty found the obscure graves of Bensaddi and his daughter. No inscription marked the spot; no friend resorted to it with tears. The sexton, after some consideration, pointed out the two hillocks, side by side. "This," said he, "is the father's and this the daughter's." "This, then," said I, "is my Judith's grave!" It was all that I could say. I shed a thousand bitter tears on the holy earth, and, having thus recorded my grief, I went to Bordeaux.

Near the last of September, I embarked with my colonists for Philadelphia, where we landed after a voyage of five weeks. Here I chartered a schooner to carry my colonists, my water pipes, and various articles of furniture to Charleston, the port most convenient to Seclusaval. I intended to go by land directly to my native country of Rockbridge and, after seeing my friends there, to continue my journey to Seclusaval, to travel thence no more until I passed "the bourne from which no traveller returns."

In Philadelphia I made a safe investment of the greater part of the money obtained for my gold mine. The stocks which I purchased then and afterwards would, altogether, yield me a revenue of more than six thousand dollars a year.

❧ IV ❧

The Lady in Black

In Philadelphia I took up my lodgings in the hotel where Judith and I had spent the ten most interesting days of my life, where in sadness and in delight we had lived like brother and sister, and where we finally separated with hearts intertwined and bound together in bonds of the purest and sweetest affection. Now, after an interval of three and a half years, I found myself again in the same house but with feelings and under circumstances, O how changed!

I desired on my arrival to visit the parlor which we then occupied but was told that a family of strangers with a sick lady were now in possession. Five days afterwards, when I was about to depart for the south, I again inquired about the parlor, and was told that the family were just leaving it and would go off in the carriage and sulky at the door. The same moment I saw a gentleman and four ladies passing out in travelling dresses. One of the ladies was dressed in deep mourning and wore a thick veil. My curiosity was excited. I also went out to look at the party. The lady in black was behind and got in last. She seated herself so as to face my position, but the veil concealed her face. Just as the carriage began to move, she drew her veil aside, and what was my astonishment to recognise in her features a strong resemblance to Judith Bensaddi! Her whole person agreed with the description of my buried Judith; her raven locks, her black eyes, her oval face—all were like my lost one. But before I could scan the resemblance, to see if it were perfect, she was driven off, and I was left trembling, amazed and unsatisfied. So far as I could judge, she was exactly like, probably the very lady, whom I had seen on the French ship when I was going out of the harbor of New York. I could not believe that this was my poor Judith risen from the dead; yet, laying all fancy aside, the resemblance was so evident that I was sorely perplexed.

When my stupor of astonishment had somewhat abated, I went to the clerk at the bar and inquired the name of the family. He told me that they were the family of Doctor La Motte of South Carolina, returning home from a tour in the north. I asked if the lady in black was a daughter of Doctor La Motte. "No," said he, "I think she is the governess of his daughters and that her name is—let me see—oh, here it is in the register—Miss Bersati." Here was another curious circumstance, the resemblance of the names yet a difference too. A painful curiosity to know more of this lady was excited, but how to learn more was the difficulty, for nothing was known here of the family except the few particulars already mentioned. I could not discover even the quarter of South Carolina in which Doctor La Motte resided.

I paid a mournful visit to the now vacated parlor. There was the identical sofa on which Judith and I had so often sat while she nursed my sore ankle; there the very spot where we had mingled tears and throbs and all the joys of our innocent love on the night when we parted. I now left the hallowed spot with an aching heart and in a few hours more was on my way again, by Lancaster, to my native Rockbridge. I gave my parents and friends—my *alma mater*, my native hills and vales—a visit of two weeks and then, as I supposed, "a long and last farewell" and proceeded southward to shut myself up in my own Seclusaval, there to live and there to die a mourner and recluse. Not that I had made a vow to do so or that I intended literally to imprison myself in my mountain-bound retreat, but there I expected to abide in seclusion from the wide world and to make excursions beyond the limits of my estate only when some important occasion should summon me away.

I arrived first at the village near which the female academy was located. I received a hearty welcome from my friends there and was gratified to see the walls of the academy in a state of considerable forwardness. The books and apparatus, bought in Europe for the institution, had just arrived and were stored away until they should be wanted. The next day I proceeded to Seclusaval and found everything going on well. My beautiful cottage was almost finished. The parlor and library were already furnished; the hillsides about the house were all trimmed and arranged in their garden style; multi-

tudes of shrubs, trees, and plants of various kinds had been growing in pots and boxes through the summer, ready to be set in their
destined places in due season so that by the next spring the garden
would be complete. The other grounds and buildings would be in
their finished state of improvement by the same time so that Seclusaval would, the next season, exhibit innumerable beauties to
charm the senses and to make it one of the most delightful scenes of
rural beauty in the world.

When my good steward, Baylor, led me into the parlor of my cottage, I remarked that he had arranged the furniture very tastefully.
Among other things in this room was a pianoforte of German man-
ufacture, which I had bought in New York, with other furniture, on
my way to Europe. I had taken a fancy to this instrument because its
tones were remarkably sweet and because in appearance it resembled
the one in Charleston on which my lost Judith had played the airs
which so entranced my soul. But why should a lonely bachelor have
an instrument which he could not play? "Because," said I to myself,
"perhaps some lady visitor may two or three times in a year awaken
its silent strings and cheer my lonesome habitation."

When I saw the instrument now in its place, I said to Baylor, "This
piano, I suppose, has never yet made music in Seclusaval." "Yes, sir,"
he replied, "I was just going to tell you about it. Just a week ago today, I was directing the men about a terrace in the garden when I happened to cast my eye down the valley, and behold, a carriage and a
sulky were coming up the lakeside, full of ladies, except the sulky,
which had an old gentleman in it. A young gentleman on horseback
led the way. They stopped several times and looked all round as if
they were admiring the scenery—and well they might admire it, Mr.
Garame. When they came near the foot of the garden, I went down
and asked them if they would not drive up to the cottage. 'Have you
a good road up the hill?' said the old gentleman. 'O, yes,' said I, 'two
of them; you had better drive up this way by the glen side, and you
can come down by the other side. You will then have all the beautiful views from the hill.' So I led them up by the glen road. They kept
looking about every way and praising the landscape—as they had
reason to do, you know, Mr. Garame. When we got into the park, on

the hill here behind the house, they stopped several times to enjoy the glimpses and vistas through the trees. You will say that I have improved them since you went away. I have cut a glimpse for the top of Craggyhead and a vista for Rocky Nook cottage over the valley yonder. Well, when we got to the foot of the great tulip tree, out yonder, and the whole valley and mountains burst on their view at once, they cried out, 'Oh, how beautiful.' There was a lady in a black mourning dress that seemed to be all in raptures at the landscape. When they had looked a little and I could speak without interrupting them, I invited them into the house. They came into the parlor, but for some time they could not rest for going to the door and looking through the window over the valley. Presently, I asked the favor of the ladies to play on the piano and tell me if it was in good tune. First, a young lady in white played a tune very prettily. 'That is a very sweet instrument,' said the black-eyed lady, 'and it is in very good tune.' Then she went and played herself, and such delightful music I think I never heard. She sung a mournful song, 'Mary's Dream'; and when she had finished and left the piano, I saw tears falling from her eyes. The old lady, Mrs. La Motte, then began to ask me about you. She said the people at the village below had praised Mr. Garame's beautiful valley so much that they had come up just to take a look at it. She finished by saying that you must be going to take a wife as you were making such a beautiful home. 'No, indeed,' said I, 'he told me that he intended to live a bachelor all his days.' 'Why, what is the matter?' said she, joking, 'is he a woman hater?' 'No,' said I, 'he is an admirer and friend of the ladies; but I think from what I have heard him say that he once fell in love with a London lady, and somehow their love did not prosper, and, having lost her, he expects never to love another.' When I said this the beautiful lady in black suddenly burst out a crying and ran out into the yard to hide her feelings. The rest of them went out too, and after they had comforted the lady in black, they returned into the parlor and said they must go. I had refreshments brought in. At first they only tasted them sparingly; but I told them to make free and help themselves plentifully, for you would not be pleased with me if I let genteel strangers go away without partaking liberally of the good things in Seclusaval. Then they ate and drank freely; and when they left the house, I mounted a horse and rode with them about the lawns and took them up to the dark cascade. When we came back, I proposed that they should take a little voyage on the lake; they consented to be rowed into the Echoing Glen. When they again mounted their carriages to drive away, the old gentleman stayed behind a little, talking with me about the valley. Presently he alluded to the lady in black, and I found out that his object was to apologise for her breaking out so when I mentioned your being crossed in love. He said that Miss Julia Bersati, the lady in black, was in deep affliction, that she had lately lost her father and lost her only brother before and had, like you, been unfortunate in love. This was no doubt the reason, he said, why she was so affected when she heard of your case. He told me that she was a very amiable and accomplished lady, bred in London, and once in prosperous circumstances there, being now reduced to distress among strangers. A lady of tender sensibility, she was easily overcome by her feelings when anything reminded her of her misfortunes. When he had finished his apology for the strange behavior of the lady in black, he thanked me for my kindness and followed the company."

Such was my steward's account of the lady in black, and the reader will easily conjecture the impression that such a tissue of strange coincidences made on my mind. In spite of what I had heard and seen in London, I was almost persuaded that this lady in black could be no other than Judith Bensaddi with her name slightly changed, probably for some motive of concealment. There was one circumstance which had escaped my notice in the tumult of my feelings when I first heard in London of Mrs. Brannigan's death. Judith had a sister married to a Christian gentleman whose name I had never heard; nor had I heard the name of the gentleman to whom Judith had engaged herself. Sir David Monteith, being unacquainted with Mr. Bensaddi's family, might possibly be mistaken in supposing that Mrs. Brannigan was the daughter who gave up her own fortune to pay her father's debts. This noble act was certainly done by Judith, whose uncle had left to her the fortune that she gave up. So that there did seem to be a possibility after all that my Judith might be alive. I regretted exceedingly that in the sudden perturbation of my feelings I had not thought of Judith's sister while I was at Sir David Monteith's and that I had left London without inquiring, or thinking to inquire, more particularly about the two sisters. Being left in some doubt now concerning my Judith's fate, I was prone to hope that the striking coincidences, both personal and historical, between this lady and my lost one were not accidental. Judith, I felt sure, would never have chosen to visit my dwelling without a previous explanation to me; but I could imagine plausible reasons to account for this circumstance, so inconsistent with the well known delicacy of her feelings. She could not object to coming with her employer's family without giving a reason that would betray what she would rather conceal, and, knowing that I was from home, she had no reason to object. Nor could she presume that the Mr. Garame of Seclusaval was the same person as the poor student of Rockbridge, whom she had known and loved three years before.

Putting all these facts and conjectures together, I was so nearly persuaded that the lady in black was my Judith as to feel the most tormenting impatience to solve the mystery. But in vain did I attempt to trace the course of Doctor La Motte or to discover the place of his residence. The tavern keeper at the village could give me no information; no one in the neighborhood was possessed of the knowledge that I sought. I concluded then to write letters to acquaintances in different parts of Carolina and to get my friends to do the like so that, if possible, I might from someone obtain the desired information. At least fifty letters were written by me and for me, but four weary months passed away without a ray of intelligence. Nobody seemed to know Dr. La Motte. At last a correspondent in Charleston informed one of my friends that Dr. La Motte with his family had a few days before embarked at that port for France but that no such lady as Miss Bersati was with them. This correspondent had learned that Dr. L.'s residence was on the island of St. Helena upon the sea coast south of Charleston. I determined to go immediately to the place and obtain what information I could respecting Miss Bersati.

On the first of March I mounted my horse and put him to a full trial of his speed and bottom. In eight days I reached Beaufort where I found that Dr. L. was well known. At his extensive plantation, ten

miles from Beaufort, I was able at last to get a clue that would proba-
bly guide me to my object. When Dr. L. left home for a visit to
France, he obtained a situation for Miss Bersati in the family of Mr.
Naudain, a relation of his, in the neighborhood of Purysburg on the
Savannah. Thither I went in eager haste and arrived at the house
about noon on the tenth day of my absence from home.

I was politely received by Mrs. Naudain in the absence of her husband. She informed me that Miss Bersati was an inmate of her family
and was then with her daughters in another part of the house. I
showed such deep emotion on hearing this that Mrs. N. suspected
instantly the cause of my agitation, and, knowing that Miss Bersati
was in a correspondent state of mind respecting some gentleman to
whom she had been attached, the good lady did not wait for any detailed explanation, but on my expressing a desire to see Miss B., she
smiled and said that the young lady would doubtless be glad to see
me. "I will request her," said she, "to step into a private room that so
joyful a meeting may be undisturbed by spectators. Be so good as to
keep your seat until I return." I literally could not keep my seat. My
palpitating heart would not let me rest a single moment; I got up and
paced the room, then sat down again; but in another moment I was
on my feet, hurrying from one part of the room to another. Every
minute seemed an hour till Mrs. Naudain returned and asked me to
walk with her. I followed her footsteps into a long piazza in the rear
of the house and then to the end of the piazza where we entered a
passage, on the left side of which was a door standing ajar. Beckoning
me to enter by that door, she retired in silence. I stood a few moments to collect my spirits. I heard light footsteps within of a person
walking anxiously over the floor. Pushing the door gently, I stepped
in and saw the lady in black walking from me unconscious of my
presence. Her stature and figure seemed to be those of Judith. Her
hair, black and glossy as the raven's plume, agreed with my Judith's.
The lady soon heard my approach and, turning round quickly, brought
to view a face which again started the rushing tide of sensibility
through my nerves. "My Judith," I exclaimed, "my own beloved!"
and I sprang forward to embrace her. She, when she caught the first
glance of my person, uttered a faint cry of joy and started to meet

me. But before we met, I discovered an instantaneous change in her countenance. The glow of joyful surprise was converted into ashy paleness. An expression of anguish came like a flash of lightning upon her face. I was in the act of taking her into my arms when she sank at once to the floor as if paralyzed. I raised her up and placed her on a settee in the room and, snatching a cushion from a chair, put it under her head. She soon began to recover from her partial swoon. Before she was able to converse, I had time and opportunity to undeceive myself. I discovered—to my inexpressible grief and disappointment—that the lady in black was not Judith Bensaddi. She resembled her much in every striking peculiarity of feature. But a close inspection immediately detected differences that left no room for mistake. This lady's eyes were rather smaller and blacker, her complexion darker, her face longer, and the expression of her countenance was to me less benignly sweet and winning.

She rose after some minutes to a sitting posture, and, giving me a sorrowful look, she sighed deeply without speaking. "Alas, my dear stranger," said I, "we are both, I fear, sadly disappointed by the result of this interview. I have long sought you in the belief that you were a dear, lost friend. You resemble her, and this resemblance deceived me." "Oh! sir," said she, "you were announced to me as a dear, lost friend of mine; it was a mistake on both sides; the shock overcame me; I saw that you were a stranger and not my friend. My hope is gone. Alas, alas, he is dead! I shall never see him again!" Here she burst into a flood of tears. After she had wept and sobbed a few minutes, I spoke some friendly words to her and gradually led her into a conversation. The keenness of my disappointment would have been more sorely felt if the anguish of Miss Bersati had not interested my feelings and excited my curiosity. I was exceedingly desirous to learn the story of one who in so many points resembled my lost Judith, now lost again to my newly awakened hopes.

"Lady," said I after a while, "your resemblance to one whom I dearly loved, whom I thought dead, but whom I hoped again to find alive in you, makes me desirous to know something of your history. Will you favor me with an outline of it?"

"I will," said she, "if my feelings permit." "I have heard," said I, "that you are from London." "I am," said she, "but I was born in Italy. My father, Anselmo Bersati, was a professor of music. After the death of my mother, he accepted the invitation of an English nobleman and removed from Florence to London when I was ten years old and my brother twelve. He had no other children. He taught music in the nobleman's family for a while and was employed at the public concerts. His reputation grew, and he soon acquired a handsome income. He bred me to the same profession, and before I was eighteen I got a good salary as musician in the opera. My brother preferred the mercantile business and was bred to that. He was fond of travelling and three years ago made a voyage to America. He returned to London with a young gentleman, Andrew Hazleton of Charleston, whose father was a merchant in good business. I became acquainted with Mr. Hazleton; he soon attached himself to me; the attachment became mutual and resulted in an engagement of marriage. He and my brother joined their influence to persuade my father to migrate to Charleston, where they assured him of profitable employment in his profession. My expected settlement in that city induced him to consent, and the next spring, now two years ago, was fixed on for the voyage. Mr. Hazleton returned home to wait our arrival for the consummation of the marriage.

"The next spring, when we expected to embark, my father was taken ill with a lingering disease which confined him six months to the house. When he was able again to ride out, he had the misfortune to be thrown from the carriage and almost killed. At last, however, though threatened with a return of his old disease, he embarked with me twelve months ago for Charleston. But it was a sad embarkation; for, on that very day, we heard that my brother had fallen in a duel at Havana to which he had gone upon a trading voyage. The news so affected my poor father that he was taken sick before we lost sight of land. He suffered great agony during five weeks, and then, just as the American coast came into view, he breathed his last. Thus was I left a destitute orphan among strangers, and my first office on landing in a strange city was to bury my father. His long illness and my close attendance on him reduced our resources, especially as he had given my brother a large portion of his capital to set him up in trade. On my landing in Charleston, I had but small funds remaining. But I experienced great kindness from several strangers, especially from Dr. La Motte, who was a fellow passenger on the voyage.

"I must now tell you another sore affliction on my landing. I did not find Mr. Hazleton as I expected. He had written to me affectionately from time to time during the first year after our separation. He then informed me that his father had met with misfortunes in business which made it expedient for him to remove to New Orleans, where he might hope to retrieve his losses. He still urged us to come as soon as possible to America, assured me of his unchanged affection, and declared that nothing prevented him from coming to London for me but the difficulty of his father's affairs which required his aid. A few days before we embarked we received a letter from him dated at New Orleans in which he promised to meet me in Charleston as soon as he should hear of my arrival there. As soon as I was able, after landing, I wrote to him an account of my arrival and of my sad condition. A month afterwards no answer had arrived. I wrote again, but no answer was returned. Dr. La Motte then wrote to a friend of his in New Orleans to make inquiries. In four weeks he received an answer saying that old Mr. Hazleton was dead and that his son Andrew had embarked, three months before, on a commercial adventure for Brazil and might be expected soon to return. This explained the cause of my receiving no answers to my late letters and gave me some consolation. In the meantime, I resided in Dr. La Motte's family as governess of his daughters and received great kindness from the family. I waited in hope of soon seeing or hearing from Mr. Hazleton. But another and another month passed away without intelligence. Dr. L. wrote again to his friend and received for answer that Mr. Hazleton had neither returned nor been heard from. I now began to fear that some fatal accident had befallen him. I had no doubt of his fidelity to me and have never suspected him of repenting his engagement, or I should not have sought intelligence of him as I have done. In the month of August I accompanied Dr. La Motte's family on a tour to the north and returned with them two months afterwards."

Here I interrupted the fair narrator with the remark that it was on their return from the tour that I got a glimpse of her face in Philadelphia and afterwards heard of her visit to my vale of Seclusa. She gave me a look of surprise and interest when I mentioned Seclusaval. "Are you the owner of that beautiful valley?" "Yes, Miss Bersati, and it was the feeling which you showed on hearing of my disappointment in love that led me to seek this interview in the hope that you might indeed prove to be my lost Judith Bensaddi." "Judith Bensaddi! Judith Bensaddi!" said she, in a sort of amazement, "Is she the lady whom you loved?" "Yes, whom I loved and lost; did you know her?" "Yes, my father was her music teacher; he often praised her as the finest and most amiable scholar that he ever had. I saw her a few times, but I never had any intimacy with her." "Can you tell me, Miss Bersati, anything of her history shortly before and after her father's bankruptcy?" "Very little, sir; I remember to have heard that she paid her father's debts out of her own fortune, and I think that I afterwards heard of her going to France with her father and that he died there." "Did you ever hear of her marriage and of her husband's name?" "I remember to have heard some years ago that she was expected to be married to a clergyman who had baptized her; but although my father was so often at Mr. Bensaddi's house while giving her lessons, he ceased to have any intercourse with the family afterwards, and we did not often hear of them. I do not think that I ever heard of her marriage." "Did you ever hear of her death?" "I heard something of another death in the family, but I cannot say for certain that she was the one."

Thus unsatisfactorily did my inquiries terminate. Meanwhile Miss Bersati gradually assumed a more cheerful air in the excitement of conversation. I stayed until the next day and became sufficiently acquainted with Miss B. to admire her beauty, her talents and her accomplishments. I thought that she showed no reluctance to cultivate an intimacy with me. She often alluded to the beauties of Seclusaval and to her despair of again seeing her lover. I thought her an interesting lady, resembling my Judith a good deal but on the whole far inferior, especially in the undesigning simplicity of heart and virgin purity of sentiment which gave to my lost Judith her transcendant loveliness. Not that Miss Bersati was notably deficient in these estimable traits of character, but the Italian ardor of her feelings was not tempered with such a degree of unsophisticated sweetness and modesty as distinguished my Judith. Yet I sincerely commiserated her misfortunes so much like those of my beloved.

The reader, if interested in her story, will be pleased to hear that within a month after my visit her lover returned and fulfilled his engagement.

V

The Music Teacher

I returned home with a heavy heart, taking Charleston in my route that I might lay in a supply of all things needful to complete my establishment in Seclusaval, where I was now more than ever disposed to lead a solitary life "the world forgetting, by the world forgot." With this view I purchased everything now in the way of furniture and stores that my little household and my laborers would be likely to need for several years. I was liberal, if not profuse, in my purchases; I designed to be not only just but generous to my agents, tenants and dependents and accumulated such various stores that I could always have suitable presents to bestow. For my worthy steward's family I made special provision. As to my private and ordinary style of living, I resolved that it should be simple and plain; but when genteel friends or strangers should visit my lovely Seclusaval, I resolved to bring forth out of my stores the elegancies and luxuries that would make their visit agreeable for the style of my hospitality as well as for the charms of the scenery.

Thus did I think to console my desolate heart. By the first of April, I again saw the unfolding verdure of my valley, promising a glorious summer display of all that is beautiful in external nature. The house was finished in a simple but remarkably neat and clean style of architecture. It was spacious enough to accommodate a large family. The water pipes were laid, and a clear fountain spouted in the yard and ran sparkling to trace its mazy rounds about the slopes and terraces of the garden. The garden, now finished and furnished, began to bud and bloom with all the riches of a temperate climate. The meadow, sprinkled here and there with trees, single and in clumps, was clothed with a luxuriant sward of the deepest green. The pure waters of the lake were inhabited by a thousand sportive fishes, among which the trouts seemed to find peculiar joy in the cool pellucid element. The neighboring hills and dales differed from the meadow only in being more shaded with the native forest trees, which had been selected to remain for their stately magnificence, their beautiful forms or their rich verdure; but among these chosen remnants of the forest, a green turf grazed by flocks and herds began to cover and adorn the ground. Lawns here and there permitted the eye to penetrate into the bosom of the park and afforded glimpses of beautiful groves and retreats that enticed the imagination as much by what was hidden as by what was revealed.

A carriage road had been made to wind among the hills and dales towards the upper end of the valley. Passing by the Dusky Cascade before described, it pursued the dark glen that led up to the Blue Ridge but presently took the point of a low ridge that led it gradually up to the top of Craggyhead. From this road another led down into the valley on the northeastern side of Craggyhead and down that valley until it joined the road leading out of Seclusaval by the ravine.

Now, with all these varied sources of pleasure and amusement, such choice gifts of nature, such sweet embellishments of art, such stores of all that my heart could covet of the productions of human industry, such a collection of books and of philosophical apparatus, and such specimens of the fine arts as I had collected in Europe and America, which, if not very costly, were all that I desired—did I not feel happy? How many are there in this country, male and female, young and old, who fancy that the possessor of such abundant sources of enjoyment must needs enjoy them and be satisfied. Or, if these alone could not satisfy, if the pleasures of society were wanting in my valley, still I could easily allure what company I would into so charming a retreat. Many perhaps among my readers will scarce believe me when I say that after the excitement of unpacking, storing away and arranging my late acquisitions was over and I had nothing to do but enjoy the beauties of Seclusaval and the goods that I had laid up for many years, then did I begin to feel a degree of hopeless despondency such as I had never felt since I came into the gold country. While I was laboring in my profession and was full of duties and engagements, I was happy. The constant stimulus that kept my faculties in a state of activity left me no time to brood over real or imaginary evils. Now, when my work was done, my fortune made, and a home, lovelier than I had ever dreamed of in my most poetic moods, was mine to have and to enjoy according to my pleasure, I first began to feel a sense of weariness and satiety, then of loneliness. Then, as the remembrance of one favorite object unattained came up more frequently and took hold more deeply upon my mind, I became so sad and restless that I saw no other means of alleviation than to fly from my quiet paradise and mingle again with the turmoils of busy life. In fact, there was an aching void in my heart; I was alone, and *it is not good for man to be alone.*

Happily, there was one favorite enterprise of mine yet unaccomplished. The female academy was not yet supplied with teachers. A difficulty arose, and the trustees sent me a request to come down and aid them with my advice. The difficulty was this: the trustees had, after much correspondence, fixed their hearts on procuring the services of Mr. Danforth, who was teaching a female academy in New York but, thinking the climate too cold for his constitution, was desirous of obtaining a situation in the South. But as his qualifications were high, so, and justly so, were his terms. He required the guarantee of a specific sum for himself during one year and for his music teacher during three years. He would not engage in a new institution and a strange country without satisfactory evidence that a complete seminary under good management could be sustained, and this evidence was the guarantee. The trustees could obtain from the families of the country around sufficient engagements to guarantee Mr. Danforth's own salary and that of his wife; but the demand of one thousand dollars a year for the music teacher seemed extravagant, and the patrons were not willing to join the trustees in securing it.

When I met with the trustees, I found them reluctantly brought to the conclusion that they could not employ Mr. D. and must look out for another and probably an inferior teacher. When I read his letter prescribing the conditions, I noticed that he spoke in the highest terms of the lady who taught music in his school; he valued her services so highly that he would not engage anywhere without her nor without securing her an ample salary. He said that she was in no degree related to him or his family and that she was a friendless and unfortunate lady whom he would not forsake and whose talents and accomplishments would adorn any station. I was struck with the noble sentiments expressed by Mr. Danforth and conceived such an esteem for his character that I promptly resolved to make myself responsible for the music teacher's salary.

"Gentlemen," said I, "Mr. Danforth speaks like a man conscious of his deserts and, what is more, like a generous friend to the unfortunate. The high terms which he demands so peremptorily for the accomplished and unfortunate lady whom he has taken under his protection are to me the strongest reasons why we should accept them. I take upon myself the guarantee of a thousand dollars annually, for three years, to the unfortunate lady. I will go a step further and promise the same lady three elegant suits of apparel yearly if she will come three times each year and play upon the instrument that stands silent in my lonely parlor. And by way of assurance that the promise shall be fulfilled, I will send to Philadelphia tomorrow for the first three suits. Mr. Lappet sets out tomorrow for that city, and he shall be my agent. So write immediately to Mr. D. and tell him that his terms are accepted, but I forbid any mention of my name in the letter. The music teacher might feel some scruple if she knew that a young bachelor had bid so high for her. She might suspect that I have some design upon her."

The letter was written, and in three weeks an answer was received, announcing that Mr. D. and his teachers would set out in a few days for the academy.

This affair lightened the burden upon my heart for some days. I returned to Seclusaval but soon began to droop again. I busied myself awhile in superintending some improvements, either not yet finished or newly undertaken. I visited all the new farms on my estate, especially the French colony in Soyevin, the name which I gave the valley devoted to vineyards and mulberry orchards. I found them doing well. Thus I made out to spend the month of April. But when May came, my melancholy increased. The opening charms of nature in Seclusaval served only to inspire melancholy thoughts. I was still alone, and *it is not good for man to be alone.* But what could I do? Though the Houris that adorn the fancied paradise of Mahomet had all smiled upon me, not one could have touched my heart so long as the sweet miniature that I wore in my bosom daily renewed my love for the peerless Judith Bensaddi, ever to be loved and ever to be lamented.

I could stay at home no longer. I mounted my horse and rode again to the academy. The workmen were busily engaged in preparing it for the expected teachers. It could divert my melancholy but a day or two. I mounted and rode away scarcely knowing whither I would go. Once I thought that I could visit the place where I first resided in Carolina, but when I reached the fork of the road leading to it, I felt too gloomy to appear among my acquaintances there. So I turned eastwardly and travelled on without object. I was flying from melancholy, but I carried the evil in my bosom and fled in vain because I could not fly from myself.

The third day of my travel from the academy was Saturday and brought me at nightfall to an inn by the wayside, where a Mr. McTab, a Scotchman, furnished homely fare to travellers. The family had just arrived from a religious meeting which was being held at a village seven miles beyond. The meeting was numerously attended on account of the presbytery, which was holding its sessions at the place. The Lord's Supper was to be administered the next day, and a great congregation was expected to attend. I was glad to hear of this meeting and resolved at once to attend it. I felt myself in woeful need of religious consolation and hoped that by means of the Holy Communion I might at last obtain rest for my weary soul.

I accompanied Mr. McTab and his family the next morning. I found the church in a grove on the outskirts of the village. Hundreds of horses were tied to the trees and fences. Although divine service had begun, great numbers of loose persons were strolling about or gathered in groups wherever they could find logs or benches to sit on. Every door had a crowd about it, and every seat and every aisle in the church were thronged with auditors. Mr. McTab's pew being near the front door, we made out to work our way to it, and, by making some youngsters stand among our feet, we were enabled to seat ourselves. I could not see the preacher except occasionally through openings in a dense mass of heads and shoulders. The sermon was an edifying one and prepared me for joining devoutly in the communion.

When the communion service began, there was considerable difficulty in passing through the crowded aisles to the table. Therefore, I waited until the service was nearly over and then accompanied Mr. McTab's family to the table. Finding it nearly full, they took the space on the one side while I passed round to the other and sat facing them. Two or three ladies still lacked seats. The elder in attendance touched my shoulder that I might make room for them. By pressing closely together, we left a space that was scantily sufficient for the ladies. The one next to me was in deep mourning and closely veiled. She was much affected after she sat down and strove in vain to suppress her sobs and tears. She had been pressed so closely to my side that I could feel the tremor of her nerves and the palpitation of her heart. Her tokens of distress excited my sympathy. Her bereavement was doubtless severe and probably recent, whether she mourned for parent; or brother, or, what seemed more likely, for the companion of her bosom. As I did, so did she, and sorely, too, need the consolations of religion. I raised my heart in supplication for the weeping mourner as well as for myself.

When the bread was distributed, she seemed to be so absorbed by her devotions as not to observe it. I took a small piece from the plate, broke it, and put one of the parts into her hand. She took it from me and ate it as I did the other part. So, when the wine came round, I tasted first and then gave her the cup which she took from my hand. Every moment I felt a greater interest in this stranger and repeatedly implored the Father of Mercies in her behalf. I knew not why, but I was conscious of a singularly tender sensation from the soft touch of her arm and side, involuntarily pressed against mine. The feeling had nothing in it incongruous to the sacredness of the hour and the place. It was a pure sympathy for the griefs of a breast so gentle and so devout as I felt hers to be. I was no little gratified to perceive the soothing effect of the communion upon her heart, whose spasmodic action ceased. Tears flowed no longer, but a holy calm seemed to have been breathed into her soul, as it was into mine, through faith in the expiatory sufferings that were signified by the sacred emblems of bread and wine. We felt the peace which the dying Son of God bequeathed to his disciples, the spiritual peace without which the soul of man is but a fountain of bitter waters.

When we rose from the table, the ladies at my side preceded me in retiring. The mourning lady then appeared to be of the middle stature, and she wore a bonnet somewhat different from any others that I noticed. These were the only observations that I could make before we parted in the crowd and I lost sight of her. I felt a natural curiosity to know who she was but had no means of learning as I could not describe her to another person with any distinctness.

During the short intermission that preceded the afternoon service, I walked out to meditate in the woods. I felt a delightful glow of spiritual comfort. A fountain, lately closed, had been opened again by the devotional exercises of the day. I no longer considered myself a solitary, unconnected being. If I lacked one tie, of all earthly ties the closest and dearest, if, so far, I was severed from that without which human nature and human happiness are incomplete, I now felt the drawing of other bonds which bound me to many hearts, even of strangers around the communion table. I was still a member of the human family; I was also a member of the spiritual family gathered by Him who came down from heaven into a peculiar brotherhood, a brotherhood of renewed hearts, which by prayer draw sweet effluences of love from the common fountain of Deity, ever flowing from its exhaustless source to purify and to console. Alas! that so many should never seek these living waters. Alas! that so many should infuse the bitterness of their own hearts into these healing streams and call the polluted mixture "religion"!

The afternoon service was begun before I returned to the church. The sermon was an excellent one, chastely and beautifully eloquent, and strictly appropriate to the occasion but delivered with less vehemence of manner than is usual in the South. The people generally seemed to listen without interest to calm and lucid exposition, logical argument and mild persuasion. The popular mind is yet too uncultivated to relish such refined oratory. I asked Mr. McTab who this preacher was. "A stranger frae the north," said he, "ganging awa'

South." Altogether, the services of the day had a surprising effect on my mind. I left the church renewed, brightened, and sanctified, at least for the time. I thanked Divine Providence for directing my wandering steps to this presbyterial meeting. I could now go home refreshed.

As I pressed through the crowd to get my horse, I happened to hear a couple of plainly dressed old country women in earnest conversation. Their Scottish dialect first struck my attention, but the subject of their colloquy soon awakened all my curiosity. "Aweel now, Mrs. McGraw, I wud na mind that a bawbee. Ye'll agree that a Jewess may be a gude Christian when she is converted." "Why, yes, Mrs. McCracken, I grant ye, if she be truly and thoroughly regenerate; but that is nae easily done wi' ane o' them hardened Jews, Mrs. McCracken. And then I wud na mind her being a private Christian like, but I unnerstan that she is a teacher, a sort o' public character like, ye know, Mrs. McCracken. Now just think: wud ye like to put your daughter unner a Judaizing teacher? Ye know how the Apostle warns us agin sic Judaizing teachers. Think o' that, Mrs. McCracken."

I had stopped at the word "Jewess," which struck me like a thunderclap, not now to frighten, but to rouse me. I waited for some further development of the subject of conversation. But Mrs. McCracken's husband called her off suddenly. "Good e'en, Mrs. McGraw," said Mrs. McCracken. "Good e'en, Mrs. McCracken," said Mrs. McGraw; and ere I could address either Mrs. McCracken or Mrs. McGraw, they had mingled with the crowd and disappeared.

Had I met an acquaintance then, I would have inquired if they had a converted Jewess for a teacher in their neighborhood. But a few moments reflection made me conclude that it was a matter of no consequence to me. Jewesses were found half the world over, and a converted Jewess was no such rarity that the mention of one should make me fancy that my lost Judith had risen from the grave.

I returned to Mr. McTab's on my way home. The next morning, while conversing with the hostess on the occurrences of the meeting, I was about to ask her a question suggested by the allusions of the old women at the church when she anticipated me by asking if I knew that the lady in mourning who sat by my side at the communion table was a converted Jewess. I started, turned pale, and, almost breathless, answered, "No." "Aweel now, she was, but ye need na be frightened. I trust that she is truly regenerate, and I dinna think that we should feel sic antipathy to ony Christian, though she be o' Jewish bluid." "I feel no antipathy, Mrs. McTab. But what you tell me is very surprising. Does she reside in this country?" "Na, she is a stranger amang us. She came till the presbytery on Saturday with the preacher that ye heard in the afternoon. They are ganging South, I hear, till teach a seminary." "Do you know the preacher's name?" "Aye, I heard it; I think they ca' him Donfort or the like o' that." "Danforth, perhaps?" "Aye, aye, Donfurth, preceesely." "Is the Jewish lady his wife?" I asked in great trepidation. "Na, na; his wife sat next till the Jewess in white claes. They say that the Jewish convert is his music teacher—though I canna say what sort o' music she teaches—some o' their ungadly whuslin lilts, I fear, for they dinna teach psalmody in their academies, I unnerstan—the mair is the pity." "His music teacher! Did you hear her name, Mrs. McTab?" "Her name? O aye, I heard any tell it till anither; but it is sic a strange name—I canna remember—but it sounded like a Scriptur name too—Beersheba—or Belshazzar. Ach! Na, it was na jist a Scriptur name. Benhadad—it was amaist like Benhadad, but I canna forgather it." "Was it Bensaddi?" I asked with almost breathless anxiety. "Bainsawdi? A weel now, I think that was it. But I canna tell; I think now it was mair like Baalsamen." "Try to remember, Mrs. McTab, do remember, I beg you." "Ye seem to hae a curiosity about it, Mr. Garame. Ah, here is Jenny. Jenny, dear, did ye hear the Jewish laddy's name at the kirk yestr'een?" "Nae, mither; I only heard her called the Jewish music teacher."

This was all that I could learn of the family. Though unsatisfactory, it was sufficient to kindle again some trembling hope—at least it stirred up a thorny impatience to learn who this music teacher was. She was a Jewess; she was a mourner. I had caused her to come to our academy, and at the communion table I had felt that there was a tender and mysterious sympathy between our souls. These alone were points of deep interest. And then the name! Oh how I longed to know the exact form of it! I was cautious, since Miss Bersati's case had disappointed me, not to trust in resemblances.

Breakfast had been just finished, and the hostler was saddling my steed when a two-horse barouche passed by towards the west. I stepped to the door and saw that the hind seat was occupied by two ladies, one in white, the other in black with the identical bonnet of the lady in whom I now felt so intense an interest. In five minutes I was on my horse, and, ere I was aware, I found that I had urged him to a gallop. When I overtook them, a short turn in the road brought the side of the barouche into view. Mr. Danforth sat on the foreseat as driver, but the lady in black was so closely veiled and so covered from my sight by the other lady that I could make no discovery. I could easily have passed and turned to look at the faces of the party, but I would not risk a recognition of such importance in such circumstances.

Supposing that they must have taken an early breakfast and would of course stop for dinner, I laid a scheme to gain my end at the house where they would stop. The only convenient house for the purpose I remembered to be in a rocky vale, where a mill, a store and a smith shop made a sort of village. When Mr. Danforth stopped the barouche at a brook to let the horses drink, I rode past, holding my umbrella so as to conceal my face from the ladies. I then dashed on and arrived at the tavern nearly an hour earlier than the barouche.

Telling the landlady that I did not "feel well"—a true saying—I called for a private room that I might lie down. She showed me first a back room which I rejected; then she offered me a room upstairs which I declined also. She looked with curiosity into my face to see if my pericranium was sound. I asked if she had not a bedroom at the end of the front piazza. "Yes," said she, "but the sun makes it too warm at this time of day." "Give me that, madam, it suits me exactly." She gave me another scrutinizing glance and then led the way. It was within thirty feet of the gate and had a small window opening towards the road. Requesting to have some toast and tea prepared, I lay down on the bed. But I seemed to lie on thorns. I got up and prepared the window by having the sash up and the curtain down so as to leave a small opening adapted to my scheme of peeping, for I desired to see before I was seen. Meditating on the possibility that this might be indeed my Judith, I considered what I should do in case that it was herself. She was probably a widow, as her deep mourning and sorrow indicated a bereavement more recent than the death of her father thirteen months before. I conceived the outlines of a plan of action and was absorbed in the subject when I heard the sound of wheels. My heart fluttered; in great trepidation I took my seat by the window just as the vehicle stopped.

Mr. Danforth dismounted, and, hearing that the party could have dinner, he handed out first the lady in white, who walked straightway into the house. Then he handed out the lady in black, who, as she entered the gate, partially drew aside her veil. A soft dark eye and part of a lovely face made me almost faint with fearful joy. Mr. Danforth spoke to her: "How do you feel now, Miss Judith?" "Better every way than I have felt these many days" was the answer; and, as she spoke, she turned her face so that every feature was distinctly seen.

I heard—I saw—it was—it was beyond a doubt my Judith Bensaddi! Her softly beaming eyes, her sweet countenance, somewhat pale and overcast with years of sorrow but yet all sweet and lovely. The dulcet voice—the name—all agreed. I must have believed though I had seen her laid in the grave. She lived, she looked, she spoke; she was *Miss Judith*, not Mrs. Brannigan. Yesterday she sat by my side a devout Christian. I then felt the sweet influence of her presence as if Heaven designed that our reunion should commence at the holy place where we mingled pious vows, ate of the same consecrated bread, and drank of the same hallowed cup. Now, when all was evident and my fearful hope was changed to certainty, I sank down upon the floor smitten almost to death with excessive joy.

Soon after, a servant brought in my tea and toast. He found me apparently very ill, really ill with joy. I had crawled into the bed; now I attempted to rise and go to the table but stumbled and fell. I made out to get on a chair and drink a dish of tea, which revived me; but I told the servant to take out the things as I had no appetite for food. The servant's report of my illness brought in the hostess, who asked if I would have a physician sent for. I told her that I was getting over the fit and could do without medicine. "There is a strange gentleman here who knows something of physic," said she. "He desired me to ask if he could be of any service." "I shall be pleased to see him," was my reply. She left me, and the next moment Mr. Danforth entered the room. I told him that my illness was going off and needed no further treatment but that I wished to have a few minutes' private conversation with him. He cheerfully assented. I locked the door and after some introductory inquiries and remarks requested him to tell me what he knew of the late history of his music teacher. "My reason for asking," said I, "is that I once knew the lady and was much attached to her. I recognised her as she came into the house and was astonished to see her, because on a visit to London, nine months ago, I was informed that she and her father had died near the same time in France."

"Of course," said Mr. D., "you were misinformed respecting her death. I presume that it was her sister, Mrs. Brannigan, whose death you heard of. I will relate to you how I came to be acquainted with her. Bad health led me and my wife to spend the winter before the last in the south of France. We resided some months at Clairfont, a pleasant healthy village near Bordeaux. We chose that village because it was inhabited by Protestants and was a place of frequent resort for invalids, especially English invalids. Here we became acquainted with Miss Bensaddi, who was attending on her sick father and sister. An English family in the village had known the Bensaddis in their prosperous days. They spoke in such exalted terms of Miss Judith and compassionated her afflictions to such a degree that I resolved to seek her acquaintance. Her assiduous attendance on her father and sister confined her almost constantly to the house; but, having gained an introduction, we assisted her in nursing the sick and soon gained her warm friendship and, what is more, acquired such knowledge of her modest virtues and talents that we felt loathe to part with her. After the death of her father and sister, which she deeply mourned but bore with pious submission, we proposed that she should come with us to America. We knew that she had nobly surrendered her own large fortune to pay her father's debts, that she was the only survivor of the family, and that she felt reluctant to go back to London, where nothing but melancholy reminiscences awaited her. I assured her that in America her talents and acquirements would gain her an ample support. She replied that her nearest and best friend resided in Boston and that she would thankfully accept our kind protection until she could meet with that friend. She declared her intention to devote herself to teaching, that she might gain an honest living and be useful to her fellow creatures. We embarked at Bordeaux and landed in New York on the fifteenth of June."

"Did you?" said I. "Then I was not mistaken when I thought that I saw Miss Judith on the deck of a French ship which our packet met in the narrows on that very day. I was then on my way to London."

"You remind me," said Mr. D., "of a circumstance which then occurred. We observed that Judith looked intently at the passengers on a ship that we passed in the narrows and at last burst into tears. When we asked what was the matter, she said that she recognised a dear friend on that ship, one whom she had never expected to see again and probably had now seen for the last time. She was obviously reluctant to mention particulars; so we did not press her, and she never spoke of the circumstance again. You, I presume, are that friend.

"In New York, I again resumed the school which I had taught. Miss Bensaddi addressed a letter to her Boston friend, Mr. Von Caleb; after long delay she received a letter from another gentleman there, a friend of his, saying that Mr. Von Caleb had gone, just a week before her letter arrived, to reside again in London. Being left in charge of his affairs at Boston, he had opened her letter. He apologised that pressing circumstances prevented him from affording her any aid but that she could write to her cousin in London if she would. She desired no aid except friendly advice, so she wrote no more but accepted my offer of employment as music teacher in my female seminary.

"She lived very retired in my family, seemed indisposed to mixed society; but in private, with my family and a few friends, she was a delightful associate while her extraordinary skill and assiduity as a teacher were of great advantage to my school and to every pupil that she taught.

"But a confined city life did not suit her natural taste and constitution. Though as cheerful as such accumulated misfortunes would permit any one to be, she evidently drooped and pined away until about the middle of autumn when we made an excursion up the Hudson, visited West Point, the Catskills and Niagara. This tour had a wonderful effect on her health and spirits. She was inexpressibly delighted with the scenery on our route and showed that a country life could alone give her continued health and pleasure. On her account, therefore, as much as my own, I was gratified with the prospect of a residence in upper Carolina, where the climate will doubtless suit me and my wife, and the vicinity of the mountains will suit the taste of Miss Bensaddi. I can see that her health and spirits are already improved by the mere expectation of living near the mountains."

"I hope that she will reside in the midst of them before long," said I under a sudden impulse. Mr. D. looked surprised and waited for an explanation. But, as yet, I gave him none.

"Do me the favor," said I, "to keep this conversation a secret for the present. I wish to remain unknown to Miss Bensaddi for a short time. I reside but twenty miles from the academy and will see you there in a few days. I must also at present withhold my name from you until I can make it known with evidence of its respectability." After he had given me the promise of secrecy, I asked him if he heard of Miss Judith's being engaged to marry a gentleman in England about three years before. He had heard it from the English family in France, who could, however, give no other account of the matter than this, that the gentleman had died without consummating the marriage. Judith had never mentioned to them anything respecting it. Though communicative on all other subjects, she had never alluded to any love affair in her past history.

Mr. Danforth being summoned to dinner, I took advantage of the opportunity to make my escape, unobserved by the party, and rode posthaste to the academy.

◆◆✦ VI ✦◆◆

The Summer Festival

I arrived at the academy a day sooner than the party of teachers. I hastily visited the trustees, told them that Mr. Danforth would arrive the next evening, and, after suggesting a few particulars of my former love affair with the music teacher, I begged them to avoid all mention of me or of Seclusaval in the presence of the teachers until I was prepared to make myself known. I besought them to humor my whim in this matter and to prevent, if possible, all knowledge on the part of the music teacher that such a person as myself existed in the country. In due time I would make myself known and would soon communicate to them privately the scheme which I had in my head. They cheerfully pledged themselves to what I requested. To prevent untimely communications from reaching the ears of the teachers, Mr. Landon, one of the trustees, took his carriage in the morning to meet them on the way and to conduct them by an unfrequented road to his house in a secluded valley of the neighborhood.

I hastened to Seclusaval and immediately set my steward and tenants to work in a multitude of preparations for a summer festival, which I told them we were to have on the first of June in Seclusaval. I astonished my people with the multitude of my orders and the eagerness of all my words and actions. They saw that new life had somehow been infused into me and wondered how I came to be so revived all of a sudden. I told Baylor to collect a dozen laborers at once and go to smoothing off and beautifying Seclusaval to the utmost. "Make the valley shine," said I. "It shall be done, sir." "Get also some carpenters to make temporary buildings for the festival; keep the sawmill going to furnish materials, and let us have a glorious festival." "Yes, sir, it shall be glorious; we are able to do it, and it shall be done, sir." That was enough; I knew that when Baylor undertook to do it, it would be done.

I next despatched letters and agents in various directions in furtherance of my scheme; and having thus put things in motion at home, I returned to the neighborhood of the academy and stopped at the house of Mr. Wilson, pastor of the church. He was an old friend and college mate and had been lately settled in the neighborhood through my influence. I communicated my scheme to him. He was pleased with it and offered me all the aid in his power. He despatched his barouche to Mr. Landon's to bring over Mr. Danforth. The distance was only two miles; Mr. D. soon arrived and was introduced to me; we smiled and shook hands cordially. I now unfolded my scheme of a summer festival to which I designed to invite all the country round and among the rest his music teacher. To carry out my views it was needful, on the one hand, that Judith should know nothing about them until the proper moment and should be for a while kept in ignorance of my being in the country and, on the other hand, that she should be prepared for the occasion and that I should know her present feelings in regard to me lest, after all, the scheme should turn out to be a painful surprise to her and a grievous disappointment to me.

After detailing the history of my love affair with Judith and explaining my object in getting up a summer festival, Mr. Wilson and Mr. Danforth readily undertook the office of preparing Judith for her part in the celebration without letting her know anything of the matter. Having visited other friends in the neighborhood and imparted to them more or less of my scheme of a festival, I returned to Seclusaval and was busy as a bee in preparations for the first of June.

In a few days I received the following letter from Mr. Wilson:

May 15th, 1824

My Dear G.—

I now inform you how I have executed the office which you assigned to me. Two days after you left us, I went with my barouche to bring Miss Bensaddi to my house on a visit. While at Mr. Landon's, I took occasion to mention in her hearing that I was a native of the great valley of Virginia and that I had received my education at Washington College. I alluded to the fine scenery in Rockbridge, especially the Natural Bridge and the House Mountain, which I had visited with a party of fellow students, and had seen from its top the most splendid sunrise in the world. The moment when I touched on this theme, I saw that she was intensely interested. Her fine dark eyes brightened immediately as she fixed them upon me with breathless attention. When I paused, she gave an involuntary sigh and, gradually sinking her head to a meditative posture, seemed to be absorbed in thought. Finding her indisposed to ask questions, I inquired if she was fond of the mountain scenery. She looked up with animation and for a minute or two poured forth an eloquent expression of her delight in rural scenes, especially in mountainous regions, and how much better she loved to dwell in this land of valleys and mountains than in a city. "Perhaps," said I, "you would like to read a description of the House Mountain written by a dear friend of mine, a native of Rockbridge, who is as enthusiastic an admirer of mountain scenery as you are." "Yes," said she, "I should be much gratified to read it." Her voice had a slight tremor as she spoke, and the color came and went upon her cheek. "Well," said I, "I have a copy of it at home that I will show you this evening."

On the way I alluded to you again without naming you. "This friend of mine," said I, "settled in another part of Carolina two or three years ago and soon acquired reputation at the bar. But his success has not made him happy. About four years ago he fixed his heart on a young lady, but by some unfortunate accident he lost her. The wound of that disappointment seems to be incurable unless Divine Providence should by some extraordinary means restore him his lost bride."

When Judith heard these words, she trembled and turned deadly pale but said nothing. She seemed afraid to trust herself to speak lest she should betray herself.

In the evening, when I and Miss Bensaddi were alone, I handed her the manuscript. When she read the title and saw your name annexed to it, she could refrain no longer but started up to leave the room that she might conceal her agitation. Before reaching the door her strength failed, and, dropping on a chair, she began to sob and weep. "My dear Miss Bensaddi," said I, "what is the matter?" "Oh, sir, I know not what to say; my feelings overcome me." "Did you see any thing in the manuscript to affect you so deeply?" "Oh yes—I cannot conceal it from you—that name— is the name of a friend who was in the ship with me when my dear brother was lost in the sea. May I rely on you not to tell how much I was affected on seeing that friend's name once more." "Miss Judith, that friend of yours and mine has told me the circumstances of that disastrous voyage. He told me also that the young lady who was then so unfortunate had won his heart wholly and forever. Pardon me, Miss B., for having taken this course designedly to bring about an explanation of your present feelings towards Mr. Garame. I had no doubt that you were the long lost object of his affections. I desire to know whether your feelings are as unchanged as his. I will now inform you that after your return to London he wrote you two letters in succession according to the agreement between you and that he feared from your silence some change of affection towards him or he would have gone himself to London. At last he received your letter announcing your expected marriage. This gave him the first intimation that his letters had not reached you. For this he is a mourner still."

When I spoke of the letters, she seemed at first to be filled with astonishment, and then she broke out into sobs and exclamations. After a little, I said, "Now Miss B., I think you must see the propriety of letting me open a communication between Mr. G. and yourself. You are both unmarried; your mutual affection is unchanged, or am I mistaken in supposing that your affection for him is unchanged?" After a violent struggle of a few moments, she wrung her hands and exclaimed, "Oh sir, I know not what to say. I have betrayed my feelings too plainly. My heart is not changed towards Mr. G. But it becomes not me to profess love for a gentleman to whose continued affection I have no claim nor right. I am unworthy of him, and I beg that you will not disturb him with any information concerning one who deserves no further notice from him."

"Miss Judith, you accuse yourself so bitterly that I must claim the privilege of being your judge. If you will state the case to me, I promise to give an impartial opinion according to the facts. If I think your self-accusation just and that you deserve no further notice from Mr. G., then I will let the matter drop where it is." She then gave me a full statement, of which I have room for a few particulars only.

The English gentleman whom she had consented to marry after she despaired of hearing from you was Mr. Wycherly, a pious and eloquent clergyman, who, after he had overcome her remaining difficulties respecting the Christian religion, accompanied her to London from the lakes of Cumberland and greatly aided in persuading her father to consent to her baptism. She received this rite from his hands. In the warmth of her Christian joy and her gratitude to so worthy and amiable a gentleman, she listened to his proposals of marriage and, mistaking the real state of her heart, yielded her consent. When she sat down, a few days afterwards, to write you the letter, she began to discover what a deep hold you still had upon her affections. Though hopeless of ever seeing you again, she found that her feeling of love towards you was of a different kind from that which she felt towards the good clergyman, who deserved her warmest gratitude and esteem but who had not awakened in her the tender sentiment of personal attachment that she still felt for you.

A few days after she had sent you the letter, she frankly told Mr. Wycherly the state of her heart and requested a postponement of the mar-

riage. He assented and returned to his residence in Cumberland. The
state of his health was rather alarming before this time. Symptoms of
consumption had already made his marriage of doubtful expediency. The
steady progress of the disease soon put marriage out of the question.
Learning the desperate state of his health, she went and did for him as
a tender and affectionate nurse all that in any circumstances she could
have done. She showed me the next day a letter of thanks written by Mr.
Wycherly's mother after his decease, in which her assiduous attentions
were warmly acknowledged.

"Now," said Miss Bensaddi, when she had concluded her narrative,
"you see that I was false to Mr. Garame because I despaired of his love
and accepted another offer when I ought to have trusted that he was only
unfortunate, not changed. And I was false to Mr. Wycherly because I
made him a promise which I could not fulfill without doing violence to
my feelings."

"Miss Judith," said I, "neither you nor Mr. Garame were false but provi-
dentially hindered from knowing each other's fidelity. Your promise to
Mr. Wycherly was made in sincerity but under an erroneous impression
respecting the state of your heart, and you did your duty honestly in con-
fessing the truth to him when you discovered it. And now, since the design of Providence is manifest in ordering that you and Mr. Garame
should once more be brought together, with hearts devoted to each other,
I put it to your conscience to say whether you can rightfully refuse to let
me inform Mr. G. of the exact state of the case. Can you thus make an
over-scrupulous delicacy forever separate two devoted hearts, and can you
run counter to the evident leadings of Divine Providence?" "That," said
she, "is a strong view of the case; I feel that it ought to be seriously considered." "The hand of God is more evident in this matter," said I, "than
you are yet aware of. This academy owes its erection to Mr. Garame's
exertions; and then without his zealous efforts, Mr. Danforth's terms
could not have been complied with, especially in relation to the music
teacher. So he was undesignedly the cause of your coming here, where
through an extraordinary combination of events you may again meet and
renew the tender relations which were so unfortunately broken off."

She was greatly surprised and affected with this information and exclaimed, "Yes, it is the hand of God. I dare not now refuse your request.
But I beseech you to communicate only so much to Mr. G. as will leave
him perfectly free to act as his present inclination may prompt. Do not, I
beseech you, expose everything that I have confessed to you. Let him not
think that I consider myself worthy of his love or that I have any sort of
claim or expectation that should induce him to do any thing not perfectly
agreeable to his wish and likely to promote his happiness. I trust to your

kindness and descretion to manage the matter so as not to involve either of us in a disagreeable predicament." I promised to act with a single regard to the honor and happiness of both parties and finally got her persuaded to leave the whole affair to the unlimited discretion of myself and Mr. Danforth, without whose consent I promised to do nothing. I have conferred with him on the subject, and we agree that you ought to know the whole truth as I have stated it.

Now your way is clear to prosecute your scheme, and I trust that God will bring it to a happy issue.

Yours, &c.

If ever a man was delirious with joy, then was I when I read this letter in my library; I danced over the floor like one intoxicated. My final arrangements were put in train immediately. I made a stealthy visit to my friends below and settled with them the scheme and order of proceedings at the summer festival. I enjoined upon them to keep the whole affair, and even the existence of Seclusaval and my presence in the country, still profoundly secret from Judith. My design was by all possible means to make it a happy day of surprises to that dear child of sorrow. On the 30th day of May, the preparations were complete at Seclusaval, and a letter from my managers below informed me that all was right in that quarter.

On the last of May, Mr. Landon, who had heretofore kept Judith very much secluded, took her in his carriage with his wife and daughter and Miss Claymore to visit the mountains, he and the brother of Miss Claymore being on horseback. The weather was fine, and the whole party in good spirits. Judith had gone through such dark years of affliction that sober cheerfulness was all that she could usually enjoy. The prospect of a trip to the wild mountains had raised her a degree above her usual cheerfulness, and her mind was prepared to derive pleasure from a ramble so congenial with her taste.

They pursued the valley that leads to Seclusaval; but, when they came to the ravine, they turned off to the right and ascended the vale at the northeastern side of Craggyhead. At a new farm in this valley they began to ascend the mountain by a winding road, not good but practicable. A little before sunset they reached a farm house, romantically situated high up on the side of Craggyhead, where a broad terrace of the mountain spread out from the base of the cliffs which supported the castle-shaped summit. Here they found the new white cottage all swept and garnished for their reception. There was a stir of cookery in the kitchen and a tidiness of apparel among the cottager's household as if they expected company. When the party stopped at the gate, they were received in the most friendly manner. On alighting and looking round from beneath some tall trees in the yard, they were detained for some time by the magnificent scenery before them. The last rays of the setting sun gilded the mountain tops while the deep vales were reposing in the gathering shades of twilight. They contemplated the wild and rugged mountains on the north of Craggyhead and the less rude features of the eastern landscape; they looked down into the half-seen vales and glens about this side of the mountain until they were called to partake of an excellent supper. After supper they went out to enjoy the soft evening air; they found the moon up in the east, shedding her silver radiance upon the green woods and the gray rocks, diffusing over the vast landscape the dreamy softness of hue which made Judith in her enthusiasm call the scene before her "the land of the shadow of life." When they had feasted their imaginations awhile on the nocturnal glories of the landscape, they went to bed in small but neat apartments, which seemed to have been furnished specially for the accommodation of such a party.

They rose an hour before the dawn and now saw the moonlight thrown back from the west upon the opposite sides of the mountains and shining into a ravine near the house. Through this ravine they were to ascend to the top of Craggyhead by a rough road, but still a safe one for a carriage, to a little fountain at the head of the ravine. From the fountain they made their way on foot and stood on the table rock of the summit just as the eastern horizon began to glimmer with the first hues of Aurora, and the moon as she went down was peeping back through the pines of the Blue Ridge. Every valley around Craggyhead was buried deeply in fog, and every high mountain stood forth, dusky and desolate, above the misty sea. It was the House Mountain scene varied. Judith recognised the resemblance and seemed entranced. "On a rock whose haughty brow frowned," not "o'er old Conway's foaming flood," but over the lovely vale of

Seclusa was Judith stationed. Her soul of liveliest sensibility kindled and glowed with ethereal animation as she looked, first this way, then that way, generally with silent admiration. Now and then her feelings broke forth in expressions such as these: "What a glorious vision! Down there! See how softly and silently the mist reposes in yon valley; 'tis like the sea of oblivion. Oh, the sun! Now the mountain tops begin to glow! How splendid are the green forests newly gilt with morning rays! How beautifully yon cliff of rocks over the valley appears with its crown of dark green pines. Behold, Mrs. Landon, the valley down here begins to show itself! That hill top down yonder—see how its beautiful trees stand out over the mist! How green and fresh the ground looks under the trees. Yonder, too, is a white cottage in a nook under the rocks with a little field and fruit trees about it. Oh! look down this glen under our feet, how wild and thickly set with trees! And yon hill at the mouth of the glen—what a beautiful park and a handsome house at the brow of the hill! Lend me your telescope, Mr. Landon—I want to see that beautiful garden on the hill side; I see roses blooming in the garden and walks and shrubberies and every thing beautiful. There is a green meadow, too, just unveiled, ornamented with trees. Let me see! The meadow is almost covered with bloom. How lovely! Miss Claymore, what is that spreading out so smoothly by the meadow side? It looks like water. It is water—a fine lake! with a boat moving over it!" Thus she noticed one object after another as each was exposed to view. Finally, after the fog had disappeared and the whole valley presented its enchanting landscapes, she surveyed it a while in silence and then asked in a sort of ecstasy if this were a real scene in the mountains or only a dream. Being presently assured that all was real, she declared it to be the most delightful place in the world and congratulated herself that it was sufficiently near the academy to admit of her coming to look at it once or twice a year.

About sunrise the party had been joined by Mr. and Mrs. Danforth and two or three other friends. At seven o'clock they were all invited to come down to the spring at the foot of the precipice and take breakfast. They found hot coffee and all the requisites of a good morning's repast. At eight o'clock they mounted their vehicles and began to descend by the road which leads down into the upper glen of Seclusaval. They frequently stopped by the way to enjoy the new views which successively presented themselves. When they reached the bottom of the glen, they found themselves so enveloped with the shade of trees and rocks that they seemed to be cut off from all that they had seen and, indeed, from all the visible and the living world of sunshine. They stopped awhile at the Dusky Cascade and admired its romantic wilderness. Pursuing their way, they wound along the southern border of the valley till they suddenly emerged from dense shades and thickets in all the disorderly luxuriance of nature into a grassy lawn, from which they caught glimpses here and there of wider lawns and of hills and mountains but only glimpses enough to excite curiosity until they suddenly reached the brow of a turfy hill crowned with a tall open grove. Here a general view of the more im-proved parts of the valley suddenly burst upon the sight and drew an exclamation of delight from Judith and several of her companions. The garden and hill of Glenview were seen to great advantage across the low grounds; on the right were the lake and meadow; above was the deep glen of the Craggyhead leading the eye up to the towering summit from which they had looked down upon the valley. De-scending the hill, they passed over by the head of the lake and wound up by the western side of Glenview into its beautiful park, through which they came forward again to the house on its brow, and here again they stopped and contemplated with admiration the best of all the views of Seclusaval, now shining in its glory as Baylor said it should.

Here some new appearances began to attract attention. In the mouth of the glen below the garden, half concealed by a grove of tall trees, were two large structures newly erected to accommodate the numerous company invited to the festival. The one was a large shed supported by framed pillars and set round closely with green boughs to exclude the sun and wind. This was furnished with two tables, each a hundred feet long; and, in the rear, the smoke and the bustle of cookery showed that the tables were to be used. The other build-ing, though a temporary structure, was formed with more regard to beauty of appearance; it was designed for such indoor exercises and amusements as might be adapted to the occasion. I shall notice this building again. It was called the Summer Hall.

Already had several parties of guests arrived, and others were seen coming up by the lakeside in carriages, on horses, and on foot, all in gay attire and with a hilarity of movement indicating that they were pleased and seeking pleasure. When Judith observed these appearances, she inquired whether Mr. Baylor (whom alone she had heard spoken of as residing here) had invited company to Seclusaval.

"Miss Judith, pardon us," said Mr. Landon, "for not having told you that there is to be a summer festival here today. We were invited to partake of it, and the rest of us agreed not to tell you until you saw the valley because we wished to give you an agreeable surprise." "All that I have seen today," said she, "has been so delightfully surprising that half the time I can scarcely believe my own senses but suspect that I am dreaming; everything bears so much the appearance of enchantment." "There is a sort of enchantment going on here," said Mr. L. "The worthy proprietor of this valley has converted it into an enchanting place, and I should not be surprised if some of us should undergo strange transformations today. I think that you are already so much under the magic influence that you may ere night be converted into something that you think not of." "If the transformations you speak of," said Judith playfully, "do not dissolve the sweet visions of this valley, I shall not suffer much." "No fear, Miss Judith," said Mr. L., in the same sportive strain, "I think the enchanter is a benevolent one and means only to give us pleasure; and if you should undergo a change, the new form of your being will doubtless be a happy one."

Now Mr. Baylor came out to the great tulip tree under which they stood and invited them into the house. He acted the landlord on this occasion with a hearty blunt sincerity, which made up for a little want of refinement in the manner of his kindness. His wife and daughter did the honors of the house. The parlor and library had been fitted up handsomely with my holiday furniture.

When the party entered the parlor, they found several acquaintances already there. Judith was asked to play on the piano. She played and sang three pieces of a cheerful character and in the best style of her unrivalled execution. She pronounced the instrument to be one of the most sweetly-toned that she had ever played upon. I owed her a dress for playing in my house; and I did not forget to pay it in due time.

The company were now joined by Mr. Wilson, the pastor, who whispered a word in Judith's ear and then took her through the hall into the library, where he handed her a letter which will explain itself. She began to tremble as soon as she looked at the inside. She read as follows:

My beloved Judith.

Words cannot express my joy to know that you are in Carolina, unmarried, and, as my friend thinks, with a heart unchanged towards me. He informed me by what means he had extracted the dear confession from you. He has also given me the outlines of your late history. Oh how my heart bled to think of the sorrows of my long lost Judith! But you were not to blame for despairing of my love when I was so unfortunate in the transmission of my letters. But thrice happy shall I now be if you will permit me to see you, to renew my suit in person, to press my long-wept-for bride to my panting bosom once more, and to solicit a speedy consummation of my ardent wish to call you mine by every holy tie and then to do what man can do to secure us from future separation and change for life. I am present at this summer festival and wait your permission for an interview.

W.G.

Here was a new surprise; she had not suspected that I was in the neighborhood. She was affected to tears by the intelligence, but they were not tears of grief. She handed the letter to Mr. Wilson. "Shall I read it, Miss Bensaddi?" "If you please; I am so bewildered with surprises and unexpected delights today that I cannot trust my own judgment. Advise me, my friend, respecting the subject of that letter." Giving the letter a hasty glance, he said, "Miss Judith, you now have from himself the ardent avowal of unchanged affection. You see the impatience of his feelings and the fear that delay may interpose some obstacle to his wishes. But before I advise you what to answer him, I must know the exact state of your heart. Answer me unreservedly, my dear friend. Do you love Mr. G. with such affection as would, in ordinary circumstances, make you freely consent to marry him?" "I must in candor confess that I do; my affection for Mr. G. is entire; he still possesses all my heart." "Well, then, as the mutual friend and confidant of both parties, I give you this advice: that you tempt not, by needless delay, the Benign Providence which now smiles upon your destiny. Open your heart at once to Mr. G., as he has done to you; and when he pleads for a speedy consummation of your union, yield, my friend—make no delay beyond what duty and necessity may seem to require. Thwart not the ardent wish of one who is worthy of you and seeks only your happiness and be not inattentive to the hand of God so manifestly pointing out the way to this happy marriage." "Yes," said she with deep emotion, "I see more and more the evident tokens of God's will in the present extraordinary crisis. I would be blind to my own good and most wickedly ungrateful to my Divine Benefactor if I could yield now to a prudish delicacy rather than to the force of such extraordinary and Divinely ordered circumstances. O, my friend, how grateful should I be to the kind Parent of all—how much do I need, at this critical moment, His good spirit to guide my actions. Pray and give thanks for me, my dear friend." She fell instantly upon her knees. Mr. D. also prostrated himself and performed in a low voice the devotional exercise that she requested.

When this was concluded, Judith appeared calmer and consented to let Mr. D. inform me that she was prepared for the interview. He came out, and locking after him the door that opened into the hall, he gave me the signal, and I passed into the library through another room. I had denied myself an interview with Judith during three weeks that I might now enjoy it and make her enjoy it the more. How I trembled with excessive emotion when I opened the door of my bedchamber behind the library and saw her sitting with her side towards me and her head reclining on the back of the chair. I could see a tremor agitating her frame also. When she was aware of my approach, she looked up with a look of indescribable feeling; then she started up with an inarticulate cry of joy. We met. Let silence cover what no language can express. Reader, thy lot hath been a rare one if ever thou did'st feel in one hour's concentrated delight a full equivalent for years of dreary absence and of hopeless sorrow.

How long it was ere we could speak, I cannot tell, perhaps fifteen minutes. My first words were "Oh, my long-lost—my recovered—my dearest Judith—will you now be mine?" She struggled for utterance a moment and replied, "My heart was yours long ago, and is, and will be while I live. But my beloved friend, if I be a bride, I must now be a dowerless bride." "None the less precious for that, my dear Judith—if anything, more precious to my heart on that very account. We shall not be destitute of the comforts of life. God has blessed my exertions, and we can trust Him for the future. So my love, do not refuse me because you have embraced a noble poverty from the best of motives. Oh, let me call you mine without delay—mine by the holiest ties." "I will, my friend, without unnecessary delay." "Thank God for that answer. Let it be this day then, my Judith, this blessed day, while heaven and earth are smiling upon us." "This day, my friend? We are not prepared." "Better prepared in respect to external circumstances than you are aware of. I have been preparing these three weeks, and all is ready if my Judith's heart is ready." "My heart is always ready—but we are here as Mr. Baylor's guests upon a very different occasion, and I never saw him till this day." "My Judith, Mr. Baylor has been preparing for our marriage today on the condition that I could gain your consent. Yes, my love, I confess that I meant to take you by surprise and, if I could, to woo and win you to my arms this sweet festal day, while life is young and our joy is fresh, while woods are green, while roses bloom, and every star of Heaven shines auspiciously upon us. Forgive me, dear Judith, for intending to surprise you thus. I meant to give pleasure; I trust that I am not giving pain." "No, my beloved friend. I seem all this day to be in a delirious ecstasy—to meet with you, to find you as I do with all the freshness and the warmth of the affection that once gave me such delight—alas! so fleeting and so soon followed by years of affliction that left me a poor orphan remnant of my family. But this hour has made me compensation." "Then crown my happiness, dear Judith, by permitting me to lead you to the altar." "I refuse nothing, my dear friend, that I am at liberty to grant, but my services as a teacher are engaged to Mr. Danforth." "That, too, is provided for, my dear Judith. Mr. D. was consulted about my schemes to win you today; he would have released you at all events if you had consented; but I sent to Columbia and have engaged him a teacher there, so that all is ready." "The occasion is very sudden; I am in a mourner's garb." "Is that the only remaining difficulty, my love?" "I do not now think of any other, and I am not disposed to multiply difficulties. If you can remove this, or if you think it of no importance, then I yield to your desire." "Heaven bless my dear bride—now I am happy. Walk with me, my love."

So saying I took her arm and led her through my bed chamber to a large closet at the end of it. There I opened a wardrobe and discovered to her three complete dresses, made secretly after her measure, fine and chastely elegant, with every appendage needful to fit her out completely. "Here are the wedding garments, my sweet bride; take your choice; I will send Miss Baylor to your assistance. I give you—let me see—it is now half-past eleven. I give you an hour to meet me with your bridesmaids down at the Summer Hall, where Mr. Wilson will be prepared to receive our hymeneal vows. Now, love, 'One kind kiss before we part' for an hour." With a blush and a smile, she gave what I asked; then, dropping on a chair, her face all covered with blushes, she hid her modest confusion with her handkerchief as I left the room. Immediately I sent Miss Baylor and a servant to the closet and hastened up stairs to equip myself for the happy occasion.

I was ready in half the time allotted to my bride and went with my attendants down to the Summer Hall to see the sports of the company. Some were walking through the garden; some were sailing on the lake in pretty boats; some fishing on the bank; some strolling among the lawns and groves and others listening in the Summer Hall to a band of musicians and preluding for the expected dance. The Hall had a plank floor and seats rising behind each other on three sides, leaving the middle space unoccupied. The vault of the roof and the walls were literally covered with branches of evergreens, wreathed and festooned, and adorned with flowers, especially roses, which were beautiful to the eye and diffused sweet odors through the surrounding air. Pots with living shrubs and plants of various bloom were set round on shelves within and outside at the broad entrance to the Hall, where a verdant bower served as a rustic vestibule to the Hall.

Fifteen minutes after twelve, the sound of a bugle called in the scattered parties. At half past twelve the bugle sounded again, and immediately a company of young ladies in white robes left the house on the hill and, winding down through the garden, approached the Hall. When they entered the flowery vestibule, they furled their parasols, opened their thick array, and discovered in their midst my lovely bride, blushing through her lace veil and radiant with all the charms of her extraordinary beauty. When I saw her now in her bridal habit, every feature expressive of the high-toned emotions of this, to her, surprising day, I vowed in my heart that she never had looked so transcendantly sweet and interesting.

I took her hand as she stole a furtive glance at me and led her to the middle of the floor, where Mr. Wilson in five minutes received our solemn vows and pronounced the nuptial benediction.

Instantly a joyful shout rang through the assembly; the band struck up hymeneal airs; and, when I had seated my bride on a chair in the midst of the floor, our joyful friends pressed forward to congratulate us. No sooner was this customary token of good will given us than a trained band of singers from the village below, headed as usual by their music teacher, Phil Gleason, rose from their seats and sang with great spirit the following stanzas:

> Human life is like the year,
>   Sometimes cold and dreary,
> Forcing many a bitter tear
>   From the sad and weary;
> But the storm will overblow—
> Blossoms follow clouds of snow.
>
> Sore, O bride, thy trials past,
>   Long and deep thy mourning,
> Brighter days have come at last,
>   Summer bids thee hail,
> Welcome to her lovely vale.
>
> Smiling see the breezy lake,
>   Smiling see the meadows,
> Wood and lawn and tangled brake
>   Smile and twinkling shadows;
> E'en old Craggyhead above
> Smiles upon thy wedded love.

Now attend, ye festive throng,
  Join the coronation,
Join the chorus of the song,
  Shout with gratulation;
Bring the wreath, the bride install,
Queen of fair Seclusaval.
                Bring the wreath, &c.

While the singers repeated the last couplet, Miss Landon, with the other fair attendants of the bride, came forward with something concealed in a basket. She first stooped and whispered a word to Judith; then, opening the basket, she took out a beautifully twined chaplet of roses and evergreens and put it on her head. This action was hailed with enthusiastic cheers by the whole assembly. Judith, with her usual grace and dignity but with tears of sensibility in her eyes, now rose and made her acknowledgments to the company. She thanked them most feelingly for the ardent welcome they gave her and for the sympathy which they manifested in her most unexpected, but nevertheless, as she said, most happy marriage. "I thank my dear young friends, too, for the complimentary coronation with which they have honored me. Though it be but a fading crown of roses, it is so much the more appropriate to one whose royal dignity on this festive occasion will so soon pass away. But oh! how shall I express the emotions which the surprising and delightful occurrences of this day have raised within me! I can only say, dear friends and strangers, may God give you all a crown that will never fade away." She then resumed her seat, scarcely able to keep her feelings from overcoming her.

Now I must inform the reader that I was myself taken by surprise when this coronation scene was acted. It was no part of my plot but an underplot contrived by Gleason and other friends, in order, as they said, to express their good will and to give me a taste of the surprise that I was so liberally dealing out to my bride. I thanked them for their good intention but was afraid that it was carrying the matter a little too far. However, it went off very happily.

Soon after this the bugle sounded to dinner. Mr. Danforth conducted the bride to the dining arbor, where two long tables were filled with guests. The dinner, though not sumptuous, was excellent, as the company seemed to think, for they complimented their entertainer by partaking plentifully of his fare. When nothing remained to be done but to drink wine and other mild beverages (for no ardent spirit was used), Mr. Landon, who presided at the first table, called out in a loud voice, "Attention, gentlemen and ladies! I have a toast to propose; after I have repeated it, let all who join in the sentiment drink standing: 'Long life and happiness to the bridegroom and the bride of Seclusaval.'" Instantly the whole company rose, and, after they had drank, spontaneously gave three cheers. I rose and made a short speech and gave my own toast in compliment to the company; but neither the speech nor the toast are here recorded.

Now Baylor, who presided at the other table, sprang up in a fit of enthusiasm and shouted, "Drink to my toast: 'The sweet rose of Seclusaval! long may she bloom and flourish here.' Nine cheers, my friends." And nine cheers made the valley ring again. After some less particular toasts were given, the company rose from the table and returned to the Summer Hall, where music and dancing began to delight those who were fond of the amusement, whilst others betook themselves to whatsoever they liked best. A party of us embarked on the lake and made a visit to the Echoing Glen, where we seemed at once to have got into another sort of region, a region of the shadow of death. When we sounded the bugle in this dark, cool recess, it seemed as if ten thousand shrill-mouthed demons had set up a yell. This romantic spot drew several exclamations of delight from Judith. When we returned to the head of the lake, we saw all manner of sports going on and everyone appearing to be delighted with the festival. About twenty of my friends now occupied the parlor of my house, where music on the piano and pleasant conversation beguiled the time.

After awhile we began to disperse ourselves in little parties over the adjacent grounds as choice or accident directed. Some strolled through the parks and lawns, some into the wild glen under Craggyhead, some into the garden below the house, while others found their way into the labyrinthine walks of the wilderness on the brow of the hill by the house. Here densely matted shrubs, vines and trees were penetrated by shady avenues leading irregularly, sometimes to little plots of open ground from which glimpses could be caught of mountain, hill, and lake, sometimes to wide lofty arcades of tall acacia or magnolia trees, festooned and canopied with luxuriant vines. Of all the spots in this romantic wilderness the most charming was a knoll on the hillside near the garden. The margin of this knoll was overgrown with an impenetrable thicket of hawthorns, pyracanthas, eglantines, and rose bushes. Within this thorny cincture was a labyrinth of Paphian bowers formed of every beautiful and blooming species of vines and trees. In the centre was a small wooden temple, circular in shape, open at the sides but covered with a dome. In the centre of the temple a fountain spouted its tiny jet so high that the water fell back in a fine white spray into a gravelly basin and ran off by a winding channel into the garden. To this charming retreat I finally led my sweet wife alone through an entrance so covered with foliage and pendent vine branches as to be invisible to one not acquainted with it. I first conducted her round the sylvan bowers, all verdant, blooming and fragrant. We then entered the little temple, and, having seated ourselves at one side among wreaths of clematis and china roses, we looked awhile in silence at the fountain, which would shoot up its foaming jet for a minute and then cease for an equal space of time.

"Well, my dear wife," said I at last, "you have now seen enough of Seclusaval to express your opinion of it. How do you like it?" "Like it! why my dear husband, it is the most charming place in the world; such a sweet image of paradise! such a nurse of pure and holy feelings! None but the virtuous and devout should ever dwell amidst such delightful tokens of Divine beauty and goodness. To have spent one day—my happy wedding day—in so sweet a place will be a pleasure to me whilst I live; and to visit this charming Seclusaval, even once a year, will add to my enjoyment of a residence in this beautiful country."

"Once a year, my love, do you say? Is that all? Do you not remember the toasts at dinner and the coronation in the Summer Hall? Are you not installed queen of this valley?"

"Yes, my husband," said she, looking up in my face, "I remember the complimentary toasts and coronation. I felt ashamed on my own account that I so little deserved the compliments bestowed on me; but, when I remembered that you were the real object of them all, I rejoiced at such striking proofs of the enthusiastic devotion of your friends and especially of Mr. Baylor, who is evidently delighted with his own generosity in giving you a wedding feast amidst the thousand beauties of his valley. He must be a devoted friend of yours."

"He is, my dear; but he ought to be my friend, for I have now to inform you, my sweet wife, that Mr. Baylor is my steward."

She gave me a sudden look of surprise and doubt.

"What did you say, my husband? Mr. Baylor your steward? Are you serious?" "Yes, love, I have reserved this surprise for the last. I have now to tell you that among all the delightful events of this day I deem it not the least that you are so well pleased with your home, for the compliments paid you today were all true and appropriate. You are the bride and the mistress of Seclusaval." As I spoke, her eyes, which were still fixed on mine, began to moisten; the tide of emotion rose and colored her cheek; the fulness of her heart was such that for some time she could not utter a word. She fell on my breast and presently sobbed out, "I have suffered many afflictions and deserved them all, but now kind Heaven has overpowered my heart with blessings."